Freedom to Die

STEPHEN SELKE

ISBN: **0994044100**
ISBN 13: **978-0994044105**

This novel is dedicated to

anyone who finds themselves in it

Levi,

Thanks for being an awesome

co-worker. Enjoy the book!

— Stephen

Chapter 1

The ride down to the pit was much too short. Micaela knew it would be and had braced her mind long before she had entered the lambently lit elevator. "The pit" was a suitable name for the hell she was about to enter. It was *hell* because whatever god was out there had turned his back on those who were doomed to its abominable function.

If the pit was hell, then Micaela was a devil. She pushed that thought aside as soon as it arose. The procedures she put the test subjects through were a necessary evil. *No, not evil—it isn't evil if it's for the good of all mankind, is it?*

In fact, she was more of a victim than the test subject in front of her was. *At least he doesn't know the terror that is to come,* she thought as she looked at the bald man who stood directly in front of her in nothing but white boxer shorts.

The man was known to her as only "Fourteen." *I wonder what his name is?* But the twenty-year-old Caucasian didn't even know his own name, thanks to the pit.

She hadn't thought about that question two weeks ago, had she? She hadn't thought about the identity of the medium-build test subject until he had become more than just another test subject.

"September 16, 2009." That was the date her pen had scribbled on her clipboard on that day—the neat pen strokes simultaneously engraving the date in her head. That was the only memorable thing that she had recorded. Any noteworthy observations were not to be recorded but put to memory. There had been a noteworthy observation that day: Micaela's needle would not pierce Fourteen's skin.

Dr. David Daniels's eyes had lit up when he had heard the news. However, it didn't take much to make Dr. Daniels's thirty-something-year-old frame vibrate with excitement. The genius was always as enthusiastic as a kid with a new toy, and he had every right to be. He was perpetually on the verge of earthshaking scientific breakthroughs. Breakthroughs like developing artificial organs, synthesizing a drug that would ward off 95 percent of the memory loss that occurs in Alzheimer's disease patients, and most recently, formulating a single injection that would stop fingernails from growing more than a couple of millimeters in length. If a cure for cancer existed, Micaela firmly believed Dr. Daniels would find it.

But they weren't researching a cure for cancer. Micaela didn't know that for certain, as she had no idea what exactly they *were* researching. Whatever it was, something had probably gone right with Fourteen, and he was subject to endless waves of testing for the next two weeks.

Micaela was swamped with tests to perform: MRIs, CAT scans, and saliva and stool tests. She also had to do things she had never done before, such as testing Fourteen's skin's resistance to heat and cold. Any blood retrieval had to be done with unconventional methods due to his abnormally resilient skin.

Her fatigue and exhaustion rose to record levels because of all of the testing she was carrying out. Yet she would have sooner taken on an even greater workload than what she was about to do.

Dr. Daniels had ordered her to take Test Subject Fourteen to the pit. The bimonthly sessions in hell had to continue. Even though the doctor had developed the procedure himself, he did not enjoy prescribing it.

Safety protocol dictated that Micaela would be accompanied by a guard at all times. During her trips to the pit, three guards would be present for her protection due to the increased risk. *Maybe they are here less to protect me and more to make sure I do what I'm told.* The thought was common for her, but unwelcome. She could tell by the grim pleasantries and the subtle sympathetic looks that they didn't enjoy the procedures in the pit any more than she did.

The trip down to the pit was a short one. The smooth and silent elevator failed in its attempt to make the descent a comfortable one.

"Walk," said Micaela as the elevator doors opened. Fourteen complied and almost robotically made his way down the corridor.

He complied because of the pit. It was there that his mind had been altered. Some people called it "brainwashing," and others called it "mind control" or "medically induced manipulation." Micaela called it wrong. Humans weren't meant to be mindless droids devoid of free will.

I'm sorry. I wish I didn't have to do this, Micaela thought as she unlocked a thick steel door and led Fourteen into a room with concrete walls. The bright lights did little to disguise the fact that a dark deed was about to happen.

"Lie down," Micaela said almost emotionlessly. Almost. She knew the guards could detect the sliver of regret that she couldn't hold back.

Fourteen didn't do anything to stop her from strapping first his hands and then the rest of his body to the table he lay on. She wished that he would have. She wanted his empty blue eyes to look at her pleadingly. She hoped for just a simple, "Stop," or even an inquisitive, "What are you doing?"

There wasn't even an ounce of resistance. Fourteen might as well have been dead.

Micaela had shaved off Fourteen's hair. The hair would have gotten in the way of the electricity.

She stuck three probes to the surface of Fourteen's skull. Each probe would deliver an electrical current to the small battery-like objects located in the test subject's skull. The miniscule batteries and the chips that they powered had been implanted in strategic locations in the test subject's mind soon after he had "volunteered."

Having chips implanted in your head is so wrong. The chips detected brain activity and somehow discouraged select brain patterns by sending out miniscule currents of electricity. Only Dr. David Daniels would have been able to develop something so complex, yet Micaela was at a loss as to why he had.

She could refuse to do it. She could refuse to administer the sleeping gas. She could refuse to power up the mind-modifying machine. She could refuse to unlock it with her handprint, key, and pass code. She could refuse to carefully turn the dials and set the timer. She could refuse to flip the switches to "activate." She could refuse to press "start."

Micaela pressed "start."

* * *

The fallen angel was free. *It's early,* thought the spirit. It knew that the end of the age had not arrived. Soon the time would arrive for the fallen angel to play its part, yet it was now that it was free.

Mankind knew very little about the realm in which the spirit resided. A few members of the species claimed to understand it. They tended to look to the science of math and dimensions, and they claimed that the "supernatural" beings lived in a dimension higher than the dimension of space and time that they existed in.

The truth was so much more complex than mankind could have ever comprehended.

Such an ignorant group of beings. I hate them.

Yet the will—the inescapable will of the sovereign Lord that the fallen angel had named "The Will"—had kept it prisoner until this point.

The realm the spirit dwelt in was intertwined with the realm mankind perceived. The spirit viewed space and time in a completely different way, yet it was still bound by them.

It was The Will that stopped humans from understanding the realm of the fallen angel. It was The Will that allowed the fallen angel to go free.

What should I call myself this time? One of the laws put in place on spirits by The Will was that the fallen angel had to adopt a name that humans could recognize. Sometimes a spirit would take the name of a trait like greed, lust, envy, or bitterness. Others identified themselves with parts of nature like wolves, frogs, or birds. Higher-ranking angels, and particularly the heavenly ones, often took on words or names of humans.

"Prefect" will be fitting enough.

The self-exalting name was indicative of Prefect's pride, a trait that the spirit shared with its leader, Lucifer. Prefect hated Lucifer, who was the reason that they were "fallen" angels, or "demons," as the humans called them. But the hate Prefect held for God was greater than the hate it had for any angel, demon, or human.

Sovereign God, the Holy One, the Ruler of Heaven and Hell: Prefect had no choice but to recognize its Creator in such decorated exalted terms. It had been designed to.

Humans had been designed to worship their Creator as well. Yet humans had more free will than angels in that regard. As far as most of them were concerned, they could choose to be ignorant and to worship whatever they wanted. Only those who lived by The Will could worship God, yet God loved all of mankind. That is why Prefect still fought. It knew some part of the Sovereign One felt pain every time one of His creations chose to worship something other than Him.

The Will didn't allow Prefect much freedom—not nearly the amount of freedom it knew it would have at the end of the age. As it surveyed the plane of space and time as only a spirit could, it weighed its options. One option was the obvious choice, which made Prefect think that it was the option for which it had been set free.

Prefect knew that whenever the more powerful enemy gave ground, it should expect a trap. Yet gaining this ground meant hurting the enemy. Prefect wasn't about to give up that opportunity.

Prefect instantly understood all of the inner workings of the man in front of him. The four others in the room knew the man as Test Subject Fourteen. There had been a modification made to the man's skin—a modification that had only been successful because of supernatural involvement.

Another modification was in place: this one to his mind. The emptiness of Fourteen's mind would allow fallen angels much lower in rank than Prefect to indwell the man, but there were none present there. *The Will must be stopping them.* This served Prefect's purposes nicely. It would cooperate with the other fallen angels if it had to, because they too wanted to hurt God. However, Prefect preferred to operate under its own power.

No more will Fourteen serve these scientists, for he is mine!

* * *

Fourteen's scream reverberated in the room. The guards instinctively drew their weapons. Micaela felt them looking uneasily at her and at Fourteen. They knew that Fourteen should have still been in an unconscious state. Micaela was frozen in fear, and Fourteen was enraged.

Micaela knew that there was no reason to be afraid. Metal clasps held Fourteen's body, arms, and legs to the table; the test subject was more immobile than he would have been if he had been wearing a straightjacket.

"Aaaaaagh!" The scream sounded demonic and sent a shiver down her spine.

"Do something!" A guard ordered. No longer immobilized, Micaela went to fetch some anesthetic to put Fourteen under once more.

Accompanying the screaming of men was the screaming of steel. Micaela looked over her shoulder and then wished she hadn't. Fourteen was bending the steel out of place.

Before she could yell, "*You* do something," the guard she knew as "Brent" fired his stun gun at Fourteen.

Twang! Steel snapped in half and Fourteen was vertical. The other two guards, Eric and Harry, fired their own guns, and two more streams of electricity collided with Fourteen's frame.

Fourteen frothed at the mouth as he swung at the guard directly in front of him. His punch was slow, but Micaela was surprised that he could punch at all while his body was twitching with electricity.

Brent stepped back, and Fourteen's punch fell much too short.

Fourteen slowly bent his knees in order to launch himself at Brent. Eric and Harry went for their secondary lethal weapons.

In Micaela's hand was the needle full of anesthetic. *What am I doing? This needle won't even break his skin! I need to get out of here!* But her path to the only door led her through the dangerous skirmish between the guards and Fourteen.

Micaela turned her back on the scene as she frantically searched for something—anything, that could be used as a weapon. *Did I just hear stones crumble?* A quick glance over her shoulder told her that she had, and she saw a five-foot horizontal crack in the concrete wall behind Fourteen. *That wasn't there before.* That only made her search for something with which to protect herself more urgent.

Loud and sharp gunshots sounded. Once more, Micaela regretted looking behind her.

"Fools," growled a menacing Fourteen, his eyes still ablaze in fury. "Nothing can pierce this skin!"

Not even bullets? At least the stun guns had affected him! Micaela's eyes momentarily focused on the door.

"You're not leaving. Not yet. We're going to have fun first." Fourteen knew what she was thinking even though he wasn't even looking at her. Instead, he was smiling grimly at the petrified pair of guards who had fired on him, daring them to make another move.

Brent, however, was looking intently at Micaela. His eyes momentarily shifted to the rear of the room. *The defibrillator! The stun guns shooting high voltage wires had affected him, so there's a good chance that the machine will be able to stop his heart. What am I thinking? That's murder!*

Fourteen reached out with one hand and grabbed the table he had been laying unconscious on only moments earlier. With only one hand, he tore it out of the ground, chunks of cement still clinging to the bottom of its legs.

Micaela ran to the defibrillator but did not yet reach for its paddles.

Fourteen swung the table at Harry and Eric, who leaped out of the way in different directions. The table ended up lodged in the wall.

I'm going to die. Unless I kill Fourteen. I need to kill him! No longer concerned with anything other than her own life, she turned on the defibrillator.

More shots were fired, that time by Brent, who was trying to keep Fourteen's attention off of Micaela.

Focus. Micaela switched the defibrillator to "manual" and set the voltage to "maximum."

Behind her, there was heavy breathing, quick footsteps, and maniacal laughter. One of the guards grunted in pain. She was scared to look.

She had to look. After turning around with paddles in her hands, she saw Harry lying motionless on the ground.

"Who's next?" It wasn't just the meaning of Fourteen's words that made Micaela's gut recoil and the rest of her body freeze with fear. It was the sheer evil sound of his voice. It was like something out of a nightmare, but it was made worse by the fact that it was real—this was really happening.

Fourteen was really ripping a leg off of the table lodged in the wall. He really did throw the leg at Brent so quickly that the guard couldn't dodge it. The leg really did pierce both Brent's upper arm and the wall.

Eric really was yelling, "Do it!"

Micaela didn't bother screaming "clear" and instead just screamed at the top of her lungs as she launched herself toward Fourteen.

Fourteen swung around to face his attacker just in time for two paddles to connect with his upper chest. He fell lifelessly to the ground.

So did Micaela.

* * *

Eric had stopped them from trying to resuscitate Fourteen. After hearing the man's story, Dr. Daniels didn't blame him. He was fortunate that one dead test subject was the worst part of the disaster. One guard was in a coma, one guard had to have an arm amputated, and one scientist had severe post-traumatic stress disorder. Those problems were costly, but at least the three of them were alive.

Micaela had fainted after stopping Fourteen's heart. It was understandable, she had just killed a person. *At least she didn't electrocute herself in the process,* thought Dr. Daniels. *Fourteen laying one finger on her would be all it would have taken.*

After the whole ordeal, there was not one resignation. The loyalty of his staff was commendable.

But the ordeal wasn't over yet. Dr. Daniels still needed to analyze the situation to determine what exactly had gone wrong.

The mind-modifying machine might have caused the chips to malfunction. That weak hypothesis was the one that made the most sense. Even though he had designed the machine, it was nearly impossible for even Dr. Daniels to understand the full nature of the effect it had on the human psyche, especially if something went wrong. But he owed it to Fourteen to try to figure it out.

He insisted on doing Fourteen's autopsy himself with no observers present.

The serum that he was developing was incredibly confidential due to its implications. Not even Dr. Daniels's staff knew exactly what they were helping him to develop.

Dr. Daniels was trying to formulate a single injection that would increase the human body's resilience by a small percentage. That small percentage would toughen the human body to near its limit. It would give a seventy-year-old a three-year-old child's ability to bounce back after a fall.

He wasn't trying to develop a serum for bulletproof skin, but his formula definitely had military implications. That, and the fact that he was doing trials on live humans, made it essential that nothing about his project was leaked to the outside world.

"Impossible," he said out loud. It was the theme for the entire autopsy.

Fourteen's body wasn't deteriorating the way a dead body should have. In fact, it wasn't deteriorating at all. There was no pulse and no brain activity, yet hours after Fourteen's death, his body temperature hadn't dropped even one-tenth of a degree. It was impossible and creepy. Not that he was willing to try it, but Dr. Daniels strongly believed that if he induced a heartbeat, Fourteen would be able to get up and walk away as if nothing had happened.

There was no way to cut into the skin. Before, they had used a drill to get blood and tissue samples. However, at the moment, no drill could pierce *any* part of Fourteen's body. *Impossible.*

An x-ray of Fourteen's head showed no trace of the chips that had been implanted there. Even if they had been completely fried, Dr. Daniels would have liked to have retrieved them. But it was as if they had simply dissolved into nonexistence. *Impossible.*

Dr. Daniels probed every possible cavity in the dead test subject's body with cameras, and everything seemed completely normal—normal for a living body. *Impossible.*

There wasn't a scientist out there who understood the human body better than Dr. Daniels did, and the man couldn't even begin to wrap his head around the case of Test Subject Fourteen.

I need more information. I need sleep. He had been at the autopsy for thirty straight hours.

* * *

One of the rules imposed by The Will was that Prefect wasn't allowed to take the life of a human being. Prefect had found a loophole in the rule and had attempted to cause one human being to take the life of another. He had attempted to kill Fourteen. By human standards, the man was dead. But the humans couldn't see what Prefect could. The soul had not yet departed from the body.

Intrigued, Prefect stayed with the body. Obviously, God wanted to keep that one alive, and that meant more opportunities for Prefect to cause destruction.

Prefect protected Fourteen's body. It protected the body from drills, knives, saws, and, a little while later, an oven. The Most High God wasn't the only one who could prevent bodies from burning in a fiery furnace.

Chapter 2

Larry awoke to the sensation that he was sinking and to the knowledge that he wasn't in his bed. *I'm dreaming,* thought Larry. The fact that his body couldn't move supported his evaluation. Yet as he gathered his senses, he wondered if his thought was accurate. His mind felt fresh; the breath escaping his mouth felt real.

Where was I when I went to sleep? His mind no longer felt fresh when he failed to recall where he should have been. The uncomfortable blurriness of his mind made him return to his initial analysis. *I'm dreaming.*

Larry smiled. The great thing about dreaming and realizing that you were was that you could do whatever you wanted to do in the dream.

What kind of dream am I dealing with? There was the sinking sensation and the fading green blur of light in front of him. *It feels like I'm lying down and am strapped inside a container.*

The sensation of sinking ended as Larry felt the container strike something. *What was that? What now?*

He couldn't think of anything better to do, so he willed himself up, pushing against whatever was holding him in place. He felt resistance, and then he was free. There was not much freedom, though, and his face smacked into something plastic. Or was it glass? Whatever the material was, it was translucent, and the weird dim light was shining through it.

Once his limbs were free, Larry used them to explore the container he was in, if it was in fact a container. He found that he could only move a few inches in each direction and that there didn't appear to be any openings in the container.

Staring at the light in front of him, he thought, *What kind of stupid dream is this?*

He firmly placed his hands against the clear container and pushed. It wasn't budging, but Larry hadn't reached the limit of his effort yet. He pushed harder and harder. He felt like he had never applied so much effort to anything in his life, but he didn't feel strained.

Then something gave.

Something wet and noticeably cold enveloped his body. *Water.* He didn't have a chance to hold his breath. Liquid invaded his mouth and pressed through his throat, so he closed his mouth and throat. *Why don't I feel pressured to start breathing again? I'm definitely dreaming.* Yet the water felt cold and tasted much like dirt; the fluid seemed so real.

Whether it was a dream or not, he would have preferred not to have the foul-tasting water in his mouth, so he made his way out of the container he was in.

The water provided very little resistance to his legs and arms as he powered his way to the surface. As his head broke into the chilly air, he concerned himself with ridding his mouth of the disgusting water before he observed his environment.

It was night, and clouds were blocking the majority of the stars from gracing the sky with their majestic beauty. The light of the moon had pierced the clouds, and it gave Larry the ability to take in his surroundings. He was in the middle of some sort of lake that was surrounded by a forest of trees. Larry wanted to make his way to land, but it was hard to distinguish which direction would give him the shortest trip, as the silhouette of trees seemed to be the same distance away in every direction.

Larry bobbed there for a couple minutes, slightly frustrated. *This dream isn't getting any better!* He wanted to be in the middle of a city or a town—he wanted to be in a place with people! *I want to be somewhere fun!*

Something caught Larry's eye. Swiveling to his left, he could make out a car's high beams. The car was slowly making its way around the lake. He started swimming toward it but stopped when he realized that what he was doing didn't make too much sense. The car he was making his way toward was moving, so the direction he was swimming in kept changing.

Switching tactics, Larry decided to head toward a small indent in the horizon of trees.

Even though the waves were giving their best attempt at tiring Larry out, he found he could swim without too much difficulty. In fact, he couldn't remember the last time he had swam with so much ease. The harder he kicked, the faster he went. So he kicked harder and went faster. Larry wasn't sure how fast he was going when his foot hit a seaweed-covered rock, but it had taken him less than two minutes to go a distance that probably should have taken closer to fifteen.

I feel like I could easily swim for at least another hour, Larry thought as he climbed onto the rocky shore. Sharp stones tried to dig into his bare feet, which refused to feel pain.

Free of container and water for the first time, Larry's attire attracted his attention. A soaked and dirty white robe that resembled the clean garments given to hospital patients stuck to his body. Under that was nothing but a matching pair of boxer shorts.

Larry's muddled memory was what had originally led him to the conclusion that he was dreaming. On top of that, he hadn't felt the burning desire to breathe when the water had infiltrated his airspace. Plus, he had been able to reach the speed of a motorboat on his way to shore. Finally, the sharp stones had failed to hurt the bottoms of his bare feet.

But his environment felt so real. He felt so awake. *Maybe I'm in a coma. I was probably laying in a hospital bed moments before I woke up here. That's why everything seems so real, and that's why I'm dressed like this. My mind is in a completely different world. This one.* His clouded drifting mind swam around in circles, desperate for a rational answer. Yet it failed to land on anything as solid as the ground that he then stood on.

I may as well press on.

"I want to worship you with the places I go," Ryan Slater sang as he navigated his slate-blue Peterbilt transport truck down a deserted stretch of gravel road. It was two o'clock in the morning, and Ryan was playing the music a little louder than usual to keep himself awake. He probably could have managed without it because he was used to driving with minimal sleep, but just staring at nothing but the road and the towering forest around him would have been boring.

Ryan was just finishing off the last verse of the worship song when he spotted a deer bolt out of the brush and into his headlights. As he quickly stomped on the brakes, it became clear to him that it was not a deer that was in the spotlight of his high beams. It was a man!

Although Ryan was a talented truck driver, stopping an eighteen-wheeler fully loaded with logs was no easy task.

The man too was slowing to a stop and finally came to a standstill in the middle of the road. If the stranger had kept on running, he would have safely made it across. Ryan had fully expected him to keep running and hadn't had time to swerve around him.

The semi ploughed into the human's body with a sickening thud, resulting in the human being sent flying like a 170-pound sack of potatoes. The truck stopped only millimeters from his feet.

For a second, Ryan could only sit in shock. But he quickly started a prayer.

"Lord, don't let him be dead." He knew that the man probably hadn't survived, but that didn't stop him from repeating his short prayer over and over again.

Larry lay on his back, his eyes fixed on one of the only clusters of stars visible in the cloudy sky. *A semi going full speed just hit me, and I feel fine. If that doesn't prove that all of this isn't real, then I'm not sure what would.*

A door popped open, and soon Larry heard the thumping of approaching footsteps. *Oh good, someone else to share this nightmare with.*

The man peering down at him was clearly exasperated and shocked. Larry casually pushed himself to his feet, and the onlooker's shock increased.

Larry wondered if he was supposed to recognize the round face of the one who stood before him. His frame was slightly taller than Larry's five-foot-eight frame, and it was noticeably wider. Slowly, the glasses-wearing black-haired stranger reached out his arm and poked Larry in the shoulder with his finger.

"What are you doing?" Larry asked as the man's hand quickly retreated to his side.

"You're…You're real!"

"Yeah. But you may not be," Larry casually shrugged. He wasn't sure how his mind could have fabricated the surprised young man; although the man appeared to be roughly the same age as Larry, he also appeared to be acting independent of his imagination.

"I…I was just part of a miracle!"

"Miracle? Nah, this is just my dream. Watch this!" Effortlessly, Larry applied pressure to his legs, boosting himself into a sprint. The gravel on the road did little to restrain his bare feet from reaching a far faster speed than they had been cruising at through the forest; he ran faster than any human had any right to.

The road took a sharp curve, but Larry didn't. What Larry did do was come to a complete stop as he collided with a tree. His white robe, which had become tattered during his trip through the forest, hung on some broken branches behind him.

"Heh, good thing this is just a dream," Larry said to himself before climbing out of the bushes and speeding back to his new acquaintance.

"Yep, a miracle alright."

"I told you. I'm dreaming this!" Then Larry had an idea. Looking to the sky, he bent his legs. With more power than any man should have had, he leapt skyward. He jumped twice as high as the surrounding trees, but unfortunately, he wasn't able to stay at that height. "I guess I haven't figured out how to fly," he said after hitting the gravel hard. "Oh well, take me to the city! I want to leap from skyscraper to skyscraper!"

The man shook his head. "This isn't a dream. Well, maybe it is. Maybe I'm the one dreaming it." He pinched himself. "That didn't work, but I suppose it doesn't work in the movies, either. I know—I'll close my eyes and imagine that we are in the city! I want to see you jump over apartment buildings too! Imagining things into existence works in some of my other dreams, anyway."

Larry followed the strange man's lead. Closing his eyes, he thought of a city. *What city is this? Is it a real city? What's the name of the city? Where do I live? Do I live in a city?* The questions in his head remained unanswered as he opened his eyes and saw the same dark forest road.

"Nope, must have been a miracle then."

Not willing to give in to the whole "miracle" idea, Larry protested. "I could be in a coma!"

"Um, I'm real."

"Or someone could have pumped me full of drugs or steroids or something," Larry continued to try to convince the man of his theory. He wasn't sure why he was trying to persuade a figment of his imagination. *Because maybe this isn't all in my head.* As fast as he could, Larry pushed that thought aside.

The figment of his imagination shook his head and then laughed. "I've heard of drugs that would enable you to successfully bench a quad. But there's not a single drug out there that would allow you to get tackled by *that* monster and get up without a scratch." He pointed to the front end of his truck.

A strange hostility rose in his mind. He didn't like semis. He didn't like truck drivers. But he couldn't think of a reason for his irrational prejudice against them. Forcing himself to set that thought aside for the moment, he persisted in his attempt to persuade the truck driver of his theory.

"But…maybe the drugs are making me hallucinate all of this."

"Well, I know I'm real, and I don't take drugs, and you're too solid to be a hallucination," Larry's "hallucination" said decisively. "Forget about it. Too much thinking on too little sleep makes my head hurt. Hop in my truck, and I'll give you a ride to town. You're not from Terrecastor, are you?"

"Nope. Not sure where I'm from."

"Well that would suck. But it's late. You might as well spend the night at my place, and we can figure things out tomorrow."

Deciding to go with the flow for the time being, Larry agreed and climbed into the passenger side of the truck.

"Oh, by the way, name's Ryan!" As he turned down the music that was playing, he laughed at how long it had taken him to introduce himself.

"Okay. I mean, nice to meet you, Ryan." Ryan's lighthearted spirit and humor made him quite likeable, and his presence somewhat eased the uncomfortable, weird stress that Larry felt. "I'm…Larry."

"Really? You sure?" Ryan joked as he shifted the eighteen-wheeler into gear.

The sad part was that Larry wasn't actually sure. *I'm not sure. No…I'm sure. I'm Larry. That's my name—Larry Tanner. It has to be.* He let out a nervous chuckle.

Ryan continued to talk about how it was an honor to sit next to a miracle man and how he couldn't wait to tell the story to his friends.

"I'm not sure we should tell anyone," Larry said.

"Why not?"

"Because…because I'd rather not get too famous right now. I mean, if this *isn't* a dream. Which it *is*." Ryan only grinned at that. "Besides, having a secret superpower has a nice ring to it."

"I guess," Ryan acknowledged. "Hey, are you saying that you expect to keep your super strength?"

"I kinda hope so. Actually, I really do hope so, even though it isn't natural. Perhaps my body isn't working right. But it's helped me so far, hasn't it? If it goes away…I don't know if there are any side effects."

Ryan smiled grimly as he continued to shift through a series of gears. Larry looked at the man. He looked at his tired yet excited eyes and at the reflection of the dashboard in the man's glasses. Everything was so real and in so much detail. One thing seemed to be a bit off, though. Ryan was a man who had just witnessed a "miracle," and he seemed to be taking it all in stride.

"So that's it? You just witnessed the most amazing thing you've ever seen, and you're fine just keeping it a secret? Just keeping on living like it didn't happen?" Larry inquired.

"I guess so. What? Am I supposed to be doing something else?"

Larry tried to look at the situation from Ryan's perspective. He was a man who believed in miracles. He must have thought that the size of the miracle meant that it had to been an act of God. Was the man religious?

"So do you think God made my body like this?"

"Of course it was Him. What else could it have been?"

I could be dreaming. No, I am dreaming. "Why would God have done this, though?" Even as he spoke the question, Larry's mind went to his own thoughts about God. He didn't know what he thought about God, but somewhere in his mind, he felt anger and hostility toward Him.

"God sometimes works in weird ways."

Larry wasn't sure why he was against the idea that God was behind his current situation. Yet some part of him rejected the whole notion of God. He no longer felt like thinking about the subject.

"So…what kind of town is Tear…"

"Terrecastor," Ryan finished the word for him.

"Yeah, I haven't even heard that name before…I think. It *is* a town, right?"

"Just another small town in Alberta. Canada. It's no surprise that you haven't heard about it. It used to be just a seasonal fishing village, but within the last fifty years, it's grown along with the forestry industry in the area. Only has the basic stuff—a few schools, a few businesses…It doesn't even have a McDonald's or a Tim Hortons!"

Larry wished he knew why that was significant. But he smiled as if he had understood.

"Is that Terrecastor?" Larry asked as the truck completed a long curve in the road and a glow of lights became visible ahead of them.

"Yep, we're almost home. One sec—I suppose I should phone my wife." Ryan pulled out his cell phone and started to apologize to his wife for waking her up.

Larry was bothered by the fact that the man was talking on his phone and driving at the same time. He didn't know why. There was obviously no one else on the road. Yet a bitterness arose in his mind. *He should not be driving distracted,* he harshly thought.

* * *

Eric stood solemnly out outside of Dr. David Daniels's office and awaited the doctor's verdict. The extremely fatigued scientist had told Eric that he needed to make a top-secret phone call.

Three others stood near Eric and avoided looking at him. They would likely share his fate. Good or bad, the responsibility for what had happened had fallen on Eric.

Eric had no clue why Dr. Daniels had assigned *him* to go with the body-hiding team. The crew of four had been charged with transporting Test Subject Fourteen's body via helicopter to "a more secure location." Hadn't he known that Eric hadn't wanted anything to do with Fourteen? Hadn't he known that Eric's objectivity had been compromised and that there were better people for the job? Had that been the doctor's way of saying that since Eric had stopped them from trying to resuscitate Fourteen, the dead body was his responsibility?

The "dead" body. Everything about Fourteen seemed so wrong—so unreal.

The helicopter trip had been uneventful for the first two minutes. At the two-minute mark, Eric had seen the body move.

"Don't be ridiculous," the others had told him. "It's just the vibration of the helicopter."

Eric had continued to stare through the clear part of Fourteen's heavy-duty coffin. He had tried to tell himself that what the others had said was true.

"No, see—he's breathing." The guard across from him had confirmed it.

The two pilots—the ones not looking at Fourteen—had scoffed at them. One of them said that the body was probably just releasing intestinal gases.

"Not at a regular breathing rate! If you don't turn around now, I'm dropping this body!" Eric had threatened. The pilots hadn't deviated from their course. His fellow passenger had aided him in carrying through with the threat. Eric would have sworn that he had seen Fourteen's eyelids start to lift a moment before he shoved the coffin out of the open door into Terrecastor Lake.

Eric tried to tell himself that he hadn't done it out of fear. There had been fear, yes, but Eric repeated to himself that he had made a logical decision. If Fourteen had been breathing even in "death," then there was a good chance that he would have been strong if he had come back to life. If he had become animated in the helicopter, then the safety of the onboard personnel could have been compromised.

I may have just saved all of our lives, Eric thought. That thought was what kept him from becoming distraught with regret. If someone discovered that body—dead or alive—there was no telling what impact it could have on the unprepared world. He knew that Dr. Daniels's confidential research and mind-modifying machine alone would have caused waves if they had been discovered. People would kill for those secrets. Yet they weren't as dangerous as the abilities Test Subject Fourteen had displayed. His powers would be fought over by all who could afford to enter the battle should they fail to remain a secret. *I may have saved our lives, but how many more have I doomed?*

Finally, Dr. Daniels exited his office, his stride weary and his face downcast. Shaking his head, he said, "He's the one person on the planet who could legitimately call me an idiot. He might as well have."

Lifting his gaze to meet the four onlookers, Dr. Daniels said, "I don't blame any of you. You are high-paid professionals, yet we are dealing with something that is beyond your pay or training. As disappointed as I am, I'm happy that you are all safe. I'm giving you all a couple of days off. The situation is now in the hands of the best of the best, so put your minds at ease."

Chapter 3

Prefect was irritated that he was no longer allowed to possess Larry. When the Holy Spirit had brought the sleeping man back to life, it had also left him with an even greater physical body than the one Prefect had provided him with. No more would electricity be able to stop Larry's heart.

Although God Almighty had touched him, the Holy Spirit did not dwell in the sad state of a man. That meant that there was still hope that Prefect could kill Larry, still hope for the fallen angel to sway him.

The less connected humans were to the physical world, the less resistance they had to spiritual influence—particularly to negative influence. Fallen angels did some of their best work when humans were fatigued, intoxicated by drugs or alcohol, deep in meditation, or in that sweet spot where they were not yet sleeping, but not completely awake, either.

Humans were in the dark about how much dominion demons had over their dreams. Prefect had more power than most other demons.

Larry's new body didn't need sleep, but Prefect was still able to send him into dreamland. It was an easy way to give Larry a little bit of his memory back. The powerful enemy of the Most High would remind Larry of his hate for his Creator.

* * *

While his physical body slept, Larry's mind was not just dreaming, but re-living past events. Just as in other dreams, Larry didn't realize it was a dream.

Larry's mom was talking to him. They were driving north on Highway 2 from Calgary to Edmonton in a dirty red Sunfire. "Larry?"

"Huh? Oh, yeah. Sounds good to me," Larry said. He wasn't really paying attention to his mom; she was only going on about where they were going to eat. One fast food outlet was the same as another as far as Larry was concerned.

"What's on your mind, dear?" his mother asked. She didn't have to divert her attention from the road in front of her to observe the fact that Larry had stopped listening to her.

"Nothing."

"That was some sermon this morning, eh?"

"Yeah, I guess." Ever since Larry's father had died of cancer, his mom had been going to church. That didn't bother Larry as long as she didn't try to force her new beliefs on him, which he felt she would do before too long.

If there had been a way to avoid that situation, Larry probably would have taken it. As it stood, though, he couldn't afford to pay for another bus ticket. The part-time job he held at a grocery store couldn't even cover the necessities like rent and school expenses for the business program he was enrolled in at the University of Alberta. So for now, traveling with his mother was an unavoidable option.

"You know, it's amazing how putting your faith in Christ can give your life meaning and direction."

"Whatever works for you, Mom," Larry replied plainly. Because he was his mother's only remaining child, he knew he meant a great deal to her. He didn't want to introduce more grief into their relationship by arguing over something as petty as religion. They had already weathered so much together; they had gone through enough pain.

"What works for me can work for you too, Larry," his mom said. "God sent His son to save everybody."

"I know," Larry declared angrily. Unable to restrain himself any longer, he went on. "He sent His son to save us because He loved us, right? Because He's such a great and loving God?" He emphasized the words "great" and "loving" with as much disgust as he could muster. He didn't let his mom say anything. "Well, I don't see anything great and loving about sending a shark to attack Jason. I don't see what's so great and loving about giving Dad cancer and killing him."

Larry's mom cocked her head like she was about to say something, but then she thought better of it and stayed quiet.

Larry immediately felt sorry; he was normally reserved and rarely mentioned his brother and father. It wasn't like him to get all emotional like that. He had known his mom was eventually going to talk about God with him, and he was disappointed with the way he had handled the situation. He looked over at his mom. She was trying to hold back tears.

"I'm sorry, Mom. I didn't mean to blow up like that."

"I'm sorry too, Larry. I know how you feel. I haven't forgotten Jason and your dad, and I know how weird it must sound when I say that their deaths brought me closer to Jesus. God often works in ways that we don't understand, but I still try to keep faith in Him because He knows what He's doing."

Larry decided that if God got people to follow Him by killing off the ones that they loved, he wanted no part of it. He was about to say as much, but he thought better of it and kept quiet. His silence only lasted a few short seconds before he let out a surprised

"What the—?"

A transport trailer that had been traveling in the left lane next to them had begun to block both lanes.

Time didn't seem to slow. Larry didn't have time to comprehend his mom's screaming as she slammed on the brakes. Larry instinctively tensed up and held on to the handle above his head.

There was no way the car was going to be able to stop in time. His mom quickly steered to the right.

The Sunfire and the transport trailer became one in a violent crash.

The tremendous blow sent Larry spiraling into the land of the living. The dream was over, but he was still tense and wincing from the onslaught of pain that the nightmare had unleashed on him. He didn't feel any physical pain, but that didn't stop the awkward tenseness in his gut and the tearless sobs.

Every memory up to and including the moment his dream had depicted had been restored, as if re-living the.moment had flipped an "on" switch in his mind. Larry's mother had been killed in that accident. Both of Larry's parents were dead. His brother was dead. The reality was harsh, and emotion swept over Larry like a tidal wave. He grieved the loss of his family as if they had all been alive the day before. It grieved him that he hadn't died too.

Although he still didn't have any memories of the events that had happened after that accident, Larry knew that a drowsy truck driver had killed his mother. The semi driver had nodded off. His mother had died because of a stupid truck driver.

Was that how God repaid someone for turning to Him? By simply killing him or her off in a freak accident?

Hatred and bitterness arose out of the depths of grief that swamped Larry. He felt hatred toward God and bitterness toward careless truck drivers.

Of course, he knew it was unfair to be prejudiced toward truck drivers in general. Ironically, another truck driver had hit him the last night, but Larry couldn't blame him.

Who could have been mad at Ryan Slater? He and his wife, Jenny, had graciously opened their home to him without a second thought.

Larry almost smiled as he recalled how Jenny had practically commanded him to take a shower. He had been more than willing to comply, as he had felt gritty and had smelled like algae from being in Terrecastor Lake.

It was a good thing he didn't have hair that could have been soaked with the foul-smelling lake water. *When did I shave my head?* It was one of the many memories that he still couldn't recall.

At least he knew where he lived and worked. He was a student in Edmonton. He couldn't decide whether he would have preferred to be a nobody with no past and no pain or to be a somebody with a morbid past. Regardless, having an actual identity would give him direction.

Footsteps from the floor above forced Larry to do his best to clear his mind for the moment. He had an objective—he needed to get to Edmonton.

The soft dim light of day spilled through the closed blinds and filled the room that Larry was in. However, what really got him moving was the beautiful smell of bacon that had made its way into the guest room.

Larry sat up and surveyed the room he was in. Everything was so tidy. There was a desk with a computer on it in front of him, there were papers stacked neatly in a corner, and there were pens and pencils inside of a shiny black elephant figurine. On the bedside desk beside him, there was a tissue box and an alarm clock that looked like they had been placed and angled deliberately. Both were free of dust.

Two framed pictures hung on the west side of the room. One depicted the front end of a large semi. Larry wouldn't have been surprised to learn that it was the same truck that Ryan had hit him with hours earlier. The other picture was a cute image of a kitten playing with a ball of yarn. The stark contrast between the bold, raw power of the truck and the pure, soft playfulness of the kitten was the only thing that stuck out to Larry as being mismatched in the room.

As awake as possible, Larry leaped out of the bed.

He was dressed in clothes that Jenny had given him to keep, he assumed, since he had shown up to the residence wearing nothing but dirty white boxers. Ryan's clothes were a bit big on him, so the beige T-shirt easily covered the belt that was required to keep up the faded blue jeans. But they didn't look too bad, Larry thought as he examined himself in the perfectly clean tall mirror that was attached to the backside of the door to his room.

Examining his reflection, it was hard for him to get over how odd he looked with no hair. Even the lower half of his face was free of any trace of stubble. *Strange—I don't ever remember caring enough to get such a close shave.* Perhaps his abnormal body would make it stay that way. He hoped so, although he wouldn't have minded some hair on the top of his head.

Suddenly feeling silly, Larry wanted to try something. He stuck the tip of his thumb in his mouth and bit down. He bit down harder and harder. Although he was sure that he was biting his thumb with the force of a beaver chewing on a perfectly good green tree, his thumb refused to hurt; the skin refused to be pierced.

Jenny was setting the table, and her husband was sitting in his seat sipping his hot black coffee when Larry climbed the stairs into the dining room. It wasn't normal for them to have a hitchhiker sleeping in their house, but then again, she knew the best they could do was merely attempt normalcy with their—her—history.

"Good morning, Larry. How did you sleep?" Ryan asked.

Jenny swiveled her head and looked through her black thick-rimmed glasses at their guest. It was sort of weird for her to see him in her husband's old clothes, but she couldn't let him walk around in nothing but boxers. Why he had been dressed like that and soaked with lake water was beyond Jenny. Ryan hadn't been any help and had only said, "It's really not for me to say, even if I knew." She was sure she could have pried more information about the stranger out of her husband, but she figured that there were some things that she didn't need to know at the moment. After all, she had her own secrets.

"Alright," Larry responded vaguely. "Thanks so much for letting me stay at your place. I really appreciate it."

"Oh, no problem," Jenny quickly said. "You can sit anywhere you'd like. Breakfast is ready."

23

"More like brunch," said Ryan, who was still in his pajamas.

Not too much earlier, Jenny had confronted Ryan about the sloppy clothes he was wearing despite the fact that there was company around. Her sometimes less than adorable husband had responded by saying, "It's my house—our house. I can wear what I want." She supposed Larry was his guest more than he was hers, and it wasn't a big deal. In fact, she didn't exactly look fit to go out in public either; her long black hair was still damp from her shower. Although she had thrown on the dress shirt she was planning to wear to work, she hadn't yet applied the mascara that would complement her deep-blue eyes that Ryan liked to call "mysterious."

"So what brings you to Terrecastor, Larry?" Jenny casually asked.

"Just passing through. Nice silverware." Larry quickly changed the subject as he sat down. Jenny hardly needed her exceptional people skills to discern that he obviously didn't want to talk about his past. *Interesting.*

"Silverware's from Germany, and the china's from China. We have a multinational setup today," Jenny said as she scooped hash browns into a glass serving bowl from…Walmart.

"And bacon from Canada!" Ryan said as he forked more than his share of the fried meat onto his plate.

"Would you like some coffee, Larry?" Jenny asked as she placed the hash browns on the table.

After a moment of thinking, he said, "Sure. Thanks."

"Careful—it's hot," Ryan said. He didn't say it sarcastically or jokingly. He said it as if he were seriously reminding Larry of it, while forcing himself to sound casual. *Interesting.*

Larry nodded and smiled. He proceeded to cautiously sip the coffee as Jenny made her way to her seat.

Jenny had barely sat down and Larry had just picked up his fork when Ryan started saying grace without warning. "Dear Jesus, thank you for a new day, for new friends, and for the protection and grace you provide for us. Bless this food, and be with us as we go about our day. In Jesus's name, amen."

Thanks for the grace and protection. Interesting.

During the prayer, Jenny had peeked through squinted eyes at Larry. He hadn't seemed too surprised by the prayer, and he had bowed his head slightly. But his eyes had been open, and had she detected a hint of annoyance and anger?

"Amen," she echoed. "Help yourself, Larry. Guests first. Well, that's the way it *should* be, anyway."

Ryan looked down at the pile of bacon on his plate. "Oh, yeah."

Larry politely chuckled as he dished up some food.

"So where are you heading to, Larry?" Jenny inquired as nonchalantly as she could.

"Edmonton," Larry quickly replied. Ryan displayed a minimal amount of surprise at his reply.

"Well, if you're willing to wait a day, Jenny can give you a ride to Edmonton. Right, hun?" Ryan volunteered. He was definitely taking advantage of the fact that he didn't have to be concerned for her safety, being as she was a cop.

She was more impervious to danger than he knew.

Still, she shot Ryan a quick look that said, *"Really, dear, it's not right to send your beloved wife off alone with a man you just met."* Of course, even if he had had the ability to read her more complex looks, he wouldn't have been able to at the moment. He was paying more attention to his ketchup-laden hash browns than to her.

"Sure, I'll be going past Edmonton anyway. I might as well take you, if you'd like."

"That would be great, thanks."

"No problem," Jenny said as she shot another look at her husband.

That time Ryan caught the look and defensively said, "I mean, I would love to go with both of you, but I have a Risk game tomorrow afternoon with the guys, and priorities are priorities."

During the course of the meal, Jenny did her best not to assault their guest with an unending list of questions. She learned little more than the fact he was on a "short break" from the University of Alberta in Edmonton. He was somewhat shy, but he was quite willing to engage in conversation, unless it revolved around his personal life.

Jenny tried to tell herself that it was no big deal and that he would soon become just another face in the sea of acquaintances that she had in her life. Yet her instincts told her that Larry wasn't someone she would be able to forget.

Chapter 4

An unmarked cube van drove near the man who had been pinpointed by the helicopter hovering high above.

"Test Subject Fourteen located," said the man dressed in street clothes sitting in the rear of the van. He was looking at a screen that projected several images from cameras hidden on the exterior of the van. He spoke again into the concealed mic that was fixed to the top part of his leather fall jacket, "Fourteen wearing beige T-shirt and blue jeans. No sign of unusual behavior." *Besides being alive.*

The vehicle drove slowly—but not slowly enough to arouse suspicion—past the man taking a brisk stroll along a lakeside trail.

"Engage in conversation," came the monotonic order from Agent Two-F and Three-G's boss via their earpieces.

"Yes, sir."

* * *

Larry had spent the majority of his afternoon meandering around the town of Terrecastor. The town was small enough that he could jog around the entirety of it in under an hour, part of the trip aided by the paved biking trail that slithered between the town and Terrecastor Lake.

As he made his way, his mind in a melancholic mess, he managed to make out the fact that the leaves on the surrounding trees were beginning to turn colors. *Fall already? Strange. How much memory am I missing? When was the accident? It was January—I was on my way back to school after spending Christmas holidays with Mom. What came after that?*

Hours of wandering and wondering provided no further information about his past.

At one point, Larry sat on a bench at Terrecastor's beach. He gazed across the lake, trying to focus more on the beauty of the scenery than on the futile, unending thought process that enveloped his brain. The high-pitched crying of seagulls easily drowned out the minimal noise of Terrecastor's traffic. The rhythmic lapping of the waves had a calming effect on Larry's discombobulated mind, which was dominated by depression.

Eventually, the sorrow that Larry had been holding back while he had been jogging seeped out, and he wept. He did not need physical pain to remind him of his aching heart. Although his eyes lacked tears, he still wept. He wept over the loss of his family and the loss of his memory, and he even wept over the fact that his abnormal body prevented him from grieving properly. As if to make matters worse, a pair of women who were roughly the same age as his mother jogged by behind him, discussing the sort of family ordeal that Larry knew he would not have the pleasure of experiencing.

As his melancholy rose to an unbearable level, Larry decided to get off of the bench and to switch his mind back to the fruitless thoughts he had been having before he had sat down. He needed to find a way to recover his memory. There had to be something he could do in Terrecastor.

Perhaps if I take a look at a newspaper, an event will jog my memory. With a plan finally in place, Larry headed back into town.

He didn't start paying attention to the cube van that was driving past him until it did a U-Turn and stopped next to him.

A tan man with a thin angled face addressed him through the open driver's side window. "Excuse me, sir, but you wouldn't happen to be from around here, would you?"

"No, sorry. I'm just visiting," Larry said.

"That's too bad. Hey, you wouldn't happen to have any smokes that I could buy off you, would you?"

"Don't smoke." Larry said before adding, "You shouldn't either. It's bad for you." He wasn't sure why he had added that last bit in. Although it was a phrase in the back of his mind whenever someone referred to cigarettes, it wasn't usually vocalized, especially in conversations with strangers. Larry wanted to think that he had said it because his fear of people had been reduced when he had gained his superhuman body. But he had a feeling that there was more to it than that. There was a sense of hostility in him, and he was certain that the source of his anger was hidden in his missing memories.

"It's horrible for me, but it sure makes a long and annoying delivery run more bearable. Especially when the boss gives an address that ain't on the GPS in a town in the middle of nowhere. You wouldn't happen to know where this place called Skiontia is, would you?"

"Never heard of it. Sorry," Larry responded, this time making sure to add the friendly Canadian trademark word that everybody said whether or not they really were "sorry."

"Alrighty, bud, thanks anyways. I guess I'll make my way into town and buy some smokes the old-fashioned way. Perhaps I'll bump into you again. I wouldn't doubt it, with all the circles I've been driving in. Later, man."

"See ya."

Vance Mortus was a man who didn't waste time. Ever. He was always doing the most important work the most efficient way, the way only a man with the most efficient mind could. Vance had just finished listening to the whole conversation between Agent Two-F and Fourteen.

The dialogue had been transmitted to him via a microphone hidden under Two-F's T-shirt collar. The microphone was the smallest example of the degree of access that Vance had to top-of-the-line technology. As the head of a secret organization that only took on assignments that no other covert agency could take on, he needed such privileges.

If most people had seen Vance Mortus as he sat at that moment, they would have agreed that he was not a person one would want to meet in a dark alley. In fact, most people made a mental note to avoid a confrontation with him in *any* location. It wasn't so much his intimidating, muscular, and limber six-foot frame that bothered people most. Nor was it the way that his high cheekbones continuously cast creepy shadows over his sunken cheeks. What really made people nervous around Vance was the fact that he didn't display any emotion. In fact, many of those who were under his command swore that he didn't even have emotions.

Being free of emotion wasn't a bad thing, at least according to Vance. Feelings and emotions only stop one from making perfect decisions. Being emotionless made Vance cunning, powerful, and efficient.

Vance's computer-like mind analyzed the situation that had been presented to him.

Fourteen showed that he had recovered much of his mental facilities. He was able to socialize. Obviously, Dr. David Daniels's mind-modifying device was no longer functioning.

Although Fourteen had regained some of his mental cognitive capabilities, the name "Skiontia" hadn't elicited any signs of recognition from the young man. That meant that the memories that the mind-modifying device had robbed him of were still missing.

The subject had answered with "just visiting," instead of something along the lines of "just passing through." That, paired with the fact that he was wearing used clothes that didn't fit him, implied that he had received aid from one or more people. There was a possibility that Fourteen had stolen those clothes, but then he probably wouldn't have been so willing to meander around the area in plain view of anyone who might pass by. Even the fact that Fourteen was sticking around town was indicative of the probability that someone had aided him and had given him a reason to stick around in a town that would have had no appeal to the average person.

Vance decided that he would find out who had aided Fourteen and do whatever it took to keep the situation under control.

* * *

The unmarked cube van whose driver had minutes ago stopped to talk to Larry was parked in front of an old-looking brick building. There was a dirty yellow canopy sign with the words "Grocery Avenue" on it in large black block letters. Larry knew that sign merely labeled the grocery store it decorated, and not the name of the street it was on.

Shopping carts were scattered about on the sidewalk surrounding the store. As Larry approached the building, he could clearly see an empty spot designated for those shopping carts—it was complete with a long metal rail and a sign that said Please Return Shopping Carts Here. For a brief moment, Larry wondered which was worse: the laziness of the customers or the failure of the store's staff to do anything about it.

As long as it's a decent enough of a place to have a decent newspaper.

Three-G watched as Fourteen entered the grocery store. He placed a few fancy items that could prove useful—including a long pistol—into the inside of his leather jacket. After he opened a secret door into the front of the van, he climbed out of the passenger side door and entered the building.

* * *

The voices were tearing away at Devon Olson at full force. Nobody else heard the voices tormenting him; they were all in his head, or at least that's what the professionals would have said if he had bothered to see them.

"Look at how useless you are. No wonder she didn't want you."

"You should just kill yourself."

"Pathetic—you thought you had a chance at a normal life."

"Shut up!" Devon growled, not loudly enough for anyone else on the streets of Terrecastor to hear him. "Leave me alone!"

"You can't make us!"

"It's because you're so scared of me. You won't even show yourself!"

"You little worm. You're so worthless. Why should we show ourselves to a disgrace like you? What are you going to do—shoot us?"

Devon distinctively felt the pistol that was tucked away in the back of his jeans and hidden underneath his jean jacket. It was the voices who had told him where to find the gun. It had been buried in a cookie tin under some weeds in the middle of the woods in the middle of nowhere. It was likely a hidden piece of evidence in an unknown crime.

The voices had told him to kill *him* with it, to kill *her* with it: *they* were the ones responsible for his brokenness. He had gotten as far as her house before he had realized that he couldn't do it. He might have been a psychotic fool, but he wasn't a psychopath. Why should he share the hell on earth he was experiencing with those who were blissfully unaware of it?

The voices told him to end the hell—to kill himself with it. The night before, he had spent an hour with the gun in his hand, contemplating giving in. It could all be over in a quick, painless moment, the voices had told him. Yet he had escaped from suicide before, and he could do it again. But the first time had been before the voices.

"I'd shoot you if you were real. But you're not real, and I am, so beat it."

"If we're not real, how did you find that gun, stupid?" "Stupid." "Idiot." "Retard!"

Plugging his ears wouldn't work. When he tried to drown them out with music, the voices twisted the lyrics of the music and changed the very music itself. No distraction could keep the voices at bay. Even when he was asleep, his dreams were twisted nightmares echoing the same phrases the voices haunted him with while he was awake.

"I'll beat you. There's meds out for that. You won't win."

"Go down this alley. A man down there has meds for you! See if that helps you, you loser!"

They were always telling him to do dangerous things. Yet they had been right about the gun, hadn't they been? What harm could there be in quickly walking down the alley?

The alley snaked between Grocery Avenue and Terrecastor Inn, which had recently closed down when a newer hotel had opened up on the outskirt of town. Devon made his way through the dark shadow between the two brick-walled buildings until he was standing next to a tall pine tree at the end of the alley.

Leaning against the wall of Grocery Avenue (or "Gross Ave" as the people familiar with the chain of grocery stores often referred to it as) was a young man in faded jeans and a dirty gray hoodie. He was smoking something, and it wasn't a cigarette or a cigar.

"He has the medication! There it is in his hands!"

Devon couldn't explain how they had led him to the gun, but he figured that the smell of weed in the air had made it easy for the voices to predict the man's presence there.

I hate you so much, Devon internally screamed at the voices. He was about to keep on walking when he had a thought. Smoking drugs sometimes caused hallucinations, and because he was already a crazed schizophrenic, he had no doubt that they would cause him to see things. With luck, he would see the sources of the voices, and that would give him something to pound his fists into. It wouldn't be an effective remedy, but it would make him feel better.

"Hey, man, how's it going?" Devon greeted the stranger.

"Rad."

"Right on. I wouldn't happen to be able to buy some weed off you, would I?"

"Morbar."

Devon looked at the man with disheveled long brown hair in bemusement. "Huh?"

"You get me a Morbar, I'll get you some weed." A dark chocolate bar in exchange for weed was a bizarre barter, but Devon couldn't argue with it.

"Deal. I'll be back in a bit." He turned toward Gross Ave; hopefully, he would only have to endure the voices for a few minutes longer.

"You're an idiot to be trusting that dolt." "Just take the weed—you have a gun." "You're so slow in the head."

* * *

Even though Larry had only entered the building to take a look at a newspaper, he decided to wander around a bit. He had time to kill.

His decision to stick around the store was obviously not aided by the music being played in it. He wasn't sure that slow melancholic country tunes were the best choice for a grocery store, as they didn't project a positive atmosphere. However, the music did fit his mood. His life was probably much worse than anything in those miserable country songs. *Maybe I should write a country song*, he thought with a hint of a smile. He even had a fitting hometown for a country star; after all, Calgary was home to cops in cowboy hats. All that Larry was missing was some whiskey and an old rusted pickup truck.

He was examining the substandard produce department when a young native lad zipped past him while riding on a pallet jack. Larry had enjoyed doing the same thing when he had been employed in a grocery store in the past, so he was amused by the display of unprofessionalism.

"You're pretty good at that."

"I'm the best worker here!" the man grinned. The employee was wearing a halfway tucked in yellow golf T-shirt that hung over a slightly stained wet pair of faded black jeans. The goofy worker's sloppy attire was the final clue that made it obvious to Larry that the management of the store didn't feel the same pressure to pursue the competitive edge that the city stores tended to strive for.

"No, *I'm* the best worker here," said a man who rounded the corner into the department and looked disapprovingly at the youth who was still standing on top of the pallet jack.

The native continued to grin, undaunted by the short blond-haired man who was no doubt his supervisor. "Sure, sure."

The supervisor, whose nametag read "Caleb, Assistant Manager," smiled passively as he turned his attention to Larry.

"How are you doing today?"

"Not bad—you?"

"Alright." The manager gave a nod before heading on his way.

Figuring he had seen all there was to see in the small store, Larry meandered to the cash registers, where he figured he would find newspapers.

Grocery Avenue had three conveyor belts, none of which were occupied by a cashier. But a young female employee stood at a counter underneath a hanging sign that read Customer Service.

There was a customer at her till. It was the same man who had approached Larry on the street earlier. Obviously, he had just bought the cigarettes he was craving. The strange rough-looking character recognized him in return and eagerly greeted him.

"Hey, long time no see!"

"Yeah, it's been forever," responded Larry. The stranger was certainly friendlier than he looked. "You found some smokes, I see."

"Yeah, but it doesn't seem like you found what you're looking for."

"That's because I don't even know what I'm looking for," Larry responded good-naturedly.

"Well unless it's trouble, a good time, or a ride, I'm afraid I can't help you," the man chuckled awkwardly.

"Heh."

"This one is always looking for trouble, aren't you, Chelsea?" The man asked the dolled-up adolescent behind the counter.

Agent Three-G watched as Two-F continued to engage Fourteen and the cashier in conversation. He moved into position. Reaching into the hidden pocket that held his pistol, he removed a clear plastic sticky strip. The strip had been implanted with a transmitter that was invisible to the naked eye and would allow anyone with the right equipment to track it. An undetectable low-quality microphone was coupled with the transmitter in the sticky strip. In general, Three-G preferred not to use such an unreliable sound-gathering device, but the circumstance had required something very indiscreet.

Three-G unobtrusively made his way toward Fourteen.

"Sorry, excuse me," mumbled Three-G as he brushed past Fourteen and stuck the clear plastic strip unnoticed onto the back corner of his oversized T-shirt.

Fourteen absently said, "Oh, sorry," and moved a couple of inches closer to Chelsea and Two-G before continuing the mindless drivel.

"Or is trouble looking for you?" he asked Chelsea.

"Something like that," replied the young blonde as Three-G made his way out of the store.

Larry had hoped to look at the newspaper that sat in a rack next to the customer service desk, but it became clear to him that he wouldn't be able to with a bored cashier watching him intently and waiting. Deciding to avoid the awkward situation all together, Larry exited the grocery store soon after the overly friendly stranger did.

As he left, though, he glanced at the front page of the newspaper on the top of the pile. He was able to make out the date. October 1, 2009. January to October. He was missing nine months' worth of memories.

The young native employee who Larry had seen earlier was then outside collecting the carelessly placed shopping carts. He had a large number of carts chained together. Larry watched as the young man grunted and attempted to move all of the carts.

"Going for a new record. Fifteen!"

"I bet you I can push all of the carts on this sidewalk," Larry said.

"Five bucks!" The employee held out his hand.

Larry shook on it. He didn't have any money, but he knew he would win the bet.

Larry's thinking that day wasn't in vain. He knew he didn't want anyone to find out about his strength or invincibility. Even though he couldn't be certain of how the world would react to his superhuman abilities, he knew it probably wouldn't be good. His fantasies about secret organizations killing each other to get at him and learn his secrets didn't seem unrealistic. Perhaps they would somehow blackmail him into living life in a hidden prison. He suspected that that was the only way a prison would be able to contain him.

He wanted his strength to remain confidential for many reasons, so he chided himself after he made the bet with the Grocery Avenue employee. *I can't be doing this kind of thing too often. I have to make sure that no one is around to see me if I want to have fun with my strength. I suppose this bet won't hurt if I appear to really strain myself.*

* * *

Devon wandered over to the cash register with a king-sized Morbar in his hand. He stuck the strange currency for weed onto the counter, and while he pulled out his wallet, he asked, "What's the damage?"

Suddenly, the girl's face twisted out of proportion, and she started laughing hysterically. "Damage? You're talking to me about damage! You're so damaged it's not even funny!"

Devon closed his eyes and opened them again. The girl's blond hair was then a mane of fire, and her blue eyes had turned into a pupil-less, searing red. *It's just the demons. She probably just said "two nineteen." I definitely need to get some help. Later.*

In order to determine the total a different way, Devon turned his head to look at the till's screen. The screen showed the words "YOU FAIL."

"Here, keep the change," Devon laid a five-dollar bill on the counter.

"Thank you very much," the girl, who was then back to normal, replied sweetly.

Devon smiled. She was so much cuter when she didn't look like a fiery hell-spawn. He glanced at the screen. His total was under two dollars.

"You're welcome."

A deep rumbling voice spoke in his ear and sent shivers down his spine.

"Okay, Devon, you win. We'll have the girl instead. She is much more vulnerable."

There was a flutter of giant wings as Devon observed a creature fly out of his body and toward the young cashier. The beast was as tall as Devon, and with its demonic horned head, it looked not unlike a gargoyle.

"No, get it away from me!" screamed the girl. She held up her arms in front of her as if that would deter the foul creature.

Without thinking, Devon pulled out the gun from the back of his jeans and pointed it at the demon. "Hold it!"

The demon laughed. "Don't worry, you useless piece of trash. I won't hurt you. Just give all of the money in your till to the nice man with the gun."

Devon tried to speak, but he couldn't get any words out.

With incredible speed, the cashier opened up her cash register, threw the whole tray of money inside of a shopping bag, and double bagged it.

Why would the demon have told the cashier to do that? *Unless...*Devon mentally screamed. He had lost all control.

After two minutes of gathering shopping carts, Larry found himself easily pushing twenty-four carts down the sidewalk. He hoped he was showing an appropriate amount of effort. He stopped when the front end of his shopping-cart train edged dangerously close to the end of the sidewalk.

"You need to push it in the store," the employee said.

A light post and a concrete garbage bin on the edge of the sidewalk were in Larry's way. They would prevent him from turning widely enough to get the shopping carts into the store. It was rather unfair of the employee to introduce that new stipulation, but Larry supposed that it had been an unfair wager to start out with.

"It's a tie. I didn't know that I was supposed to push the carts in the store too!"

The employee, who wasn't wearing a name tag and whose name Larry still didn't know, helped him separate the shopping carts so that he could push the first few into the store.

There was another obstacle in Larry's shopping-cart adventure: the door to the store wasn't automatic. He hesitated.

"Just push it in!"

Larry wasn't sure that that was good advice, but he decided he'd take the employee's word for it. He slowly pushed the shopping carts through the door, which easily swung open under the weight of the shopping carts. As he passed through the store's entryway, the motion caused the adjacent exit door to automatically open. *So the door is automatic going out, but not going in? Not the greatest incentive for customers to shop at the store,* Larry thought.

One more door stood in between the shopping carts and their home inside of Grocery Avenue. It was on top of a ramp, and Larry couldn't figure out whether there were any customers nearby. Then he remembered how quiet the store had been when he had been inside. It wasn't likely that there would be someone in his way. Besides, they would most definitely hear him coming. Plus, if customers were exiting the store after going through the cash registers, they wouldn't approach the exit from the space that the door would open toward. He bashed the shopping carts through the second door.

With the stolen cash in one hand and the gun in the other, Devon turned toward the exit of the store.

"Hahaha. You thought you were free, you foolish boy." "You can't run from us."

Frustration, anguish, and panic all had their talons in the schizophrenic man. He wasn't exactly sure what had happened, but he would have guessed that the voices had taken over his body long enough to use him to rob the store—long enough to turn him into a criminal.

"That's right—you're a criminal now. You're scum!"

No! I'm not scum. I'll beat you yet! I'm going to turn myself in and get help. Then we'll see who is the scum!

Just as he was about to reach the exit, however, a long train of shopping carts noisily blocked his path. A gargoyle was pushing the shopping carts.

"I won't let you leave!" sneered the gargoyle.

"I'm sorry," Larry politely told the man who was making his way toward the exit. The customer wasn't approaching from the direction he should have been approaching from. Then Larry saw the gun in the stranger's right hand, and there was definitely a till drawer in the shopping bags in his left hand. *Now this is messed up.*

The robber pointed his gun at Larry. "Out of my way!"

Although Larry wasn't afraid of the medium-sized man with the beginning of a black beard, common sense dictated that if a man with a gun tells you to do something, you do it. Larry intended to cooperate with the thief. Yet he couldn't outright leave his position, because then the employee behind him would see that he had space to bring in his own train of carts and would get in the robber's way.

"There's no need for violence. I'm going to slowly turn around and tell my friend behind me to get out of your way as well."

"I'll never get out of your way. And your puny gun will do nothing to me!"
Devon aimed at the hideous beast's chest and pulled the trigger.

Chapter 5

Something small and metallic hit Larry in the chest and then clinked to the floor. He looked down at the spot where the bullet had hit him. There was no pain, and there was no blood; there was no bullet wound. But a new hole in his T-shirt proved that he had indeed been shot. *Cool, I'm bulletproof.*

The loud rattling of carts behind him told him that the young employee had abandoned the carts to escape to a more favorable location. From that angle, he wouldn't have been able to see Larry get shot, but he would have been able to hear their dialogue and the gunshot.

He looked around to see if anyone besides the gunman had seen him get shot. Someone else had. Caleb was staring in disbelief and crouching behind a wooden display showcasing baguettes. Larry couldn't spot the cashier who had been running customer service when he had been in the store.

I suppose I'll have to talk with Caleb later and ask him to keep this a secret, Larry thought as he looked back at the shooter. He looked just in time to see him squeeze the trigger once more. A bullet struck Larry in between his eyes. He blinked.

Knowing that they were beyond negotiating a peaceful ending, Larry leaped toward the man to persuade him to stop in a more physical manner.

The invincible demon flew toward Devon with lightning speed. In less than a hundredth of a second, Devon's malfunctioning brain told the rest of his body to brace itself. A few hundredths of a second later, his body followed the order—but it had been the wrong command. Even if his brain could have come up with the right response, involving the legs propelling the rest of the body out of the way of the incoming beast, the legs wouldn't have had enough time to completely carry through with the action.

Devon didn't have time to feel the pain caused by being on the receiving end of the tackle. His head connected with the ground a fraction of a second after his body did, giving him sweet relief from the nightmare of consciousness.

* * *

Prefect watched in delight as a fellow fallen angel toyed with the man named Devon. Like Prefect but on a much smaller scale, it was one of the few demons that were able to alter the physical perceptions of men. The cashier hadn't seen any demons, except for the one in Devon's eyes when the man had become possessed. The Will had been extra lenient in that situation.

Prefect knew that everything happened for a reason. He despised how the Lord Most High used the torture the demons inflicted on their victims for his own magnificent glory. God was truly amazing. And annoying.

Of course, most humans wouldn't have attributed what Devon had gone through to a demonic attack. As Devon had said, "there's meds for that." The medication altered the part of the brain that aided demonic intrusion. Humans were getting smarter and beginning to understand the human body that angels had always understood. Prefect and his fellow demons were more than happy to let the humans use the success of their medication to support their unbelief in the supernatural.

* * *

Having the ability to adapt to and control any possible scenario was one of the requirements to work under Vance Mortus, regardless of specialization. Vance had employed men who were fluent in over eleven languages and skilled in the art of manipulating people. Agent Four-C didn't specialize in that field.

Agent Four-C was a skilled computer technologist, which was indicated by the *C* in his name. It didn't matter what kind of computing device he was dealing with—Four-C would know how it worked, how to build it, and how to disable it. He could program a device to hack past any firewall; he could build a robot watchdog that could shake its paw and chase a rabbit. In fact, he could probably design a robot rabbit that could hack past any firewall.

Agent Four-C didn't have a name; he only had a number. His number was a reminder that who he was as a person didn't matter. It was also indicated how he was ranked within Vance's crew. He was the fourth-best computer technologist. However, even the fifth-best agent—the lowest-ranking agent in Vance Mortus's crew—was far more skilled than anyone outside of his clandestine organization.

Unlike a few other agents who worked for Vance, he did not have the ability to read people so well that he could almost know what they were thinking before they knew. But adapting and controlling was part of his job.

There were only three agents in Terrecastor with Vance Mortus. The rest of the people in the organization were in various locations keeping the world stable. Besides Vance himself, Four-C was the only one in the town who had yet to come into contact with the target. So it fell on him to stabilize the bizarre unfolding situation.

From the sky, Mortus and Agent Four-C were able to observe Fourteen stop the robbery using infrared cameras. Their job would become more complicated if the news of Fourteen's strength—if he retained it—got out into the public. Four-C needed to make sure he controlled the information gathered by the local law enforcement, the RCMP.

When controlling a situation, it was helpful to be recognized as someone with authority. The simplest way to accomplish that was with a badge. Before he had been lowered from the helicopter that Vance was piloting, Four-C had quickly grabbed his FBI badge. Even though he was in Canada, it would be more believable to any witnesses for an FBI agent to come down from a helicopter than a member of the RCMP.

He dropped onto a gravel lot that was being used as a secondary parking lot for the surrounding businesses. After identifying Grocery Avenue's large bay door and steel back door as potential exits from the building and making a mental note of the smell of an unrecognizable variant of marijuana, Four-C jogged around to the front.

A young native employee of Grocery Avenue stood at the door. A chain of grocery carts was between the native and the second set of doors.

"We're closed," Four-C heard the employee tell him from the other side of the door.

"FBI," Four-C held up the corresponding badge to the door. "Let me in."

The young man studied the badge for a moment as if he would have been able to tell whether it was a fake. It was fake. However, it was also connected to an ID that would show up in FBI databases. It was connected to a legitimate field officer named Colin Duprey, a man who was on assignment in an undisclosed location.

Seeing that the young man wasn't fully convinced that the five-foot-four man standing before him was an officer of the law, he pulled back his black leather jacket. He revealed the holster of the gun sticking out of his jacket's lining and put his FBI badge back into the same pocket.

"Caleb, the FBI is here!" the young man yelled into the store before he unlocked the door.

"Good man," Agent Four-C said as he stepped into the store. "What's your name?"

"Watson."

"Okay, Watson, I need you to stay here and to not open the door for anyone. I don't care who else shows up, whether it be the police, the store's manager, or owner. Just tell them that a law enforcer who outranks them told you to say that and that the only person allowed past you is Jenny Slater."

"I know who she is," the man said as he turned the door's dead bolt back into place.

While he had been en route to Terrecastor, Agent Four-C had been ordered to bring up information about Terrecastor and its people of interest. As the newly appointed administrator of the local law enforcement, Jenny Slater was automatically a person of interest. Agent Four-C had a much more powerful and piercing search engine than Google, and he dug up almost all there was to know about Jenny Slater. She was so much more than what she claimed to be. Agent Four-C intended to use her decorated past as leverage to contain the situation.

"Good," Four-C responded as he made his way through the entryway. "And try not to talk to anyone not in uniform."

The first body to greet Agent Four-C after he entered the store was the horizontal one of the thief. Fourteen was visible a short distance away discreetly talking with an employee. Four-C could more clearly hear the young cashier behind customer service on the phone with the police. All of their eyes were on him, and he made a show of examining the robber's body and checking his pulse by placing one hand on his neck. With his body between his observers and the robber, he discreetly used his other hand to dig a sedative out of a hidden pocket in his jacket and plunge the needle into the man's arm. *He's not going to be waking up anytime soon. One witness down, and one more to go.* He quickly put the needle back into its hiding spot. *And Fourteen.*

Fourteen and the employee were then approaching him. As he looked up at them, he said, "I'm Agent Colin Duprey of the FBI. This man is wanted for questioning. I tracked him to the store and was going to apprehend him upon his exit—except he didn't exit. Looks like he tried to rob the place. I'm sorry, if I had suspected that this was a possibility, I wouldn't have let it happen. Are you four the only ones in the store?"

"Yes," replied the man whose name tag identified him as "Caleb."

"Okay, I want to question each one of you separately so that your own stories aren't influenced by the accounts of others. Caleb, why don't you go over by that young lady on the phone? Only tell her what you absolutely need to, alright?"

"Okay, sure," Caleb said. He quickly strode away from Four-C and Fourteen.

"The police will likely want to talk to me when you tell them an FBI agent is here," Four-C said to Caleb. "Just tell them my name is Colin Duprey and I'll talk to them when they get here, not before."

"Alright, will do."

Four-C stood up and placed himself between the unconscious man and the gun that lay a short distance away from him. He addressed Test Subject Fourteen. "What's your name, sir?"

"Larry."

So he knows his name. "Last name?"

"Tanner." *He didn't want to tell me that.*

Vance Mortus was observing their conversation from the helicopter. Both the image and the audio of the conversation were being gathered by a hidden camera on Four-C's black thick-rimmed glasses. Vance's computer-like mind would analyze the situation, and he would radio any additional messages over to a speaker that was also hidden in Four-C's glasses. But no additional orders had come so far, and so Agent Four-C knew what he had to do.

"From your perspective, tell me what happened."

"I was bored, so I was helping bring in carts. When I got through the doors, I realized I was in someone's way. I apologized, and when I saw his gun, I told him I was going to get out of his way, but he took a couple shots at me. But they must have been blanks or something, because I'm alive and not bleeding."

Agent Four-C didn't need to have a specialized skill set to know that Test Subject Fourteen was hiding something from him. He had little doubt that there was a bullet hole or two behind Fourteen's crossed arms. *I'm willing to bet...whatever is in my pocket that there are a couple of ruined bullets in Larry's pocket. He wants to sweep the whole thing under the rug. Good. Smart man. We can use that.*

Caleb was in between a rock and a hard place.

He had walked into the scene early enough to see the bald customer get in Devon's way with the shopping carts. Devon was the nephew of the store manager, and he had been one of Caleb's supervisors when he had started at the store a number of years ago. That fact made it more confusing for Caleb to see him carrying a gun in one hand and a drawer full of cash in the other. Was Devon just playing a prank on him?

Well, the joke would be on Devon because Caleb had decided to call the cops on him. He had placed one hand in his pocket on his cell phone.

But it hadn't appeared like Devon had wanted Caleb to witness the prank. There hadn't been a hint of a smile on his face when he had pointed his gun at the bald man. The man behind the carts had looked like he was quite willing to comply. Caleb had felt that drawing any attention to himself would have antagonized Devon and intensified the situation, so he had ducked behind a display in the bakery section and had kept an eye on things.

Devon hadn't sounded like himself when he had shouted at the customer to move out of his way. But that was nothing compared to moment he had pulled the trigger.

Caleb had seen the bullet drop out of a new hole in the man's shirt. But the victim had just stood there, free of any trace of a wound. He hadn't clutched his chest, hadn't collapsed, and hadn't groaned in pain. Caleb had clearly witnessed the second shot, and no hole had appeared in the stranger's forehead.

After the customer had tackled Devon, he had quickly scooped up the two bullets lying on the ground and had placed them in his pocket. He had then headed straight to Caleb and had said, "You tell a soul that you saw me get shot, and I swear I will end you and your family."

Caleb knew questions would be asked, and the idea of lying was repulsive. The whole situation was messed up. How much of it had been real? If it had been real, the only thing that could have protected the customer was God—as far as Caleb knew, anyway.

The situation was so much larger than Caleb. He decided to do what he could about the present and let God take care of whatever was beyond him.

"We'll talk, but I need to get those doors locked," Caleb had said. The bald man with earnest blue eyes had nodded. Caleb had then shouted, "Chelsea, call the cops! Watson, it's safe to come in. Lock the doors!"

His hollering had resulted in a flutter of activity from both places. Chelsea had been hiding behind the customer service counter, and although Caleb didn't know where he had been hiding, Watson had heard him too.

Caleb had looked at the man who had threatened him and his family. Perhaps it was because of the adrenaline that had flooded his system, or perhaps it was because he knew where his soul would end up should he die, but the man's threat hadn't scared him as much as it could have.

He had said in a hushed voice, "I'm not scared of dying, and neither is my family. However, I'll do my best to keep your secret anyway. The thing is, the whole thing is on camera."

The customer's stance had gone from threatening to pleading. "Erase it!"

"Caleb, the FBI is here!" Watson had said.

Caleb had apologetically looked over at the customer. He had known that he couldn't erase the recorded video without getting caught. "I'm sorry. Hopefully, the quality isn't good enough to make out anything important."

Caleb had felt relieved when the man had said, "Fine, just don't tell anybody, please."

So Caleb was between a rock and a hard place. The rock was his promise to the man who had stopped the robbery. The hard place was the fact that he knew he would have to give an account of what had happened.

He had hoped that his questioner would be Jenny Slater, because she was the one RCMP officer with whom he was friends. She was married to his best friend, Ryan. But the arrival of the FBI agent had dissolved all but the tiniest bit of his hope.

Regardless of the turmoil and worry that swamped Caleb's mind, he showed none of it as he calmly comforted Chelsea, who was still on the phone with the police. He smiled kindly as he said, "Thanks Chelsea, you did good. We're safe now."

The emotionally shaken girl was teary, but she smiled back as she continued talking on the phone. "I don't know. I didn't see what happened—I was hiding behind the counter. Here's my supervisor. He can answer your questions."

* * *

A couple of cop cars with flashing lights had arrived at the scene before Jenny Slater had. Yet none of her coworkers had entered the building. Apparently, there was an FBI agent in there who would only allow Jenny Slater to enter the building. One FBI agent. *What the FBI doing in Canada? This doesn't make sense.*

The "FBI" agent had a gun, and that alone had convinced Watson to not unlock the door for any of Jenny's coworkers.

The time was twenty after four in the afternoon. In another hour, the blackness of night would force its way into the sky. By then, Jenny would normally have been done with work. In another hour, she would have probably visited Grocery Avenue to pick up some last-minute groceries to make a decent meal for Ryan and his guest. *So much for getting off of work early today.*

Excitement lit the eyes of the other officers. It was the first reported robbery all year, and it was the only one that had involved a man with a gun since Jenny had started working in Terrecastor three and a half years ago.

"If you don't hear from me in twelve minutes, come in. Until then, don't let anybody in or out without my permission. Don't worry—I'll be back soon," Jenny said with a smile to Corey, the officer who was still trying to negotiate his way past Watson.

Upon seeing Jenny, Watson opened the door. "Hey, Jenny, we've been robbed!"

"I know. Thanks for guarding the door for me. We'll get a report from you, and then I'll tell Caleb to let you off of work early today, alright?"

"Sounds good to me," Watson grinned. He was such a likeable young lad.

"Keep the door unlocked. The only ones allowed in are other cops." Jenny moved quickly and confidently into the store. There was no way to know what she would be seeing next, but if anyone was competent enough to handle it, she was.

Devon Olson lay unmoving on the ground. Next to him was a mess of coins and bills—and a gun.

Why would Devon rob Grocery Avenue? Jenny was familiar with all of the troublemakers in town, and Devon wasn't one of them. She knew who the young man was because she had spotted him stumbling home after a late night at a bar a couple of times, but she didn't think he was the sort to resort to violence.

But the sight of Devon was overpowered by Larry's presence next to him. Worry blanketed his face. "Hello, Jenny. I didn't mean to hurt him."

What was Larry doing there? Was he just there by chance, or was he somehow connected to the robbery? Everything about Larry seemed strange, yet Jenny couldn't see anything but innocence in his eyes.

"Hey, Larry. It's alright. The paramedics are on their way. Where are Caleb and the FBI?" She would eventually try to understand how Larry fit into the situation, but first, she needed to deal with the man who had stopped Watson from letting in the RCMP.

"We're in here," said a short man with buzz-cut black hair and glasses. As he spoke, he stepped out of a small office that was at the top of the six steps located at the front of the store. "We were just reviewing the footage of the robbery. Come on in."

"I'd rather talk out here first," Jenny refused steadily.

"My name is Special Agent Colin Duprey of the FBI. I outrank you, Jenny Slater of Seattle, so this is my investigation, I'm afraid," responded the self-proclaimed hot shot in the black leather jacket. Jenny judged the man to be in his mid-thirties. Although he was adopting a casual stance, his tone of voice conveyed that he was not the least bit intimidated by Jenny and that he knew exactly what he was doing. That didn't bother Jenny nearly as much as his word choice had. *Jenny Slater of Seattle. He knows where I moved here from, and that's supposed to mean something to me. I wonder if he knows...It certainly would explain why he asked for me specifically.*

The man who claimed to be Colin Duprey continued. "As I have already told Mr. Larry Tanner and these fine young employees, I wish to talk to everybody separately. The culprit of this robbery is of great interest to the FBI and is connected to sensitive information. We should only be five to seven minutes."

The whole situation was bizarre. Jenny cautiously followed the man into the office.

"Hey, Jenny," greeted Caleb as he looked over his shoulder toward her. He was sitting in an office chair and was angled toward a monitor that displayed a full-screen view of Grocery Avenue's exit.

Caleb would forgive her for not saying hello back. Instead, she addressed Colin. "Do you have your badge on you? An identification number?"

"Shut the door, please," the man plainly said as he reached into his jacket.

"You didn't answer my question." Jenny didn't take her eyes off of Colin, as there was a possibility that he was reaching for his gun. If he was, in fact, reaching for a gun, Jenny didn't want the cashier who was watching from customer service to witness the violence that would follow. Plus, it would stop Larry from entering the room and giving Jenny two people to deal with. After all, Jenny couldn't shake her gut feeling that the two people were connected. Two mystery men had appeared in the small town in the same twenty-four-hour period, and their appearance had been punctuated by an attempted armed robbery. It couldn't have been a coincidence. Jenny closed the door behind her.

A second later, Colin had a gun trained on Caleb, and Jenny had hers trained on Colin.

Chapter 6

Jenny and Colin steadily focused on each other. Each one of them was trying to get a read on the other. Neither fear nor menace was present in Colin's eyes. Instead, confidence shone through as he began to speak.

"You're not going to kill me, Jenny."

"If you pull your trigger, I'll pull mine," Jenny answered coldly.

"Oh, of that I have no doubt. But you won't kill me. You'll shoot me somewhere that won't instantly kill me, and since you've already sized me up as someone you could take on, you'll apprehend me."

"I've killed before," Jenny said.

"I know, but you won't kill again. That's why you left the CIA, wasn't it?"

Jenny mentally flinched. Who was this man, and how did he know so much? "What are you talking about?"

"Caleb, did you know Jenny was in the CIA?" Colin said without taking his eyes off of Jenny. Caleb, who was sitting frozen in fear due to the gun against his hair, managed to say a soft "no."

"She was one of their top agents, but she then she met Jesus and had enough of all of the lying and killing, am I right, Jenny?"

Only a few trustworthy people knew her specific sentiment against the pitfalls of her former job. Most of the people who knew her from her past life were merely aware that she had fallen in love with a Canadian and had moved away to be with him. Of course, those who knew about both her history in the CIA and her newfound faith would have probably been able to put together the pieces. But the man had more conviction than someone who was just making assumptions would have had. He knew too much, and although Jenny desperately wanted to find out what else he knew, she also needed to get Caleb out of harm's way as soon as possible.

"What do you want?"

"I eventually want for both of us to put down our guns and have a dialogue as people on the same team. But first, I need Caleb to do something for me. Caleb, I want you to hit 'play' for me. Jenny, I would watch the screen carefully if I were you."

Jenny felt it was safe to assume that Colin wasn't going to shoot Caleb if she took her eyes directly off of him, so she slightly swiveled her pupils to focus on the monitor, still keeping Colin in her field of vision.

The security footage had very poor quality. Everything was pixilated, and the feed only displayed a little more than one frame per second. Jenny was aware that the majority of the other video cameras around the store were either horrifically out of focus or not operational at all.

Larry, whose bald head made him easy to identify, entered the scene behind a chain of shopping carts. It wasn't as easy to identify Devon Olson, but it was obvious that he had a gun in one hand and a double-bagged drawer of cash in the other. In one frame, Devon had his gun fixed directly on Larry, and in the next, Larry was in midair with his arms around Devon.

"Okay, hit pause," Colin Duprey said as the screen showed Larry walking away with his hand in his pocket. "When I talked to Larry, he said shots were fired, but he didn't tell me where the bullets ended up. Caleb, where did those bullets hit? Your life depends on your ability to tell me the right answer."

Caleb was only silent for a short moment before he said, "There's no need for violence. Why don't you just investigate the crime scene to find out?"

"What do you say, Boss?" Colin said as he used the hand not holding his gun to retrieve a cell phone from his pocket and flip it open.

A new voice came from the cell on speaker phone and entered the conversation. *"You can take your gun off of him now, Colin. This man isn't afraid to die. But this isn't over. Jenny, my name is Vance Mortus. Does that mean anything to you? Yes or no."*

The voice was robotic in nature, and the words sounded like they almost could have been words that the man had programmed the computer to say. Yet the name Vance Mortus assured her of the fact that the voice she was hearing was very real in nature.

Even within the CIA, the name Vance Mortus was only known by a privileged few. Or perhaps it wasn't a privilege to know that if Jenny failed to complete her assignment, the CIA would have had no choice but to contract a man named Vance Mortus to get the job done. He was a man who didn't make mistakes—a man who was willing to do whatever it took. Vance Mortus would have had no qualms about killing thousands of innocent people for the greater good. Regardless of what was going on in the office, Vance Mortus's involvement meant that something that would have a massive global impact was at stake.

Jenny lowered her gun as Colin lowered his. "Yes."

"I'm sitting in a helicopter with guns pointed at Grocery Avenue. If you don't answer my question correctly, Caleb, I will kill that young cashier. I can see her through the window. I will also kill the group of law officers outside of the building. Yes or no, Jenny, am I a man who is capable of doing something like that?"

She knew that Vance Mortus would do it without feeling a smidgen of regret. "Yes."

"We don't have time to investigate, Caleb. You have seven seconds to tell me where the bullets ended up, or many innocent people will die."

A large timer appeared on the computer's screen.

"7...6," The timer counted down. Caleb closed his eyes, no doubt in prayer. *Come on Caleb just tell him what he wants to know!* Jenny thought.

"5...4..." Caleb's eyes were still closed. Jenny's heart beat painfully in her chest. Vance was only doing this for the greater good. What was taking Caleb so long? Jenny spoke with all of the authority she could muster.

"Tell him!"

"3...2..." Silence from Caleb.

"1...0"

"Time's up."

Chapter 7

"You pass," said Vance Mortus. His emotionless words caused a tidal wave of relief to wash over Jenny. Vance's next words hit Jenny with a tidal wave of a much different nature. *"But if you tell anyone that Larry Tanner is bulletproof, you and whoever you told will die. Jenny, that goes for you too. We'll be in touch. Proceed, Colin."*

"Here's what's going to happen," Colin said without missing a beat. His animated voice was a welcome change from his superior's creepy tone. "You're going to let the other officers into the store, and you're going to conduct this investigation like it was just your run-of-the-mill robbery. Caleb, you will say in your report that the robber took shots at Larry, but nothing more than that. Jenny, you will defer to Larry's story that the shots were blanks. After all, it is the story that makes the most sense given the lack of bullet holes.

"I will leave the premises with the unconscious body, and you will tell the others that it's because I have reason to believe he has been poisoned and that I need to get him to a facility with the antidote as soon as possible. The helicopter that Vance is piloting has been disguised as an air ambulance, and when the paramedics arrive, they will help me load him on it.

"It's unfortunate that the store's video recording system is full of bugs and that the security footage has been corrupted beyond recovery." Colin retrieved a device that looked like a memory stick from the computer's USB port and put it in his pocket before going on. "Larry Tanner escaped from a top-secret research facility. Before we take him back in, we need to find out who aided him and make sure nobody else knows his secret. Jenny, see if you can persuade Larry to give away who helped him."

That little tidbit of information about Larry unraveled a huge knot of confusion in Jenny's mind. Yet it didn't give her relief, as her husband was intertwined with the series of events.

A new knot formed in Jenny's stomach as she realized that her husband would be the next one put through Vance's cynical test. There was the very real possibility that Ryan would not "pass" the test.

Thinking quickly, Jenny did her best to grasp some control on the situation. "It would help me to know how you know that Larry is receiving aid."

"Among other reasons that I won't disclose, there is the fact that he's wearing clothing that he didn't have in his possession yesterday. He has no money, so either he stole it or someone helped him out. Since he isn't fleeing the area, it is much more likely that someone supplied the clothing."

"Alright, I have an idea. Leave it to me." Jenny gave Caleb a sympathetic smile before exiting the room. There was a reason that Jenny was one of the privileged few who knew about Vance Mortus's existence: she used to be one of the CIA's best agents. In an instant, an idea had formed in Jenny's mind. She would save her husband.

She quickly radioed the other officers and told them to proceed into the store. She made sure to tell them to leave the FBI agent alone and said that she personally wanted to question Larry Tanner, the key witness.

It was fortunate for Mortus that Agent Three-C was facing Jenny and Larry. Otherwise, he would have missed the subtle look of confusion on Larry's face when Jenny approached him and said, "Hello, Larry. I'm Sergeant Jenny Slater. I was wondering if you could answer a few questions for me." Larry's face told Vance that he was already familiar with Jenny and that he was confused about why she was introducing herself to him. The Slaters were the ones who had aided Larry Tanner.

There was no doubt in his mind that Jenny's plan was to contact her husband and to tell him not to say anything, as Caleb's silence had seemed to keep him safe. If Ryan Slater heard that from his wife, Vance's method of getting a reliable response from the man would become time-consuming, and Vance always got the job done in the quickest and most efficient way.

He immediately radioed commands to his agents. "Two-F, Three-G, find Mr. Slater and find out what he knows. Four-C, stop Jenny from telling Larry or Ryan anything."

* * *

Ryan would have liked to have hung out with Larry all day, but there was this strange thing called "work" that had gotten in his way. He was on his way out to retrieve another load of logs from the same site he had been at the day before.

His cell phone started to ring in its somewhat-hands-free device: his cup holder. He pressed "answer" to accept the call via speakerphone.

"Hello, Ryan. You should pull over." The voice was male, unfamiliar, and straightforward.

Ryan started to shift down—not to pull over, but to make it easier for the white cube van that was fast approaching from behind to pass him.

"Who is this?"

"We have a mutual acquaintance. Larry Tanner." The idea of learning Larry's last name hadn't even crossed Ryan's mind the whole time he had been with him, but Ryan was certain that the voice was referring to the miracle man.

"What's this about?" His question was only answered by the cube van's honking. Despite his slow speed, the van hadn't taken the opportunity to pass him. *The caller must be inside that van. I'm guessing that whatever this is can't wait.* "Fine, but there aren't really any good spots to pull over right now."

"Two kilometers up, there's a turn off to a small oil rig. Turn just inside of that."

"Okay, but this had better be quick." Ryan didn't have a whole lot of patience for people without a whole lot of patience.

Once Ryan had safely parked off of the gravel road and on the grass-filled trail to the oil rig, he wasted no time and hopped out of his truck. Upon seeing a tall rough-looking man standing outside of his own vehicle, Ryan said, "How can I help you?"

"It's very simple. All you have to do is answer one question, and then I'll let you be on your way. There is something special about Larry Tanner. What is it?"

There isn't anything special about Larry. God protected him by making him super strong. I promised him I wouldn't tell anybody. Not knowing exactly how to respond, Ryan said, "Well, he seemed to be suffering from some amnesia when I was talking to him."

The intimidating man smiled and said, "Is there anything else special about him? Something much less common than some memory loss?"

"Last night, he was wandering around in the middle of the night in the middle of nowhere. I'm not sure if that's more special than memory loss or not. If you give me your phone number, I can tell Larry to get in touch with you. I'm sure he can answer your questions about him better than I can."

"You're hiding something from me, and I know why. Larry asked you to keep it a secret. That's good—you should keep it a secret and not tell anybody. Except for me. You see, last night, Larry escaped from a top-secret research where he was a test subject for an experimental drug. The effect the drug had on Larry's body was exponentially more powerful than the effect it was supposed to have had. That is the only thing I managed to gain from his doctor before he passed away. Larry stabbed him in order to escape, you see. He killed him.

"I bet you didn't know that Larry is a very dangerous man. Not too long ago, he almost killed a man at the store called Grocery Avenue. He made a nice young lad named Caleb promise not to say anything, either. Do you know the man?"

Ryan nodded, trying to take in everything that the stranger was telling him. It was so bizarre—so unreal. It was like something straight out of a movie. Had he not seen what Larry's body was capable of, he likely would have assumed that the man in front of him had been sent by some friends to play a prank on him. If only the situation were just a practical joke.

"Caleb broke his promise to Larry and told us how violent the man had become. But we already knew that much. But there's more to Larry than just a streak of violence, and we need to know what it is in order for us to help him out. We are monitoring Larry at the moment, but before we take him in, we need to know what else the drug has done to Larry's body. That way, there won't be any surprises that will end up hurting Larry or us. What has this drug done to Larry's body, Ryan?"

Ryan had promised to keep Larry's secret, but he hadn't known about him then—he hadn't known that he was violent.

The tan rough-looking man almost had goaded the truth out of Ryan with his very convincing story, but there was something more than his physical appearance that made Ryan suspect his motive. Why had he needed to pull over for this—why hadn't the man just talked to him over the phone? And besides super strength, what effect could the drug have had on Larry that would have scared the man so much? It was almost as if the man knew the answer to the question he was asking Ryan.

"I'll tell you, but I just want to phone my wife first." If Larry really had almost killed a guy in Gross Ave, then his wife would either know about it or would want to know about it.

"Stop," the man said while Ryan's hand was in his pocket searching for the phone that he had forgotten in the cup holder of his truck. "Your wife is one of the people monitoring Larry. If you phone her and start asking her questions, Larry will be tipped off, and who knows what will happen. You said earlier that this had better be quick. Well I want this to be quick too, but you're the one stalling and not telling me what I want to know."

The man was certain that Ryan knew something, which was another indicator that the man probably already knew the answer to his question. There was no reason for Ryan to break his promise to Larry and to tell the man something he already knew. He shrugged as he took his empty hand out of his pocket and spoke as casually and convincingly as he could.

"Larry was the fastest runner I have ever seen in my life. So the effect the drug had on him was probably like steroids or extra adrenaline or something. I saw him running down the road last night, and he knew it wasn't natural, but he didn't want to be treated any differently because of it, so he made me promise me not to tell anybody. But if you're going to help him, I suppose there's no harm in letting you know. Now, can we both be on our way?"

Ryan was about to turn away and start walking toward his truck, but the man's next question came too quickly. "How fast was he running?"

"I don't know. It was dark, and it was hard to tell exactly how fast he was running. Probably should try not to get in a footrace with him."

"You drive for a living. What speed was he going? Tell me your best guess."

At least seventy kilometers per hour, but I can't tell him that. Instead, Ryan said, "I'm sorry. I'm not good at guessing the speeds of people sprinting in the middle of the night. I won't be able to help you further. Have a good day."

Ryan was about to turn around again, but the gun the man had retrieved from the inside of his jean jacket persuaded him not to. The man looked as serious as the long bulky pistol in his hand. "We aren't done here. You're going to tell me what you're hiding from me, or I'll put an extra hole in your head."

For the second time in less than a day, Ryan felt fear and adrenaline saturate his body.

Ryan only had two options: he could tell what he knew or be shot. There was no way he could stall by understating Larry's strength anymore.

Closing his eyes, Ryan prayed, hoping for the luxury of a few more seconds to think before he was shot. *I don't want to die, especially not for keeping a miracle a secret. But I promised Larry…Oh, Jesus, what's the right thing to do right now?* The prayer had a calming effect on Ryan, and then an answer came to him. Before Jesus was crucified, he had stood through a mock trial. People had made up false testimonies against him. However, instead of rebuking them, showing them another miracle that would prove that he was God, or even saying something witty to get himself out of the situation, Jesus had remained silent. Ryan hoped that that portion of scripture didn't cling to the foreground of his mind because he was meant to die like Jesus had. But he knew that regardless of the case, God wanted him to stay silent.

Ryan kept his eyes closed, dropped his head, shook it, and waited for the bullet.

"Your friend Caleb had the same response at first. Then we told him we would kill a bunch of innocent cops if he didn't spill the beans, and that's when he gave in. I'm going to be honest. I have no interest in killing a bunch of cops. But I *am* an honest man, and I *will* shoot you. You're already a dead man because you didn't tell me what I need to know. But there's worse news. I'm going to tell my team to kill an innocent person for every minute that you remain silent. As a little extra motivation, we're going to start with your lovely wife. The minute starts now."

No, God, no! Not my wife! Do You still want me to be silent? Jenny and I will end up in Heaven together, but that won't be true for everyone this man kills! Please, God, make this man stop! Or give me a sign! I need you so much now, Jesus. Tears streamed down Ryan's face. *No, God, I'm sorry. I can't do it. I'm too weak! He knows about Larry anyway. I have to tell him! If You don't want me to, then You'd better stop me Yourself!*

Ryan spoke with a clarity and firmness that surprised even him, "Stop the clock. God protected Larry."

"Really. And how did God do that?"

Ryan opened his eyes. The man was closer, and the empty hollow end of his pistol was more vividly staring him in the face. "I hit Larry with my truck going full speed. Larry didn't get a bruise. He ran as fast as a car."

Agent Two-F sighed. Ryan had failed.

Chapter 8

Then again, Agent Two-F knew that there was no such thing as passing. Caleb's and Ryan's fates had been sealed as soon as they had found out about Larry Tanner's secret. Agent Two-F knew that anybody would reveal any secret given the proper manipulation.

However, Vance Mortus had reminded them that as long as Larry was alive, it was less of a risk to keep his friends alive as well. A happy secretive Larry Tanner would be easier to manage than an upset invincible Test Subject Fourteen looking for answers and willing to retaliate. Vance's team would wait until they were certain that Larry was dead for good, and then they would take care of those who had known about him.

Ryan's insistence that God had protected Larry told Agent Two-F that he didn't know about Larry's connection to Dr. Daniels and Skiontia. His Christian bias would be beneficial to both of them. After all, a Christian revival wouldn't happen just because a small-town truck driver claimed that God had worked a miracle. Verification of this particular claim would not be permitted.

"You pass," Two-F said, lowering his gun. "Here's what's going to happen. Whenever you want, you can call your darling wife and tell her the horror that you just went through. She knew it was coming, but she was powerless to stop it. I'm sure she's furious at my team and me, and you may be too. However, you won't tell anybody else what you have just gone through. Here's the thing. Larry's secret is so huge that we can't afford for anybody to find out about it. The world simply isn't ready for it.

"You might believe that it was a miracle of God, but let's say someone more evil than I got to you and started demanding that you talk. They won't see the answer the same way. You once promised Larry that you wouldn't tell anybody, and now you must promise me the same thing. If we find out that you've told anybody about Larry's abilities, even Jenny or Caleb who know about it anyway, then I actually will kill you and whoever you told. Do you understand me?"

Ryan's eyes weren't filled with anger or hate, but with sadness and relief. "Yes."

"Good. I have one more question before you're free to go. Do you know of anyone else who is aware of Larry's secret? Be honest—I will find out either way."

Ryan shook his head. "No."

Two-F could see that the man was telling the truth. So much for the easy part. It was then time to acquire Test Subject Fourteen. He replied to Ryan. "Excellent. Have a great life."

Ryan took that to mean that he was free to go. Seeing the man put away his gun and stride over to his cube van, Ryan wasted no time getting into the safety of his own driver's seat. Before he could put his truck into gear, he desperately needed to talk to his wife. Her life had been threatened, and just hearing her voice would do wonders for him and would reduce his skyrocketed blood pressure.

A text message from her awaited him. "Will be working late today. Don't worry about me. Larry probably won't be coming with me tomorrow. He's fine. Love you."

Without the beautiful, soothing music of Jenny's voice, they were just words with very little meaning. He dialed her number. There was no answer. Unlike Ryan, Jenny always stayed professional and refrained from taking personal calls while she was on duty, especially if she was with others.

After the beep, Ryan left a message. "Hey, honey, could you phone me as soon as you get this? Love you."

Ryan texted Jenny to make doubly sure that he would hear from her, and he considered driving back to check on her. His job seemed of little importance at the moment. But what had she said in the text? He had been too distracted to comprehend any of the words, so he read it again. "Don't worry about me."

Smiling, Ryan put down his phone, gave a prayer of thanks to the God who had protected them, and shifted his truck into reverse. Everything was in God's hands, and Ryan felt that the worst of it was over, at least for him. As he guided his long empty trailer onto the deserted gravel road toward the jobsite, he said a prayer for Larry Tanner and wondered if he'd ever see him again.

* * *

In addition to the darkness, the night had brought a crisp, strong breeze. Larry had little doubt that the chilly air would have bothered him nine months before. Leaves dancing in the noisy wind assaulted him as he inserted the key to the Slater residence into their door.

In the store, Jenny had given him the key to her house and her address as if he hadn't already known where she lived. Why had she pretended that she wasn't already familiar with him? She had appeared as though she had desperately needed to tell him something, but something about the FBI agent's presence was stopping her. Larry was anxious for answers, but he was also aware that Jenny had a tremendous pile of work to take care of due to the robbery.

At least it seems as though my invincibility is still a secret. Caleb must have kept silent. But what did the cameras show?

At least Larry had the presence of mind to ask Jenny if he could use her computer. He had nine months' worth of missing memories that he desperately wanted to recover. Larry doubted that his memories would be worse than the painful past he had recalled after the last night's dream.

Larry booted up the machine that sat in the couple's living room and typed in the password that Jenny had given him.

Once in the Internet browser, his fingers automatically typed out "Facebook.com" before his mind remembered why. It was a website he had visited often, although he had used it more to play games than to keep in touch with his friends. According to what he could remember, Facebook had recorded that he had over one hundred friends. Yet none of them were *good* friends. The ones who weren't merely extended family members or former coworkers were high school friends who he hadn't bothered to keep in touch with after graduation.

Muscle memory led Larry's fingers to enter in his username and password. An error screen popped up and said that the e-mail address Larry had typed in wasn't connected to any Facebook account. Larry reread his entry, making sure he had correctly typed out all of the characters. He had—that was definitely his e-mail address. Perhaps he had merely typed in the wrong password. A few failed attempts later, Larry was frustrated and gave up on trying to log in.

His next destination was Google, where he typed in his own name. There were many Larry Tanners, and he was not one of them. As far as the Internet was concerned, he didn't even exist.

His brother, Jason Tanner, showed up more easily. It must have been rare for a shark attack to lead to death, and so of course articles had been written about it.

None of the news articles allowed Larry to come any closer to recovering any of the nine months' worth of missing memories; he couldn't recall a single event during the time that he was reading about.

The vibrant and loud chime of the doorbell penetrated Larry's frustration. He wondered if he should answer the door. It wasn't his home, and its owners weren't around. Larry really didn't feel like encountering any more strangers that day.

Again, the doorbell rang. Larry crept to the door and peered through its peephole. He recognized the man on the doorstep—he was the stranger he had met on the street and in the store. Had he resorted to asking door to door for directions? Larry opened the door.

"Hello, Larry. I owe you an explanation."

"Explanation?" Then Larry realized that the man had said his name. He didn't recall introducing himself to the stranger; Larry suddenly became incredibly interested in whatever explanation the man had for him.

"You have a secret strength. Why don't we go talk inside? I don't want anyone overhearing this."

"Yeah, uh, okay. Come in." The two retreated into the sound barrier of the Slater residence. Once the door was shut, Larry asked, "Who are you?"

"My name is Jared McDonald. But my part in your story isn't really worth mentioning. I understand Jenny was going to give you a ride to Edmonton tomorrow, right?"

Larry nodded. Obviously, Jared had talked to Jenny—was that why the man knew about Larry's super strength? It was possible, but Larry was betting otherwise.

"You have experienced some memory loss, haven't you?"

How could he have known that? Jenny didn't know that about him. Ryan, maybe? No, Jared obviously knew something about him that hadn't come from either of the Slaters.

"Yes, how did you know?"

"You no longer live in Edmonton. I couldn't see any reason for you wanting to go there unless you still had memory issues."

"Still?"

"Let me start at the beginning," Jared removed his shoes and moved toward one of the nearby couches in the living room. "You'll probably want to sit down for this."

Larry sat in a chair opposite the couch that Jared had made himself comfortable on.

"Have you heard of Dr. David Daniels?" Jared quizzed.

"His name sounds familiar—why?"

"He is the man who has led the scientific community through a plethora of world-changing breakthroughs in technology in the last decade. When the people on the news say that scientists have discovered a way to slow fingernail growth, he's the guy they are talking about. Well, his latest research project involves developing a way to strengthen the body. You were a part of that project."

"So there's more people out there like me?" Larry inquired, trying to take it in. "How did I get involved in this research project?"

"This latest research project is top secret. It needs to be, because it involves human testing and procedures that wouldn't normally be authorized. But Dr. Daniels earned a fortune through his scientific discoveries. He had the money he needed to keep it a secret. Just outside of Terrecastor is a facility named Skiontia. It produces many of the pharmaceutical drugs that Dr. Daniels has developed. But what the public doesn't know is that underneath the production facility is a top-secret research facility in which he does his more sensitive research. You were a test subject in that research."

Larry narrowed his eyes slightly. So he had been a part of some illegal setup? Jared had anticipated his response, and he went on to say, "Don't let yourself think ill of Dr. Daniels. His discoveries have saved millions of lives in the past and have greatly increased the quality of life of those living. He only does tests on those who are fully aware of what they are getting themselves into and have agreed to do it.

"When Dr. Daniels's team found you, you had just lost your job. You were very alone and very depressed. Perhaps you were suicidal when they found you like other test subjects have been. I don't know, but that seems to be the kind of people who Dr. Daniels likes to work with. He likes giving people who have lost all will to live a purpose. You were promised a large sum of money for participating in the research project for a few months. You graciously accepted.

"Dr. Daniels's project wasn't making much headway until you came along. Something about your DNA accepted the serum he was developing, and your skin became incredibly resilient. Yet the effect the drug had on your skin was much greater than the effect Dr. Daniels had anticipated. He was distraught when your new skin demanded more work from your heart, which caused it to go into overdrive. If you weren't being carefully monitored, you would have died of a heart attack. Your heart failure a few months ago caused part of your mind to fail as well. That is likely why you are having problems with your memory. You were on life support for a while, a machine doing the work that your failing heart couldn't. Dr. Daniels didn't want you to be connected to a machine for your whole life, but in all of his genius couldn't fix the situation using conventional means. A heart transplant wouldn't have saved you, as your body would have been too hard on any new heart.

"Dr. Daniels decided to turn to another means to save you. He never only has one project on the go, and while he was developing a way to strengthen a person's skin, he was also working on a way to strengthen one's muscles—all of the muscles, including the heart. It was a risk to give you this drug that was still in its development stages, but you agreed to it. You said you would rather be dead than spend your whole life trapped in bed, kept alive by a machine. So the experimental treatment was administered.

"The treatment worked, and you were able to operate independent of the machine. However, the drug had one nasty side effect. It kind of turned you into a monster. You lost control of your brain facilities and started raging like the Hulk. Nobody could pin you down or stop you. Your skin couldn't be pierced by any needles so you couldn't be restrained by any conventional methods. I'm sorry to say that although you didn't kill anyone, you seriously injured people. Out of self-defense, one doctor was forced to stop your heart using defibrillator paddles. She saved her own life, but ended yours, supposedly."

Jared paused for a moment to let Larry take in his explanation. The story was fit for a science fiction novel, and Larry would have rejected it altogether if it hadn't fit so nicely with what he had experienced in the past day. It explained his tough skin and his super strength, as well as his memory problems. What it didn't explain, however, was why he hadn't drowned when he had woken up on the bottom of Terrecastor Lake.

"You were aware of the secrecy of the project, and at the beginning of your involvement, you agreed to make a Facebook status saying that you were deleting your Facebook account, taking an extended vacation, and traveling the world to get your mind off things. That way, your extended family wouldn't start asking about your disappearance. Dr. Daniels's team couldn't just send your possessions to your next of kin without raising questions, so they sold off what little personal belongings you had. All of that was apparently explained in contracts you signed before you began. I wasn't told how much money you would be given, but it must have been substantial for you to have agreed to all of that.

"Anyway, when the time came for your body to be incinerated—er, cremated—your body didn't burn. Nor did it deteriorate like a normal dead body. It was as if another jolt of electricity to your heart would have revived you. But Dr. Daniels's crew was too scared to do that, of course, because they didn't want to revive the incredibly dangerous and potentially unstoppable monster you died as. So Dr. Daniels decided to send your body off to a distant location where it wouldn't be discovered. However, your body started to move on its own while in transport, so a panicking helicopter crew dumped you into Terrecastor Lake. And you can pretty much fill in the rest from there."

Larry sat in silence for another five minutes, trying to take it all in. All of it was so bizarre, but the pieces were fitting together. Finally, he said, "Okay, where do you come into this story?"

"Dr. Daniels hired the organization I work for to track down your body. He told us that if you were alive, we needed to make sure that the secrets you held remained secrets. When I engaged you earlier, I simply wanted to assess whether you had control of your mental facilities. We are incredibly fortunate that you do. However, your body also maintained its superhuman strength, and that is an issue."

For a moment, Larry pondered what kind of methods Jared's organization would have used to make sure that the secrets he held "remained secrets." Yet whatever strategies were in place were necessary ones. "So I'm alive and sane. What's your plan?"

"I don't need to tell you that I can't force you to do anything you don't want to do, but I want to strongly suggest that you come with me back to Dr. Daniels. If anyone can return you to normal, he can. Whatever the case, the man owes you a great deal of money as far as I'm concerned, and he has the ability to get you back on your feet."

Getting back on his feet was exactly what Larry needed to do. As much as he liked being invincible, what he really wanted was some semblance of a normal life. From the sound of it, going with Jared to see Dr. Daniels was the only way he would achieve that.

"Okay, Jared, shall we get going?"

* * *

Dr. Daniels's smile was broad, and his eyes were opened wide in ecstatic excitement as he personally greeted Test Subject Fourteen.

"Welcome back, Larry! It's so good to see you alive and in such great shape!"

"Yeah, well, you know. I guess I have you to thank for that." Although Larry was attempting to smile, his own enthusiasm was practically nonexistent.

Reading between the lines, Dr. Daniels received the message loud and clear: Larry knew that his "great shape" was his fault. Still, he carried on the conversation in an upbeat manner.

"It seems as though I am responsible. If only I know how it turned out like this. I greatly appreciate your choice to return. I hope to do what I can to set things right."

"What are you planning on doing?" Larry's curiosity was less passive than it had been when he had first entered the project. Unlike the Larry Tanner who had stood before Dr. Daniels months before, this man had the power to do something devastating if he heard something he didn't want to hear. There was no doubt that if Dr. Daniels hadn't been a proven genius, Vance Mortus wouldn't have entrusted him with the task of dealing with Fourteen.

"Well if you don't mind, I plan on seeing if I can get any answers from your body as to why it adopted such abnormal attributes. As to what I can do for you after that, well, we can discuss that. It depends on what you want to do with your life. If you're still planning on getting a business degree, I will uphold my end of the bargain and pay fully for your education and living expenses for the next few years. That is, of course, if you haven't changed your mind."

"Throw in a cash bonus for killing me, and you have yourself a deal." Larry said it lightheartedly, but Dr. Daniels could tell that he was quite serious. He could also tell by listening to Larry and by looking into his eyes that he was a soul who was lost and without a set ambition. Even at that moment—perhaps even more than before—the young man felt powerless to do anything but give in to the cards life had dealt him.

Of course, the doctor had never meant for him to re-enter the public realm. If things went smoothly, Larry's ambitions—or lack thereof—wouldn't matter because he would be dead. Dr. Daniels took no pleasure in that fact. But his own life had dealt him a hand of cards that had allowed him to help out humanity in a huge way, and sometimes sacrifices needed to be made for the greater good. Yet there was no way that Larry was going to find that out.

"Yes, I believe that's only fair. I'll throw in an extra million dollars." A trivial million was far less than what he had paid to hire Vance Mortus.

Technically, Vance and his small team had already completed the task Dr. Daniels had contacted them to complete. Test Subject Fourteen was back in the secret basement of Skiontia under the watchful eye of Dr. Daniels, who had abandoned all of his other projects to fully study the resurrected test subject. Yet Vance Mortus's involvement with Larry Tanner wasn't over. The mission wouldn't be complete until Larry Tanner was dead for good and all of the civilians who knew the truth behind his secret were taken care of.

Chapter 9

"This is a camera I'm going to lower down your throat," Dr. Daniels explained. Unlike the autopsy, Dr. Daniels didn't have the privilege of experimenting on an unresponsive body. Fortunately, Larry's curiosity had yet to cross the border into suspicion. "This tube that it's attached to is going to deliver a substance into your stomach, to see how it will react to your stomach fluids."

The adrenaline that had kept Dr. Daniels energetic over the evening had worn off, and the intensity of the situation was beginning to drain him. It was then three in the morning, and Subject Fourteen gave no indication that he had any trace of tiredness or fatigue in his body. Time had flown by as Dr. Daniels had personally conducted a plethora of tests, all of which had ended in fascinating yet unenlightening results. But he would have time to study the test results more closely later—hopefully soon.

Saliva was the only bodily excrement that Dr. Daniels had been able to gather from Fourteen. The test subject had been unable to provide any urine or stool samples. Although Larry had confessed to eating brunch and to swallowing his share of lake water, he admitted that not only had he failed to feel hungry or thirsty many hours later, but he also hadn't needed to relieve himself.

"What kind of substance is it?" Larry asked passively.

"It's a mixture of xyloascorbic acid, or vitamin C, and a number of different electrolytes not too different from the ones found in your typical sports drink," Dr. Daniels lied. The truth was that the smallest portion of the fluid he was about to drain into Larry contained enough poison to exterminate a herd of buffalo.

Dr. Daniels doubted that his first attempt to kill Larry would work. Earlier, when he had tried to retrieve a sample of the man's stomach fluid with a completely inert specialized plastic device, Larry's stomach acid had instantaneously disintegrated the device. Test Subject Fourteen's body wanted to remain in exactly the same state, and it held up against whatever Dr. Daniels threw at it—including electricity. Defibrillator paddles would not pause Larry's heart a second time.

As he had feared, the poison failed to do anything to Larry. The liquid disappeared into Larry's stomach acid. There was no sizzling, no gas bubbles formed, and there was no evidence of any chemical reaction when the two liquids connected. It was as if the poison had entered a liquid black hole. It had gone from existent to nonexistent on impact.

It was as if God Himself were protecting Larry. Dr. Daniels despised the thought as soon as it entered his mind. Although he would have classified himself as agnostic, he held that there was a very tangible and physical explanation behind everything in nature. Disappearing poison went against the law of conservation of energy, which stated that energy couldn't be created or destroyed. Simply saying that God had done it was not acceptable to Dr. David Daniels.

Yet so far, it was the only explanation that made any sense. Although Dr. Daniels knew that yesterday's witchcraft was today's science, he couldn't shake aside the notion that there was a higher power deeply involved in Larry's preservation. That would make killing Larry even more difficult.

* * *

Cashiering at Grocery Avenue wasn't a boring job, but it was a mindless one. It took Larry little effort to transfer the skills he had gained at the grocery store he had worked at in Calgary to the store he then worked at in Edmonton. So while Larry robotically scanned items and instinctively punched in numbers and codes, he had ample opportunity to let his mind wander.

School was finally out for the summer, so Larry had taken on full-time hours. The pay was just high enough that he could afford his rent and the bare necessities like food and bus passes. He couldn't afford to drown his grief in alcohol.

Larry had a feeling that he was going to become somewhat of a workaholic for a while. It wasn't like he had anything else to do: he had no homework over the summer, and he hadn't made any close friends during his year at the University of Alberta. At work, he kept to himself for the most part; there wasn't too much motivation to spark up conversations with the other employees during the short periods when he had the opportunity to do so.

Larry wished that he had gone to school at the University of Calgary or even at SAIT instead of at the University of Alberta in Edmonton. At least in Calgary he might have actually kept in contact with his old high school friends. Instead, those friendships had dimmed right after graduation because his postsecondary workload had allowed him very little free time to gain anything more than acquaintances. Perhaps if he had had at least one close friend, he would have had someone to help him get over the loss of the only remaining member of his immediate family.

As he waited for another customer, Larry miserably sprayed down his conveyor belt with glass cleaner and then wiped it off with paper towel. He was dead to the task: only working on routine.

His mind was focused on how he could go on. The accident had only been a few months ago, and the funeral was still fresh in his mind. More members of his extended family had made the trip from Ontario and the United States for his mother's funeral than for his father's, which had not been much earlier. Of course, his cousins, uncles, aunts, and other distant family members had felt obligated to invite him to stay with them. Although those offers had been sincere, no one had expected Larry to actually take them. He was an independent adult; he already had a place to stay. Staying with those relatives would not have been better than staying with strangers. No, Larry would have to endure the grieving process by himself.

Larry added more packing bags to his bag rack, and his thoughts meandered toward his mother and her religion. He wondered about whether she would have still been alive if they hadn't argued in the car. He doubted it. Larry believed in a god, but he didn't believe in the same God that his mom had. All Larry knew was that there was a higher spiritual being out there playing around with the lives of innocent people. He most certainly couldn't have been a God of love as Christians would have had him believe.

A young Inuit woman approached his till. Larry recognized her—he wasn't so distracted by his thoughts that he couldn't see that it was her second time in the store in the last hour.

Smiling at the lady, Larry said good-naturedly, "Forget something?" That verbal engagement didn't require any additional brain usage or attention. A repeat customer was quite commonplace, and Larry had often recited that phrase.

"Sort of," the young woman replied, returning his customary smile. "My husband just phoned me and asked me to pick up smokes. Could I get a Morx Light King-Size please?"

As Larry obliged and retrieved the pack of cigarettes, the thought of asking her for her ID never even crossed his mind, at least not until she was halfway out the door. The mistake didn't seem worth remedying. She had looked twenty-two or twenty-three to Larry, and she had said that she was married. No big deal.

No big deal, until the store manager called him into his office. The all-too-familiar sickening feeling in his stomach returned as he lost his job for selling tobacco to a minor.

The grocery store was a shrinking image behind him as he walked home. When there was no one close by, he couldn't help but cry out in anger, "Why do You hate me, God?!"

* * *

There, that's better, Prefect thought in satisfaction as he reintroduced Larry to more bitterness toward God.

However, Prefect hadn't felt the least bit victorious after this latest endeavor. The Will had allowed Prefect to show Larry the place that Prefect had wanted to show him. But Prefect had only wanted to do so out of its own volition. In the end, nothing Prefect did could be solely out of its ambition. It was all because of The Will—because of the Glorious One, the Sovereign Ruler. Prefect cried out in the tongue of angels, attempting to curse God in a language that had been designed to worship Him.

* * *

Although Larry had accepted the dismal history that Jared and Dr. Daniels, the flood of memories brought on by his dream intensified his feelings of depression. With every recovered memory, there was a new reminder of how worthless his life was.

Larry hadn't been searching for a job for long before Dr. Daniels's team had found him. Larry had received a phone call a couple of hours after he had submitted his résumé to a website that had distributed it to potential employers. Apparently, an organization's computers had selected Larry as an eligible candidate for a research project for which he would be handsomely paid. The words the caller had said were words he would have expected from a robotic telemarketer or from a scam in an e-mail. However, there had been a real lady on the other side of the phone, so Larry had been compelled to take the offer seriously.

Larry's first big hint that it was no average research company was the fact that the lady who had phoned him had arranged to go to his own apartment for an interview. His misgivings about taking part in a top-secret project had been easily overweighed by his eagerness to make ten thousand dollars each month. Adrenaline and eagerness had caused the rest of the hiring process to become somewhat of a blur. Affirmatives had been given, lines had been signed, and Larry had found a new summer job.

Larry finally had a rough idea of where he was, but he hadn't the first time he had taxied to Skiontia. After spending four and a half hours in the back of a windowless van, Larry hadn't been sure whether he was even still in Alberta. Terrecastor and Skiontia were not even three hours outside of Edmonton, so his previous trip had been lengthened. That had been an additional precaution—an additional deception.

Deception. Larry didn't know why that word had come to his mind. During his time with Dr. Daniels, the man hadn't seemed like the sort who would lie to get what he wanted. Sure, he had adopted measures to keep his project a secret, but there was nothing cynical about that. Larry was living proof that the project's confidentiality was a necessity.

I wish I had just had a normal life—or even that I had access to one in the future. You'd think that being invincible would make me feel like I could do anything I wanted to do.

As he sat up, Larry thought, *Well, right now I feel like I'm probably not going to be able to get back to sleep.* Larry wasn't sure how he had managed to fall asleep in the first place.

He was still wearing the same jeans and bullet-punctured shirt that he had been wearing the day before. Lifting his shirt collar, he sniffed underneath his shirt. *I guess I also don't sweat or have body odor. Plus, I don't have any hair that can get greasy, so I probably won't have to shower as much.*

He no longer had the morning pangs of hunger, so there was nothing stopping him from beginning his day.

In the corner of the room, there was a neatly folded set of clothes for him. There was a navy-blue fleece turtleneck, a long-sleeved shirt, and a pair of track pants. Larry opted for those items over his own clothes, as they were free of bullet holes and looked like they would be more fitting for his high-energy movements.

I guess I'll need to go outside to really let loose.

Dr. Daniels was already up when the staff member in charge of monitoring the video feed of Larry Tanner phoned him to say that Larry was getting dressed. A member of Vance Mortus's team had been monitoring the same feed and had notified him as soon as Larry had woken.

Even though it was somewhat irritating to have Mortus constantly watching over his shoulder, it was comforting to know that someone would be able to compensate for his own weaknesses. Despite the fact that he was a world-renowned genius, he certainly wouldn't have been able to deal with Larry on his own.

Dr. Daniels threw on some clothes, grabbed a prepared satchel, and rushed out of the door. He was nearing Larry's own door when it opened.

"Good morning, David. What time is it?" Larry asked upon seeing him. Dr. David Daniels had insisted that Larry use his first name to make the process even the slightest bit comfortable for the test subject.

David glanced at his custom-designed wristwatch. "About ten after three in the morning."

"Really? Why are you up?" Larry asked.

"I could ask the same thing of you," Dr. Daniels redirected as casually as he could.

"I couldn't sleep."

"Same here. I actually just retrieved a few things that are going to help me. Can I offer you a book to read? Tea, maybe?"

"No, thank you. I don't think that would help. I was actually just planning on going for a walk."

As long as he doesn't intend on walking outside, thought Dr. Daniels. *But the more I make it seem like he doesn't have much freedom, the more he'll want to leave.*

"That sounds like a good idea. Since there isn't much to see around here, some of my staff like hopping on a treadmill and throwing on the TV. It helps to clear the mind."

"Actually, I would rather just walk outside."

"I'd feel more comfortable if you stayed inside," Dr. Daniels talked slowly, stalling for time. A tracking device and a bug had been woven into Larry's shirt. Mortus had supplied them so that he could constantly keep tabs on the invincible man. "That way, if something goes wrong with your body—say, some unusual side effects—we'll be right here to treat it."

"I'll be fine," Larry said nonchalantly.

"Oh, you're very likely right. Just in case, why don't I give you this cell phone?" Dr. Daniels pulled a cell phone out of the satchel he was carrying. Like Larry's clothes, the cell phone's purpose was to transmit Larry's location and words. "It's my spare cell phone, so it has my other cell phone's number in it. Just call 'me' in the contact list if you need anything while you're out. In fact, why don't you keep it? I've never really needed to use it anyway."

After saying thank you, Larry took the phone.

Okay, Vance, it's your show now.

* * *

Silently, a shadow that was invisible in the night sky glided over the briskly walking man. When the man's pace picked up to an abnormally fast run, the shadow easily kept up. The blanket of leaves and branches in the heavily wooded area did not deter the shadow's keen eyes.

Chapter 10

It was a cloudy night, and the stars were having problems peeking through the cloud shadows in the sky. The few stars that managed to reveal themselves were blocked from Larry's vision by the branches of the towering spruce trees that surrounded him. Although it was hard for Larry to see in the darkness, he figured that would play to his advantage as no one would be able to spot him.

In fact, why don't I have a bit of fun? Larry launched himself upward.

He was planning on coming to rest at the very peak of the nearest tree. Once he hit his target, Larry experienced the flaw in his plan. Tips of trees were not designed to support the weight of humans.

"Whoa!" Larry exclaimed as he landed on the highest branch of the tree. Except he didn't actually *land* on it. The broken tip of the tree in his hand did little to slow his descent. The branches he crashed through on his way to the ground didn't help much either.

Larry felt a mixture of twigs and mud press against his bare back. At some point during the trip down, his shirt had managed to obtain a substantial tear. He stuck his hand inside of his pocket and pulled out a very broken cell phone. *Oops.*

Vance watched as Larry tore off what remained of his shirt, unknowingly casting aside technology worth as much as a couple hundred T-shirts. The cell phone and the wires woven into Larry's track pants had also been rendered useless by his failed attempt at climbing a tree.

However, there were still eyes on Larry. There was no escape.

* * *

Ollie might not have been the sharpest saw on the shelf, but he knew from experience that when he was high, he had to keep his interaction with the public to a minimum. That was why he had recruited a young man to buy a Morbar for him the day before. When he had heard gunshots coming from inside Gross Ave, Ollie had decided that the best course of action was to vacate the area.

He sat with his back against the trunk of a tree and let his mind gravitate back to the hard, firm ground of reality.

"Whoa," Ollie said to himself at last. "That was the trippiest one ever." Ollie was no stranger to hallucinations, yet his visions had never been so vivid and so distinct. In fact, his feet were resting on the solid dirt of reality, but the memory of his latest hallucination seemed to be clearer than the forest around him.

"You know, man, you should really lay off the drugs," Larry insisted to the man sitting in the air that was saturated with the pungent odor of what seemed to be burned weed.

"Oh, so now you can see me," the man dressed in a dirty gray hoodie and jeans responded.

How out of it is this dude, Larry thought. "Why wouldn't I be able to see you?"

"Don't know, man, that's what I thought. I was watching you awhile, and now you see me."

Very out of it. "I just got here, man. You really need to quit doing drugs, it screws up your mind." There was no doubt that if Larry had encountered that man a few months before, he would have merely walked past him wordlessly—he would not have wanted to cause any trouble. Yet Larry had become uncharacteristically bold, and the transformation was obviously a result of his altered flesh.

"How'd you get here so fast?"

"What do you mean? Get here from where?"

"I don't know what it was. It looked like you were in the hospital or somethin'. You were talking to some man."

"A doctor?"

"He kind of looked like a doctor. Except his hair was all messy."

Larry looked at the druggie's disheveled hair. *You're one to talk.*

"You said that you wanted to go to the bottom story. He was like, 'This is the lowest level,' and then you were like, 'Don't try to pull one over on me, bro. I remember. I wanna go downstairs,' or something like that."

Without knowing why, Larry's brain tried to organize the information it was receiving at that moment. There was a man heavily under the influence of drugs who had no doubt hallucinated something prior to Larry's arrival. Perhaps he still was seeing things. Larry had never seen the man before, yet the man had said that he had just finished watching him in the hospital. Perhaps the stranger in the woods had known him during the period of time his memory was still missing. Maybe he had been involved in Dr. Daniels's secret project at one point, and maybe the "hospital" he had mentioned was actually the facilities hidden underneath Skiontia.

Larry asked, "Do you know who I am?"

"Nah, man," a degree of worry flashed on the man's face before he casually continued. "Should I? Are you, like, some famous dude?"

"I hope not," Larry responded, mildly amused. "But if I bump into more strangers having dreams about me, then maybe I should start looking for an agent."

"Hey, man, you're...real? Like, you're not a hallucination, are you?" His tone of voice implied that he hadn't been convinced that Larry was a real person until that moment.

He's just figuring that out?

Larry stuck out his hand and introduced himself.

It was unfortunate that The Shadow wasn't able to listen to Larry's conversation with the stranger in the woods. Agent Three-G was once again stalking Test Subject Fourteen.

The rustling of the nippy night breeze through the branches created enough noise to cover Three-G's careful footsteps. When he finally drew close enough to listen, he could hear the man Larry had referred to as "Ollie" sharing his life story. They were in the middle of the woods. Larry was shirtless, and the air stank of a variation of weed, and yet the two were talking as casually as they would have at a house party.

When Larry eventually said farewell and left, Three-G pulled out his tranquilizer gun and aimed it at Ollie. Even though Three-G hadn't heard Larry reveal anything confidential, it was still possible that he had before Three-G had arrived. The agent needed to make sure. He pulled the trigger.

* * *

What is the Most High up to? Prefect wondered. The words Ollie had spoken to Larry hadn't merely been some drug-induced hallucinations: they had been prophetic.

It was no accident that many demonic religions (a few of which Prefect had had the pleasure of starting) involved the use of drugs for "spiritual encounters." By doing so, the cursed God-blessed race rolled out the red carpet for Prefect's team.

Of course, the One Who Is Worthy of All Praise would sometimes choose to take advantage of a man's altered state of mind and would personally show up. Prefect knew that that had been the case with Ollie. There had been a host of evil spirits accompanying the man, but none of them had had the ability to prophesy. Even if Prefect hadn't had the ability to see the future, he would have still known that Vance Mortus would have his hands full as a result of the meeting between Larry and Ollie.

* * *

Larry had nothing better to do, so he was once again wandering next to Dr. David Daniels toward the cell that served as his bedroom. He couldn't stop thinking about his conversation with Ollie. Somehow he had spent a great deal of time visiting with the "hippie" in the woods. The random meeting had been bizarre, and so it had easily fit into the pattern of his recent days. Larry smiled. At least his encounter with Ollie had been entertaining. He was glad he had decided to go for a walk.

Before his meeting with Ollie, Larry wouldn't have considered himself an outgoing guy. *Perhaps I should be. I could probably meet all sorts of interesting people.* It took only a moment for Larry to discover the flaw in this plan. The more time he spent around other people, the more likely it was that his secret would somehow be exposed. For example, the day before, he had only spent a moment around other people before he had begun easily pushing a heavy load of carts and repelling bullets.

He couldn't risk anyone else learning about his secret. For all he knew, Caleb, Ryan, and possibly Jenny could be locked up somewhere simply because they knew too much. Not knowing what had brought on that thought, Larry had the sudden urge to go see if they were okay.

"May I offer you a fresh set of clothes?" David interrupted his train of thought. "It looks like you were having a bit of fun. Is that marijuana I smell? Don't tell me that you have a secret stash somewhere and that you're not sharing any with me."

Larry would have had no problem explaining to Dr. Daniels why he had returned wearing one less article of clothing. However, he wasn't certain he even wanted to mention Ollie. *Ollie probably wouldn't want me to. He was hiding in the middle of the woods for a reason. I need to redirect the conversation.*

Then Larry noticed Dr. Daniels's messy hair, and a seemingly silly idea came to his mind. *Whatever, I'll just go for it. Afterward, I can just blame it on a stressed mind not working properly.*

"I want to go to the bottom story."

"This is our lowest level," David quickly replied.

Wow, that's just what Ollie said he would say. Then again, that's also a predictable response, because we are probably on the lowest level. Might as well say my next line. What was it again?

Larry spoke the words that came to him. "You can't hold the wool over my eyes. I remember."

Was that a look of shock on David's face? Was it fear? Whatever it was, it quickly disappeared. "What is it that you remember?"

This will probably work. He's momentarily too distracted by my faulty memory to care about the fact that I smell like weed. Hopefully, I can come up with something good before the next time he asks me about it.

"I want to go downstairs."

"I suppose that if you are intent on going there, I should probably go with you. After all, the whole thing is my fault," Dr. Daniels seemed distressed for the first time since Larry had met him. Before, he had had a childlike excitement akin to that of a youngster in Disneyland. But at the moment, his face resembled a kid who had been caught red-handed stealing from the cookie jar.

"I'm listening," Larry said bitterly. He assumed he would have reason to be at least bitter after he heard about whatever Dr. Daniels had to confess.

David turned away from Larry and to his left, and then he turned a key in a door that Larry had assumed led to an empty cell identical to his own. He followed David into the room that was exactly what it had appeared to be.

"I have one request. Please hear me out. Then you may take whatever action you feel is necessary." The distraught doctor retrieved a cell phone from his pocket and punched in a series of buttons.

Larry couldn't mask his surprise as a section of the wall parted and revealed the inside of an elevator. David perceived his surprise, and he looked more horrified than anything else.

Dr. Daniels had made a fatal error. He had tried to control the situation without fully assessing it. Perhaps anyone else, and especially someone as tired as he was, would have made the same mistake. Well, Vance Mortus wouldn't have; he didn't have emotions like fear that could cloud his judgment.

Unable to get past the fact that his loose tongue had just threatened the security of the entire world, Dr. Daniels said, "You…didn't know about the elevator. You don't remember anything."

"I remember enough." He was bluffing, but Dr. Daniels was finally managing to keep his fear in check, and he could clearly see that Larry didn't actually remember "enough."

"How much do you remember?"

"How about we take this elevator down, and you hope that the story you tell me matches what I know." There was no backing out. To the pit they would go.

Chapter 11

Perhaps he could get away with telling only a partial truth. Dr. Daniels started his improvised story as he and Larry descended.

"I am responsible for your memory loss. Because of the sensitivity of the nature of this project, I couldn't risk anyone finding out about it, so I hooked you up to a machine that would erase any memories of this place."

"Can this machine give me my memories back?"

"No, but"—Dr. Daniels paused, not to think, but to give Larry the impression that he was thinking—"perhaps, for your sake, that is a good thing."

"What do you mean 'for my sake'?"

"Well, part of your missing memories include an incident where you essentially turned into a mindless monster and did something you would regret if you could remember it. Your missing memories are protecting you from a great deal of emotional stress, and you already have more than your share of stress as it is."

Larry's anger level had not increased as much as it could have. For the moment, he was quiet, and apparently trying to process all of the information Dr. Daniels had presented him with.

However, when Larry stepped into the room with the mind-modifying machine, he became livid. "You were brainwashing me!"

Dr. Daniels's worst fears had come true. He wasn't sure exactly how Larry's memories of the pit had returned, but he was scared for his life.

He knew that he had no one but himself to blame for the mess. He had invented the mind-modifying machine, and he had given Larry his super strength; Dr. Daniels would accept whatever the monster he had created had in store for him.

"I trusted you!" Larry roared as he leaped toward the machine. Using his fists as sledgehammers, Larry pulverized it. "This thing shouldn't exist!"

Dr. Daniels didn't have a lot of conversation options. Saying that the machine was a necessary evil would only infuriate Larry more. He could only think of one thing that could possibly calm Larry down. With as much sensitivity in his voice as he could muster, Dr. Daniels said, "Larry, look at the wall."

With fury in his eyes, Larry whipped around and looked where Dr. Daniels was pointing. A steel bar stuck out of the cement wall. "What about it?"

"Do you remember doing that?" Dr. Daniels inquired.

"No, but what does it matter? You were still mind controlling me! You had no right!"

"Would you kill one man to save ten?"

"Maybe I should kill you," Larry retorted with an angry look.

"Then you would be no better than I am," Dr. Daniels said. "You may want to kill me to stop me from doing this evil thing again. I am willing to brainwash a few to save thousands. Maybe you're right—perhaps this machine shouldn't exist. But do I deserve to die for trying to do the right thing?"

"I'm not going to kill you. But I don't care what it takes—I'm going to make sure that this machine never gets used again. Are there any more of them?"

"No, I only had this one made."

"You're lying!"

Dr. Daniels shook his head. "I don't even want to think about what would happen if the mind-modifying machine fell into the wrong hands. That's why there is only one, and that's why the only remaining blueprint for it is in my head."

Larry didn't know what to think or what to do. Standing in front of him was a man who had not only almost killed him, but who had also kept him as a mindless, obedient zombie. He had taken away his free will; in a sense, he had removed part of what made Larry human. Somehow, David had deluded himself into thinking that all of that was alright!

Larry knew that he wasn't the only one who had fallen victim to Dr. Daniels's evil methods. That's what all of this was: it was evil. The man in front of him looked like an innocent man who had nothing but good intentions, but what he had done was the work of Satan himself.

Larry knew that it would take little effort for him to end David's life. All it would require was a single punch.

But Larry knew for certain that he couldn't kill another person. So the question of what to do with the deranged doctor remained.

He couldn't turn David in to the authorities without revealing his own involvement with the man. That's what it came down to: justice or keeping his strength a secret.

Perhaps the day would come when his secret would be exposed, and on that day, Larry would bring to light David's dark deeds. But for the time being, Larry wasn't ready to face international attention.

"If I find out you are doing any more research at the expense of another human being, I will break both of your arms. Do you understand me?"

When David nodded, Larry continued. "Here's what's going to happen. You will give me my old set of clothes, and I will leave. You will leave me alone. You will not have me followed, or I will break both of your legs. Agreed?"

Given the situation, Dr. Daniels had done as well as could have done. It was true that Vance would have done a better job if he had taken Dr. Daniels's place, but Vance had not seen the need to give him special orders.

However, it was apparent to Vance that the doctor's involvement in the deteriorating situation had come to a close. But there were still a number of options available that would keep the situation under control.

Vance radioed David Daniels's earpiece. "Tell him that you don't have the authority to keep him from being followed."

After his message was relayed, he continued. "Tell him that it's not in your control, and that if he doesn't like it, he can speak with me."

A few seconds later, Vance was taking directly with the ticking time bomb via Dr. Daniels's cell phone. "Larry Tanner, you are a risk to international security, and so you will be monitored regardless of your wishes."

"No, you will leave me alone, or else you will end up losing Dr. Daniels!"

Dr. Daniels was a valuable asset to the world, and Vance Mortus would have preferred not to lose him as collateral damage. It was a good thing he knew that Larry was bluffing. "Your willingness to hurt the scientist proves our need to monitor you. However, if you complete specialized training that will allow you to operate in public without making a scene, I will promise to leave you alone."

There was silence. Larry would be able to tell from the lack of emotion in Vance's voice that killing the doctor wouldn't benefit him. Test Subject Fourteen's next words hardly surprised him, for Vance had known the outcome of the conversation before it had begun.

"What kind of training?"

"You will have the most qualified trainer in the world. The sooner you get trained, the sooner we can both get on with our lives."

"I'll do it."

There had been no question in Vance's mind. There were variables to be weighed and played, but Vance's calculations didn't leave any room for error. He would personally train Larry. After that, he would kill him.

Chapter 12

"I don't like that look that you have," Jenny said reproachfully.

Rebecca Hiltman looked past a strand of her red hair to her friend in the driver's seat. Despite Jenny's stern expression, she grinned. "What look?"

Shifting the car up a gear, Jenny emphatically replied, "The look that tells me that you are actually looking forward to all of this!"

By "all of this," Jenny meant the fact that Rebecca's planned visit to her friend had become an extended work assignment.

She and Jenny had been best friends since they had met as CIA recruits. They were such good friends, in fact, that Rebecca didn't even mind that Jenny had excelled at everything she had done, risen through the ranks, and left her in the dust. That didn't keep Rebecca from feeling a healthy amount of envy toward her friend. Her own duties weren't dull, but Jenny had always gone on the more exciting missions.

Jenny had just finished explaining to her that "whether she liked it or not," she had a task so important that failure would result not only in her death, but also in the deaths of countless others. Finally, she was on a mission that fully catered to her inner desire for an exciting, adrenaline-filled adventure. That was the whole reason she had joined the CIA in the first place!

"Well, I guess part of me *is* looking forward to this. I mean, a bulletproof man. Like, wow. How could I not want to see that for myself?"

"Becca, you don't know Vance Mortus like I do. It seems like he's on our side, but he's really on his own side. He knows that Larry Tanner's secret must be kept a secret, and he will do anything to accomplish his goal. *Anything.*"

Rebecca's grin faded when she saw that she wouldn't be able to easily brighten her friend's spirits. It wasn't normal for Jenny to be that solemn—at least not the Jenny she had known. Part of Jenny's carefree spirit had disappeared when she had gotten married.

Rebecca wished that that were the extent of the changes she saw in her friend. A fatigue like she had never seen before was apparent on her friend's face. It was more than just tiredness brought on by a lack of sleep, although Jenny's makeup didn't fully disguise the bags under her eyes that told Rebecca that a lack of sleep was part of it. The tone of voice that Jenny had used when she had said "anything" the second thing that had hinted at the fact that she had experienced firsthand the lengths that Vance would go to.

"What happened, Jenny? You don't seem like yourself today," Rebecca prodded with an added sensitivity in her voice.

"I just told you what happened," Jenny said. "We are teaming up with a psychopath in order to cover up a secret that could have huge international implications."

"But you've covered up secrets like this before, right? Secrets you couldn't even share with me. That's part of our job. You're good at it! You told me yourself that you could look into the eyes of the antichrist himself and not blink. But something has gotten to you, the fearless spy."

"I did say that, didn't I?" Jenny managed a small smile. "I said that right after I became a Christian. I have God on my side, and He is bigger than any situation. There's no reason for me to be afraid of anything as long as I trust in Him. Thanks, Rebecca, for reminding me of that."

Rebecca wasn't going to let Jenny change the subject, especially not to religion! "What happened, Jenny?" she asked again.

"Things change when you get married," Jenny began. "Everyone has people they care for, but not in the same way. I love my husband so much, and now I have something new to worry about. Before, when you were my only best friend, I cared about you as a friend. But we both had our own separate lives, and we were living for ourselves. I had no problem going on dangerous missions because I was only putting my life on the line. Sure, there were other lives on the line as well, but no one I was in a relationship with. Not a deep relationship, anyway. You know what I mean? There are relationships where you care about people, and you would be sad if they died. Then there are relationships where if something bad were to happen to them, it would be like getting stabbed in the heart and not ever being the same again."

"I know what you mean. Go on."

"I guess a big part of it is that now I know exactly what's in store for us after death. Anyway, you want to know what happened. Yesterday, after that whole incident with Larry happened, I got home from work to see my husband alive and well, and you can imagine how relieved I felt."

"Why wouldn't he have been okay? You're the one who knew about Larry. Vance had no reason to hurt him."

"He knew something," Jenny answered softly. "He was the one who originally found Larry. I could tell right away that he was hiding something from me, but I didn't press him to tell me. Whatever it was, it wasn't doing him any harm. If anything, he seemed happier. But last night was different. I came home, and the first thing he did was give me a hug. He didn't want to let go. When he eventually did let go, I could see tears in his eyes. Something had happened to him. Vance had gotten to him—he must have. Ryan wouldn't tell me what happened, but I could just tell."

Rebecca let a moment pass before asking, "Does he know you're CIA?"

"*Was* CIA, and not as far as I know."

"So what are we going to tell him about why I'm sticking around for more than just a short visit?"

"Simple," Jenny said. "You used your connections in high places and requested to be transferred to Terrecastor so that you could work with me."

"Right, because I seduced Larry into wanting to keep me around," Rebecca nodded.

"I didn't say anything about seducing him!"

"You said that Vance wanted me to become really good friends with him, right? The closer the better. Is he at least cute?"

"He's nothing special."

"Hmm…" hummed Rebecca as she contemplated the meaning behind Jenny's response.

"And it's okay if Larry doesn't ask you to stay, because unbeknownst to the rest of us, you're actually a CIA agent. Because you were in the area and you know me, you were assigned to help the CIA's man train Larry. As soon as his training is complete, you're planning on returning to Seattle."

"It may be hard for me to return to my old life if I end up being Larry's girlfriend, don't you think? After all, the whole situation seems to be quite delicate, and I don't think I'd want to break Larry's heart."

"Rebecca," Jenny said emphatically. "I know I'm no longer your senior in rank so I can't order you around. I know that you can do whatever you want. But I want you to trust me as a friend: things will go smoother for both of us if you do as I say. Your life could very well depend on it."

Normally, Rebecca would have paid minimal heed to anyone who had tried to boss her around without the authority to do so. However, Jenny had always been there for her, and even though they were the same age, Rebecca had looked up to her as the older sister she had never had.

"Got it."

"It would also be safest to assume that Vance Mortus and his team will be monitoring us twenty-four-seven, no matter where we are or what we're doing. He is a control freak. This car is probably already bugged, and they've probably heard everything we have said."

Some of the color drained from Rebecca's face. "So then Vance heard you warning me about him and his bugs."

"I didn't say anything I wanted to hide from Vance," Jenny said. Rebecca imagined that her words had been directed toward Vance as much as they had been toward her. "Vance already knows my sentiments about him, and there's no use hiding it. It's not as though we were conspiring to disobey his orders, which is what he is really concerned about."

Jenny looked over to Rebecca, and seeing that she had successfully introduced her friend's nerves to a healthy dose of fear, she continued. "But on the bright side, Becca, think about all of the catching up we can do. You were always jealous that I didn't get to spend that much time with you, and now we can spend so much time together that you'll become sick of me."

"What makes you so sure that I'm not already sick of you?" Rebecca jested before the two started laughing.

* * *

When Larry had left the Slaters' home with Jared, he had left a note saying that he had found another ride to Edmonton. Before the couple could ask any questions about his return, Larry had said that he simply needed a place to stay awhile and that he didn't feel like talking about what had happened. As he should have expected, the Slaters had nevertheless graciously welcomed him into their home once more. That time, however, Larry could sense some unease in their demeanors. The difference in Ryan was more noticeable. The previous morning, Ryan had witnessed his strength and had continued on like he had just watched a good movie. But the truck driver's casual disposition seemed more guarded.

Guarded or not, Ryan threw an arm around Larry as soon as he saw how depressed he looked. Larry was more than depressed; he was completely broken.

Ever since his mother had died, Larry had floated along in life, guided by the currents of other people's desires for him. His life lacked meaning or value, which had made him the ideal candidate for Dr. Daniels's unethical research project. But his life had become a burden for other people, too. He wondered if the world would be a safer place if he didn't exist.

"We're here for you, Larry. Stay as long as you need," Ryan had said. It had meant the world to Larry. Dr. Daniels appreciated Larry because of the value he gave his research. Ryan's tone conveyed to Larry that the Slaters believed that he had worth beyond what he could contribute to science.

The stranger, who Larry had mentally nicknamed "the eyes in the sky," had promised that his personal trainer would find him sometime within the next two days. Larry was thankful that he had yet to meet the trainer, as he was still pulling himself together.

He spent his morning in much the same way as he had spent the previous morning: he wandered around Terrecastor, trying to sort his mind out. By the end of his walk, he had gained some composure. He was an invincible man, and he would take on any trials that life had for him with a brave face.

When Larry re-entered the Slater residence, any boldness that his bodily strength had given him had completely disappeared. Jenny had returned with the guest she had picked up from the airport. The guest happened to be the most the most beautiful woman he ever had the pleasure of meeting.

"Hey, I'm Rebecca," said the attractive woman who was sticking her hand out to greet him. She had short red hair and sparkling emerald-green eyes.

"I'm Larry, nice to meet you!" Larry was certain that if he had not had abnormal skin, he would have been blushing as he shook her hand. Yet her smile managed to give him a nervous, excited feeling in his gut. It was the first truly positive feeling Larry had experienced since he had seen Dr. Daniels's mind-control machine.

Rebecca's presence in his life gave him a renewed passion to live. It was time to start living for himself. The fact that he was so important to the security of the world should have granted him special privileges. Couldn't he ask for anything he wanted and receive it? Larry didn't know what he wanted in the long run, but for the moment, he knew he wanted to get to know Rebecca.

"Can I get you two something to drink?" Jenny asked, barely denting Larry's train of thought.

"Do you still have that cinnamon apple tea?" Rebecca asked. "I brought you even more from the States in case you don't."

"Thank you! For some reason, Gross Ave isn't able to carry that stuff. Larry, would you like some?"

"Sure, sounds good," Larry said without thinking. He was too distracted by Rebecca to care.

"Okay, why don't you guys make yourselves comfortable in the living room while I get it ready?"

Larry followed Rebecca into the Slaters' stylish yet unsophisticated living room. He sat on a love seat across from the couch on which Rebecca was making herself comfortable.

"So you flew in from the States?" Larry did his best to engage in a conversation with the beauty he was trying hard not to stare at.

"Yeah, I'm from Seattle. Do you live in Terrecastor?"

Jenny interrupted their small talk. "Looks like I'm going to need that tea you brought after all. It's okay—stay seated. You're my guest. I'll go grab it."

"Thanks, Jen."

When Jenny was making her way downstairs, Rebecca started talking to Larry in a lowered voice. "Jenny doesn't know this, but I'm actually CIA. I was initially coming here for a short visit, but on my way here, the CIA gave me a spur-of-the-moment assignment. Apparently, there is this bulletproof man in Terrecastor who needs training."

Larry didn't know what to say. The gorgeous woman was going to be his trainer? Did that mean that "the eyes in the sky" were the CIA? Could he trust Rebecca? Oh, how he desperately wanted to trust her.

"Does Jenny know about your secret?" Rebecca asked after a short moment.

"No," Larry said.

"Alright, you can trust me. I won't tell her. I know that you've gone through a lot of hard things lately, so if you want someone to talk to, I'm here for you."

At that moment, Larry's greatest desire was to just vent out all of his feelings and thoughts. However, it wasn't the time or the place for that, and he had yet to see how trustworthy Rebecca was. It was hard to have faith in anyone so soon after his experience at Skiontia.

"So you're my personal trainer?"

"As cool as that would be, I'm not your main trainer. He'll be in touch with us soon enough. I'll let you know. However, I will be assisting in the training process. I'm looking forward to working with you."

"Me too," said Larry. He a hard time sorting out his thoughts about Rebecca. He was too dazzled by her charming smile.

Jenny had played her part and had planted bugs in her own home. Vance's team had provided the bugs, and they were not merely listening devices. Vance Mortus was able to monitor the entire conversation between Rebecca and Larry. It became obvious that Larry was infatuated with Rebecca. That very infatuation meant that Vance's master plan would play out more quickly. Depending on how many unknown variables came into play, Larry would be dead by the end of the year.

* * *

It wasn't the mechanical whine of the refrigerator that kept Larry awake. Nor was it the fact that the couch was an uncomfortable substitute for the guest bed that Rebecca then occupied. The simple fact was that Larry *couldn't* sleep—he didn't have the ability to. His body didn't get fatigued, and so it didn't need the rest that sleep provided. However, night supplied a gratifying respite for his mind.

Rebecca was a welcome presence in Larry's thoughts. Her fiery red hair kept his heated thoughts about Dr. Daniels and Skiontia at bay. His brain had a hard time distinguishing the sound of her voice from a beautiful musical melody. It relaxed the storm of anger and anxiety in his mind.

But could she be trusted? Had he not deemed Dr. Daniels a decent dude until his demented designs were discovered? Was she not employed by a group of people who were used to acting and manipulation?

Yet she was friends with Jenny, a woman who Larry had only met because of a random encounter with her husband. Larry had determined that the Slaters were trustworthy people—as trustworthy as anyone could be, anyway. If Rebecca was friends with Jenny, she couldn't have been that bad of a person, right? And he was lucky enough to have the opportunity to spend a great deal of time with her.

Forcing his mind off of Rebecca before his thoughts traveled down a path he wasn't willing to go down yet, he ended up wondering what kind of training he would be going through. After all, his very habits would have to be broken down and built up in a whole new way. Larry thought of how Ryan had repeatedly found ways to remind him that certain foods were hot or so hard that he couldn't chew through them. How long would he need to train before he could enter the world on his own and live something resembling a normal life?

A loud snore from the direction of the master bedroom brought Larry's attention back to reality. He looked at the clock. It was only one in the morning. He felt like going for a walk.

Larry quietly tiptoed outside into the cool fall air, allowing himself to watch the dance of fallen leaves being tossed about by the breeze. During the day, those leaves, which had been painted orange and red by autumn, looked so alive and radiant in the sunlight. Lit by moonlight, they almost looked sinister and restless, moving in unpredictable ways while everyone slept. In the morning, the neighborhood residents would awake to a shifted world that would be different than the one they had left the day before.

A movement in the shadows, not of a leaf but of a man, caught Larry's attention. The man was tall and was walking toward him with a confident gait. The intimidating man in a black leather fall jacket looked to be in his mid-to-late fifties, but his upright stance told Larry that his wrinkles were more from experience than from weakness. A smile spanned the man's narrow face as he looked directly into Larry's eyes.

"Hello, Larry. I was wondering when you would show up!"

The man spoke lightheartedly, and he had a kind facial expression. But his gray eyes concerned Larry—they were eyes of a man who knew much and feared nothing. Well, there was one thing the stranger should have feared, and that was Larry Tanner.

"Who are you?"

"Jordan Bolmer, the man who will help you get back on your feet without becoming more famous than you want to be. Pleasure to meet you." Larry detected a distinct accent—possibly a Dutch one—in the man's confident voice.

Perhaps it was Jordan's imposing figure that made Larry feel inclined to outline the status of their relationship. "I'm *already* on my feet. The only reason I'm doing this training is so that you and whoever your bosses are will leave me alone and let me live my life in peace. I trust that my training will be short and that you'll soon be satisfied that I require no further attention."

"My time is valuable as well as yours, my friend. The sooner all of this is over, the sooner we can both go on to better things. However, I plan to make the best of our current arrangement. I hope you will as well. Maybe we should continue our conversation in a more private location."

So far, the man hadn't said anything disagreeable, but Larry kept his guard up. There was no doubt in his mind that the man was a skilled manipulator. Larry needed to make sure that he maintained control of his life and that he was only doing what he actually wanted to do.

"Where did you have in mind?"

"Why don't we talk inside of my car?" Larry followed Jordan a short distance down the sidewalk to where the man unlocked the doors of a new-looking silver Cadillac. Inside, Jordan laid out the plan for the next few months. Nothing Jordan said was disagreeable. In fact, Larry found himself looking forward to the days ahead. It would be the reboot his life needed.

Chapter 13

"Turn right here," Jenny dictated.

"Just where in the world are you taking us, babe?" Ryan asked as he smoothly maneuvered the massive thirty-eight-foot recreational vehicle onto a narrow gravel road. "I don't think this vehicle was made to travel off of the pavement."

"I told you. We're going camping in the middle of nowhere," Jenny said from her seat next to her husband.

Caleb chuckled. He was sitting farther back with Larry and Rebecca. Originally, the Slaters had only planned to take Rebecca on their camping trip. But that was before Larry had showed up.

Caleb didn't consider himself much of a camper, and he would have been just as happy to stay home and kill his newfound free time by himself. He had free time because Grocery Avenue was in the process of getting demolished. Surprisingly, a mysterious owner had bought the store and the next-door Terrecastor Inn, and he was going to combine them into a larger Grocery Avenue.

The shocking new developments were explained when Caleb found out that the bulletproof man who had stopped a robbery days earlier was staying at his friends' place. He also learned that the man who was going to train Larry was CIA, had bought the two buildings, and was going to build a secret training facility underneath the new store. Once the building was rebuilt, Caleb would be promoted. He was going to be the new store manager, and his primary job would be to keep an eye on Larry, who would be working as his assistant. Jordan figured that the job would provide Larry with a degree of normalcy. At the same time, it would give him a chance to practice hiding his strength in public.

What would happen if Larry failed to hide his strength in public? Caleb thought.

"Well, Rebecca, it's your friends who lent us this RV, so you're the one who will get the blame if it gets scratched up. Just say the word, and I'll turn this bad boy around," Ryan said as the vehicle bounced and rattled along.

"I'm sure my friends won't mind. They're pretty loaded," Rebecca said.

Knowing that the CIA had paid for the expensive vehicle, Caleb smiled. He looked across the aisle to where Rebecca and Larry were comfortably sitting side by side. Caleb had recognized Rebecca from Jenny's wedding, although he had been much too shy to introduce himself to the beauty at the time. Didn't she have a boyfriend? The way she and Larry were looking at each other and laughing...

This whole situation is awkward. Rebecca was actually CIA, just like Jenny used to be, but neither Ryan nor Larry knew about Jenny's ties to the agency. Ryan and Jenny both knew about Larry's secret, but they were keeping it a secret from each other, even though they both suspected that the other knew. *It's just like something out of a wild novel.*

"I wish I had friends like that," Ryan said half-jokingly. "What kind of work do they do?"

"That reminds me—I have something to tell you," Jenny jumped in.

"Is it big?" Ryan asked lightheartedly but with some measure of seriousness.

"You could say that."

"You're pregnant?" Ryan jested, which resulted in a sharp elbow nudge from his wife and laughs from their passengers.

"Rebecca is going to be moving to Terrecastor," Jenny declared before Ryan could throw in any more wild or embarrassing guesses.

"Why would you want to go and do that?" Ryan inquired loudly.

"Why not? I happen to have a good friend here, and I want to work with her as a cop here," Rebecca answered. "There's honestly nothing for me in Seattle anymore."

I'm going to guess she doesn't have a boyfriend, Caleb thought. Then, glancing at Larry, he thought, *At least for now.*

"It definitely won't be as exciting here as it is in the city," Caleb added to the conversation. "You might get bored."

Rebecca grinned and flashed a look at Larry. "I'm not too worried about it."

* * *

A snapping sound from outside of the tent woke up Rebecca. She sneezed. *Great, I have a cold.*

It was her own fault. She hadn't dressed warmly enough for the cold October air. It had been easy for the chilliness to creep up on her because she had been distracted by Larry. Whenever Jenny and Ryan weren't looking, Larry would show off his super strength to amuse her and Caleb.

Larry would grab stones and squeeze them until they crumbled into dust in the palm of his hand. He would also do backflips and summersaults in the air. After seeing Caleb attempt to skip stones at a nearby lake, Larry had thrown his own stone. However, his aim had been too high, and the stone had sailed over the entire lake. Caleb had started laughing and had said, "I can just imagine someone coming across a tree with a stone lodged in it in the middle of nowhere and getting super confused."

The most memorable feat of all had involved a bear. Rebecca had gone with Larry to collect firewood, which Larry had insisted on doing even though they had perfectly good dry wood in the RV. They had walked a ways through the bush and had somehow found themselves within ten meters of a large grizzly bear. The bear had seen them first and was growling at them.

"Cool," Larry had said as he had rushed toward the bear.

"Don't kill it!" Rebecca had pleaded.

"I'll try not to!"

When Larry had reached the bear, it had stood up on its hind legs and had roared. Larry had laughed and had thrown a few mock jabs toward the bear.

"So you want to box, do you?"

The bear had responded by landing on Larry, who had then lifted it up.

"Aw, he just wants a hug," Rebecca had jested from a safe distance.

"Or maybe he wants to dance," Rebecca had thought she heard Larry, whose mouth had been muffled by bear fur, say. The young man had lifted the bear and had spun it around. Gently, Larry then lowered the bear to the ground. The bear was then on all fours. It had looked at Larry, had growled, and then had made its way off in the opposite direction.

"See you later," Larry had called after it.

Rebecca had hoped she wouldn't see the bear later, especially without Larry next to her. She had slept with a pistol in reach.

Sneezing again, Rebecca looked over at her tent partner to see if she was still asleep. The top of Jenny's hair was sticking out of a sleeping bag that was buried in a mountain of blankets. Her slow peaceful breathing assured Rebecca of her slumber. Shivering, Rebecca buried herself under her own blankets. Hours before, she had mocked Caleb after he had opted for the more comfortable RV, but Rebecca was tempted to ditch the tent for the RV herself.

Rebecca's jealous thoughts of Caleb were interrupted by some rustling coming from outside the tent. *Relax, Rebecca. It's probably just a squirrel or some birds.* Grizzly bears roaming her thoughts, Rebecca couldn't keep from checking. After grabbing her gun from the inside of her clothing bag, she unzipped the flap of the tent and peeked out.

Entering the other tent was Larry, who emerged after a moment with clothes in his hands. As he began to slip into his jeans, Rebecca retreated and quickly changed into some clothes of her own. She then took off after Larry, who was sneaking into the forest.

"Killing time?" Rebecca said in a hushed voice as she caught up to the man. She knew that Larry didn't sleep. He was probably beside himself with boredom while he waited for his friends to wake up.

"Yeah, I suppose I should get used to it. But it's not so bad. I already swam a few laps around the lake and danced on its floor."

"I would have liked to have seen that," Rebecca said.

"Yeah, but I didn't learn my lesson from Lake Terrecastor."

"What do you mean?"

"I came out covered in dirt and smelling like seaweed. I probably still stink like it."

"You kinda do," Rebecca admitted with a giggle and then a sneeze.

"Bless you."

"Thank you."

"Any time," Larry cheerily said. "Then I climbed trees by bounding to the top of them. I'm getting better at jumping to just the right height. Probably not a useful skill in the real world, though."

"Well that's why we're in the middle of nowhere—so you can have some fun without worrying about being seen," Rebecca said.

"Heh, maybe I should just get a bigfoot costume and live out here. Then whenever people spot me, no one would believe them."

"Ha-ha. Except bigfoot doesn't leap over trees," Rebecca laughed.

"Well I guess I would be adding on to the legend, then."

"How high can you jump?" Rebecca asked.

"To be honest, I don't know. I stopped tree jumping because I was making too much noise, and I didn't want to wake anyone up. I didn't want to make even more noise by jumping really high. If I did, I'd probably take out half a tree on my way down," Larry answered.

"Well if the others aren't awake by breakfast, you should go and try."

"Maybe."

They walked in silence for a bit before Larry said, "Oh, there's my clearing."

"Your clearing?"

"That's where I just laid for a while, staring into the sky. For whatever reason, it helped me think even more than walking. It's kind of like I was projecting my thoughts into space, allowing me to see them more clearly than when they are trapped in a knot in my head. Maybe I'm just weird."

"You're not weird," Rebecca assured him. "Well, not because of that, anyway. What did you think about?"

"Life. My life and life in general." After Rebecca didn't say anything, Larry went on. "I mean, how could God have let all of this happen to me? Why did He?"

"Maybe God didn't. Maybe it all just happened by chance, and you were the unfortunate victim," Rebecca suggested.

"I wish that were true," Larry admitted. "Maybe I could blame my dad's cancer on bad luck and my mom's death on a stupid truck driver. The shark attack seemed like a cynical act of God, but I suppose Jason was swimming with an open wound, which didn't help matters. Maybe I was Dr. Daniels's target because it made sense to recruit people with less connections to the rest of the world. Maybe my tough skin actually came from his research.

"But…The next part doesn't make any sense without God. I never have to sleep, and I never feel hungry. When I do eat, the food just disappears into some sort of black hole in my stomach, never to be seen again. Rebecca, I could stand at the bottom of a lake for hours if I wanted to. I don't need to breathe. I feel like nothing in this physical world can kill me."

For a moment, Rebecca was quiet, and not just because she was attempting to remain sensitive. Even though she had seen extraordinary examples of Larry's strength, hearing the young man speak those words and accepting them as truth were still surreal experiences. After a few seconds had passed, Rebecca responded as delicately as she could.

"Well, is that last little bit really a bad thing?"

"I don't know," Larry answered. "That's why I was thinking about life. If I can't die, what should I do with my life? I might not feel God's presence, but I can't find any other logical explanation for my abilities besides Him. But I refuse to follow a God who is fond of taking away someone's life and forcing him to live as torture. God is cheating."

"Cheating?"

"He has taken away my free will. I can't choose to die. It's like He's forcing me to follow Him."

God and religion were things that Rebecca hadn't cared much about in the past. She thought that God might be good for some people, but He wasn't real enough to her; He might have been real, and He might not have been real, but His existence didn't seem relevant to her. Talking to Larry, Rebecca was forced to face the compelling evidence that God was not only real, but also was presently physically working in the world.

Rebecca wasn't looking forward to death, nor did she want Larry to die, but she knew it would have bothered her if something had encroached upon her own free will. Once again, she tried to keep things positive.

"Well, the way I see it, you still have your free will. You're choosing not to follow Him because of what He has done, right?"

Larry nodded. "Yeah, I guess. I don't know why, but for some reason, that doesn't make me feel any better."

* * *

Free will. It was something that even Prefect didn't fully understand. However, it understood the concept on a much deeper level than the two foolish humans he was eavesdropping on did. The Almighty, the Sovereign God, the Immortal King of all Kings had much more control over everything than Larry and Rebecca knew. If only they had known how much the Holy Supreme Ruler had His hands moving them and events to do His bidding.

Prefect was jealous of their naïveté. It felt the will of God at a much more real level than the two humans did. It was like there was a narrow tunnel around it that gave it very little freedom of movement. When it moved forward, it was only because the All-Powerful Master *let* it move forward; when it moved, it was because of permission granted to it by The Will.

But Prefect would move forward nonetheless, especially since that meant hurting the Enemy.

* * *

An airborne winged shadow of the physical realm picked up the entire conversation between Larry and Rebecca. By listening to Larry Tanner and Rebecca Hiltman, Vance was able not only to gather data on the nature of Larry's abilities, but also to assess his relationship with Rebecca. Larry's attitude toward life, God, and Rebecca was in the perfect spot. The pieces of the puzzle of Vance's master plan were all smoothly sliding into place.

Chapter 14

Rebecca's eyelids lifted, and for a while, she didn't move as she allowed her mind to orient itself. After their camping trip had ended, Rebecca had wanted a long hot shower more than anything else. But after she had plugged her dead cell phone into the outlet next to her guest room bed (which she supposed was "her bed" as she would be staying with the Slaters awhile), she had sprawled out on top of the bed's covers, still wearing the dirty, stinky sweater and jeans she had worn for too long without a good wash. Before she knew it, she had found herself in a vivid dream.

She had dreamt that she was back in the States was and camping with her parents. Jenny, Ryan, Caleb, and some high school friends were there too, as her dreams always seemed to find a way to incorporate completely random, unrelated people. Rebecca was trying to sit down and talk with her parents, because just seeing them invoked in her a loving emotion. Jenny dragged her away to sit around the fire pit.

"Come on," dream Jenny had insisted. "Caleb is about to tell us all a story."

"But it's not even nighttime yet," Rebecca argued. But then she looked at the sky. At some point in the middle of her sentence, the sky had darkened. She gave in and made her way to the fire pit, and her parents followed behind her.

"I'm going to tell you the story of *bigfoot*," Caleb began. He began his story, but before Rebecca knew it, Larry was there. Except Larry was a monster like bigfoot, and he had a giant tree in his hands.

Larry swung the tree around, and it collided with Rebecca, her parents, and all of her friends.

As Rebecca painfully lifted herself off of a collapsed tent, Larry came stomping in behind her. Rebecca screamed. She was too paralyzed to run away but too scared to look behind her at Larry. Suddenly, she felt his breath on her neck.

"Don't scream," he said. "I would never hurt you. I just want to be your friend."

It was such a bizarre dream, but Rebecca supposed that all dreams were bizarre. Her mind told her she was lying in an awkward position on a bed. She knew she was awake because the light was shining into the room in such a way that everything was lit in a crisp and clear manner. She wasn't in the United States anymore. Her parents were hundreds of miles away, and Larry was calmly checking out the new Grocery Avenue with Caleb.

Her head still groggy, she made her way to the bathroom to splash some water on her face and to evaluate the damage her nap had done to her hair. On the way there, she realized that the past three weeks had not been unlike a dream. Larry's abnormal strength wasn't something a mind rooted in reality would have been able to easily process.

Why am I fixing my hair if I'm just going to wash it right away? Rebecca thought before she returned to her room.

Before grabbing some fresh clothes to change into, Rebecca picked up her charged cell phone and turned it on. She saw that she had a number of missed calls.

Dad. His name came up a number of times in her missed calls list. *Weird. I was just dreaming of you.*

Over the past couple of weeks, listening to Larry talk about his life story and about how he had lost his family had caused Rebecca to think about her own family. Rebecca too had become an only child when her younger sister, who had suffered from a rare heart condition, had died at a young age. Her parents had lost yet another baby through a miscarriage, and that had concluded their attempts to have another child. Even though Rebecca's parents were both still alive, she was glad that she was at least partially able to relate to Larry. There was no doubt in her mind that she would have been devastated if the other members of her small tight-knit family had disappeared.

Well, her family wasn't as tight as it should have been or as it used to be. The close bond Rebecca had had with her parents had faded soon after she had become an adult. Not only had she inherited her red hair from her parents, but she had also been gifted with the fiery personality that redheads were known for. Her dream of becoming a CIA agent had clashed with her parents' opposition to the idea. They didn't like the risk it would pose to their only beloved daughter. A few years later, her parents had introduced another impediment. Jesus Christ had taken Rebecca's place as the one her parents loved the most. That had changed Mr. and Mrs. Hiltman to the very core, and Rebecca found it increasingly hard to relate to her converted parents.

Her communication with her parents had decreased to sparse and brief conversations, so her father's repeated attempts to contact her intrigued her. Suspecting she wouldn't enjoy the conversation, Rebecca returned the call.

"Hey, Rebecca, so good to finally hear from you," her dad answered. *"Enjoying your vacation?"*

"Yeah, it's been exhilarating. Sorry for not returning your calls earlier. I barely had any reception because we were camping out in the middle of nowhere. What's up?"

"Remember how Mom and I have been waiting for visas to go work in the Middle East?"

"Yeah?"

"Well we finally have valid visas. To go to Iran."

"Iran! Why there?"

"We were pretty surprised, too. We were hitting closed doors in a number of countries. But then the door to Iran opened, I'm sure it was God who opened it."

"No, God did not open that door," Rebecca argued. "They kill Christians there! You got in because they really needed English teachers or something. Do you even speak Arabic?"

"We do speak a little. We've started learning ever since we felt called to go to the Middle East. I will be going as an engineering consultant. Only the members of a church that we are supporting over there will know that we are Christians."

"You weren't called to go to the Middle East. You just feel like it because you became extreme Christians, and that's the most extreme option."

"I figured you probably wouldn't understand. When are you getting back from your vacation? We leave in a week. It would be nice to see you before we go."

Rebecca felt a maelstrom of emotions, including worry, anger, and frustration. After taking a moment to try to calm herself, she said, "I actually wasn't even planning on returning to the States for a while. But you can't go! It's too dangerous!"

"Rebecca," her father said, his voice was far calmer than hers. *"Do you remember when you said that you were joining the CIA? We were opposed to it because it was too dangerous. Do you remember what you said to us?"*

"This is different!"

"You said that you were an adult and that we had no right to control your actions. You said that you wanted the freedom to live the life that you chose. Well so do we."

"I have training that prevents me from getting hurt, Dad. My job comes with risks, but there are safeguards in place. I didn't even really go on dangerous missions. I was just a glorified cop. What you are doing has no safety net. If you're incredibly lucky, you'll just be shouted at a lot and shipped out of the country when the government finds out why you're really there. You're not like me. I was asking for the freedom to live. You're asking for the freedom to die!"

"Honey, I'm not asking you to agree with our decision or support us in it. But it would be nice to see you before we go." Her mother had joined the conversation from a different phone.

Rebecca didn't know how to respond. She loved her parents, but she knew that if she went back to see them off, the visit wouldn't be a pleasant one. The emotions she felt would be amplified when she looked at their faces.

"How long will you be gone?"

"The plan is to go for six months, but nothing is written in stone."

"I'm sorry, I'm not able to leave here for a while. Try to make the trip a short and safe one. I'll see you when you get back. I love you."

* * *

The new Grocery Avenue looked out of place in the small town of Terrecastor. Dwarfing all of the nearby buildings, the grocery store's structure was twice as big as the old version had been.

"This is so cool," Caleb exclaimed. He was so excited that he seemed like a seven-year-old at Christmas or a tourist visiting Niagara Falls. The look on his face reminded Larry of his brother, Jason. During their camping trip, Larry had noticed how similar Caleb was to his deceased brother. He had the same constantly positive demeanor, he walked quickly, and he had the ability to get under Larry's skin, but not badly enough to make Larry angry with him for any extended period of time.

"Dude, it's just a grocery store," Larry put in.

"Imagine going from being a passenger in a station wagon to being the driver of a Dodge Viper. That's what this feels like," Caleb said.

That sounds like something Jason would have said, Larry thought.

Larry laughed. He highly doubted helping Caleb run the grocery store would be as thrilling as driving a fancy sports car. "If only you were the owner of the car," Larry added as the one representing the store's owner walked up to them.

"But the owner is the one who has to pay all of the bills," Jordan Bolmer said with a smile. "Glad you like it. Wait until you see the inside."

If Caleb had looked like a kid at Christmas before, he then looked like a youngster at Disneyland.

"It's not as if we put all of our efforts into the training facility and just quickly slapped together a store on top of it," Jordan explained. "Everything in this store is designed not only to accommodate Larry, but also to run an efficient, profit-generating business for our organization."

Jordan could see a hint of stress in Caleb's smile at that point, so he reassured him. "No pressure, Caleb. We're not counting on you to run the perfect store. Remember that your primary job as store manager is to keep the store's and Larry's secrets. Everything beyond that is just a bonus."

Larry could see that Jordan's words had added to Caleb's stress, so he diverted the conversation. "You said this store has a special design, but it looks normal to me."

Then Larry got a crash course in store design. He was already familiar with the subject but was surprised about how much knowledge Jordan had. It seemed like there was no question that Jordan didn't have an answer for. Jordan not only explained how the departments were arranged in a way that would get the customers to spend more money, but he also explained how even the wiring and plumbing was set up in the store. Larry wouldn't have been surprised if Jordan had designed the building himself.

"You sure know a lot about the store," Larry pointed out.

"I was around for the construction of the building, and so I picked up a fair bit about its design. You'd be surprised by how having knowledge about random things like grocery stores comes in handy in my field. And that leads me to the second part of our tour—the part where I show you where you'll be picking up some random, and some not so random, knowledge of your own."

Jordan unlocked a door and led Larry and Caleb down some concrete stairs to a bunch of pipes and machinery.

"I thought all of the compressors were upstairs," Caleb said.

"They are. These aren't compressors. These are your backup generators, which you'll rarely need, so there's no reason for anyone but you two to be down here. This is where things get downright awesome."

After walking to a tool cabinet in the back of the small area, Jordan pressed his hand against the wall. "This part of the wall looks like it's cement, but it's not. It's actually made of a metal that looks at your hand print."

Jordan removed his hand and placed it against the same spot twice more. "You have to do it multiple times as a safety feature."

Click! The wall swung away as a door and revealed a deep, dark empty space.

"Shoot, forgot to put lights in. Sorry, guys, the tour is over. Come back tomorrow," Jordan said with a serious expression on his face.

Larry wasn't buying it. "Nice try."

Jordan laughed and flipped on a switch, and the vast basement was lit. Part of the basement was a gymnasium-sized room that looked taller than Larry had expected it to be.

"Wow, how did you build all of this in just three weeks?"

"With a lot of money and manpower," answered Jordan. "Actually, more than half of the time was spent just digging and getting the foundation and walls in place. We needed to make the building resistant to flooding and earthquakes."

"We don't have earthquakes in this area," Caleb remarked.

"You never know. Perhaps in a hundred years, even this peaceful part of Canada will see war, and in that case, it would be nice to have some stability when bombs shake the ground," Jordan replied. "We figured that since we were going to sink a lot of money into this facility, we might as well think in the long term. This will be a useful facility even after Larry is finished training. Well if he doesn't wreck the place, that is."

Larry and Caleb both chuckled.

Jordan's dry sense of humor was present for the rest of their tour of the training facilities.

Shocking both Larry and Caleb, Jordan asked, "So, Larry, are you ready to visit your new home?"

"I didn't know I needed a home," Larry said.

"Then what will you tell people who ask where you live?" The question was rhetorical, and Jordan didn't wait for an answer. Instead, he started walking away from the doors through which they had entered the training facilities.

"I live underneath the store?" Larry asked.

"Nope—next to it. Did you two not see the house right next to the store? Right where Terrecastor Inn once stood?"

Larry looked at Caleb, and they both shook their heads. "I was too distracted by the new store," Caleb admitted.

"It must have been hiding behind the building," Larry put in.

"There is a secret entrance to your house from here. I would like to caution you at this point to always leave the same building you enter. It would look suspicious if you always appeared at work without using the front entrance."

"Makes sense."

Larry was more astonished by his house than he had been by either the grocery store or the training facilities. It wasn't the fact that the house had a bed or an extensive home entertainment system. It wasn't the fact that the ornate rooms came prefurnished and decorated with assorted paintings. What shocked Larry more than the fact that he had his own personal living space were the items sprawled out on the dining room table.

"We brought you back to life, my friend," Jordan said as Larry held a driver's license with his name and picture on it in his hand. There was also a debit and credit card, some cash, a card with his social insurance number, a birth certificate, and a wallet to keep it all in.

"Is this…"

"Real?" Jordan finished Larry's sentence. "Well let's just say that no amount of inspection would be able to prove that it wasn't."

"What, no passport?" Caleb joked.

"I have friends in high places that can get you a passport, but that won't be necessary. You won't be traveling for a little while. If you do, I'll probably be out of a job. That's why we didn't give you a car or a garage. Don't worry—your training will be over before you know it, and then you can buy whatever car or garage you want with the million dollars in your bank account."

"Million dollars?"

"Courtesy of a certain doctor who I believe promised you that sum."

Dr. Daniels. Well, I guess he at least owed me that.

"You can have a good life for yourself, Larry. A much more comfortable life than you'll have if you became famous in the wrong way."

So just go along with things, and don't mess things up. Larry could easily read between the lines. He didn't like being manipulated, but he would go with the flow for the time being. The instant he felt that the training was dragging on longer than it should have, he would be out of there, and the CIA wouldn't be able to do anything to stop him.

He voiced as much. "Well, I'm guessing you're not planning on wasting my time, so there's not much to worry about."

Vance Mortus didn't waste time. Ever. Every single word he spoke and every move he made was calculated and deliberate. He was speaking with a false Dutch accent and in a casual manner in order to persuade Caleb and Larry that he was on their side. By pretending to be Jordan Bolmer, Vance had given Larry an authority figure, but one who wouldn't antagonize him into rebelling.

Most leaders of covert organizations did not involve themselves in field operations the way Vance did. However, most of those organizations had missions that actually failed. Vance Mortus had never failed to complete an operation because he had the best people for every job, and out of those people he was by far the best. The more involvement he had in an operation, the more control he had over its outcome. The Larry Tanner situation required maximum control, so Vance Mortus's involvement in the mission had to be at the deepest level. There was unacceptable risk factor in relying on any of his men to do this job, which required absolute perfection.

Chapter 15

"Ready to start?" Jordan stood before Larry and Rebecca underneath Grocery Avenue.

"I'm ready for anything," Larry replied. He looked at Rebecca, who seemed to be bothered or distracted by something. Whatever it was, she wasn't showing the enthusiasm Larry had expected her to show.

Rebecca must have detected Larry's concerned glance because she cheerfully chimed in, "Ready!"

"I thought that we might begin with a few strength measuring tests." Jordan walked over to where an assortment of items was laying on the ground. After selecting a two-inch-thick steel bar and handing it to Larry, Jordan said, "Try breaking this."

"No problem." After placing both of his hands around the very center of the bar, Larry snapped the steel in half.

"Wow," said Rebecca. Larry was glad that he was still able to surprise her even after the feats of strength he had performed during their camping trip.

"Okay, as the next test may involve some collateral damage, I want you to stand in the bunker room."

Larry remembered the "bunker room" from their tour. It was called a bunker not only because it could protect the people inside of it from a bomb (Larry held Caleb's sentiment that a bomb wasn't a viable possibility) but also because its walls were thick and strong enough to protect the outside world from anything that happened inside of it.

"Then what?"

"When you're inside, we're going to observe what happens when you squeeze steel so tightly that it shatters."

"Sounds like fun." Making a show of acting nonchalantly, Larry entered the bunker room with the piece of steel and casually squeezed it in one hand. A high-pitched sound that would have hurt Larry's eardrums had they not been impervious to pain emanated from the steel. As the steel squealed, it stretched, and part of its length escaped Larry's grasp. The portion of steel remaining in Larry's hand crumbled. Shards of metal escaped Larry's fist through the gaps in between his fingers, and they flew at high speeds around the room.

Larry brushed off the pieces of metal dangling from his clothes with his free hand. "Well that was new."

"That was amazing!" exclaimed Rebecca as she and Jordan entered the bunker room.

"You got anything harder, Jordan? That was too easy," Larry boasted.

"Follow me," Jordan said smoothly. Larry stared in disbelief; his trainer had not shown any signs of being surprised.

"We know you're strong," Jordan said once the trio was standing in front of a cement block. "But I'm interested in seeing how fast you can summon your strength. This next exercise includes the both of you. Larry, I want you to hold Rebecca's hand."

It would be my pleasure, Larry thought. He acted as casually as he could as he complied. Larry was instantly intensely aware of Rebecca's hand in his. He was aware of its warmth, its softness, and the way her fingers gracefully slid through his.

"What now?" Rebecca asked, her words breaking his thoughts. Was that annoyance in her voice? Was she, too, pretending to be nonchalant? Or did she actually not feel anything special when she held his hand?

"As quickly as you can, Larry, I want you to let go of Rebecca's hand and do your best impression of a karate chop on that cement block," Jordan said.

Larry could detect a bit of worry on Rebecca's face. He, too, was a bit worried. If he summoned his strength too early, he would crush her hand. *No, that's not going to happen. This will be easy.* As gently as he could, he removed his hand from Rebecca's loosening grasp. He shouted "hi-ya!" and lowered his hand all of the way through the cement block. He made sure to place his body between the cement and Rebecca to protect her from any flying pieces.

A severed iron rod stuck out of the crumbled remains of the cement block.

"Very good," Jordan said.

"Heh, it looks like I don't even need training. I can control my strength."

Without warning, Jordan threw a strong uppercut that connected with Larry's chin. The punch launched Larry backward onto his back.

"What did you do that for?" Rebecca asked angrily. Larry smiled—maybe she did have feelings for him after all.

Jordan responded with the tone of a professor. "It's one thing to manage your strength, but it's another thing to manage your weakness. Larry, your weakness is your invincibility. That blow would have at the very least dazed the average person of your size. We need to train you so that if something happens to you, you can respond in the expected way. If you're solid and strong, we need people to believe it's because you've been trained how to fight."

"So you're going to teach me how to fight?" Without using his arms, Larry launched himself to his feet, but not before doing a couple of midair summersaults.

"That technique was horrible. It appears that I'll have to train you on how to do proper acrobatics as well. Your strength means that you don't have to work as hard to balance as everyone else does, so your very form shows your strength. You do want to keep your strength a secret, don't you?"

Larry nodded and bristled. He hated to be reprimanded. He was the strongest man in the world, and that man should have watched his tone around him!

Rebecca must have sensed what Larry was thinking, so she optimistically said, "Acrobatics—that sounds like fun! Well it's sure a good thing that you don't get tired, because it looks like you have a lot of work ahead of you. I can't wait to see what you'll be able to do in a couple of weeks!"

Smiling, Larry thought, *Well I suppose I can bear Jordan just so long as I have Rebecca around. She's so cute.*

* * *

"Wow, what am I going to do with all of this space?" Caleb wondered out loud. He was standing next to Larry and was helping him arrange shelf labels on the bare shelves. They were following the layout that the members of Grocery Avenue's corporate office had given them. Meanwhile, other members from that office were hanging up signage elsewhere in the store.

"It seems to perfect to me," said Larry.

"Yeah, but you're used to working in a big-city store." Caleb held a piece of paper in front of Larry to make his point. "Look at how many different kinds of yogurt drinks they want us to sell. I get that it's the new big thing and that people in Edmonton probably just love it, but here it barely sells. Here, people buy what's cheap."

Larry smiled. Caleb was engrossed in his work. Despite his occasional griping, Caleb was having the time of his life.

"Oh well, let's just hang the labels to make the head office people happy," Caleb continued. "I'll fix it later, we got a whole store to do right now."

It was going to be a long day, and only a small amount of the store's staff would be helping. The rest of the staff would come back to work the next day when the actual groceries were supposed to start arriving.

Most of the staff members who had worked at the previous building had stayed to work at the new store. The previous store manager hadn't, although Larry didn't know whether that was because he was embarrassed by his own nephew's involvement in the armed robbery or because the CIA had persuaded him to leave on different terms.

Chelsea, the blond cashier who had been working at the time of the robbery, hadn't returned to work either.

"On the plus side," Caleb said, his voice vibrating with enthusiasm, "We're making real progress without having to deal with customers at the same time."

"It *is* nice." There were some things that all retail workers could relate to regardless of the size of the store that they were used to working in.

"Oh, that reminds me!" Caleb exclaimed. "It's time to test out the store's music system!"

Larry followed Caleb to the office where there was a large black box full of dials and buttons. The day before, Jordan had explained that it could play anything from a radio station to a personal iPod.

Caleb pulled out a green iPod shuffle from his pocket. "With no customers in here, I can play whatever I want!"

Larry grinned as Caleb gave the volume dial a generous twist toward the max setting. "Is that too loud for you?" Caleb asked the technician who was working on one of the office's computers.

"Did you say something?" the technician joked. "Do whatever you want. Hey, this store has a good sound system."

Larry could concur as he listened to the quality of the sound reverberating through the store. He began to follow Caleb back to the dairy section, but then something about the music's lyrics caught his attention. "I still want to want to worship you…"

"Caleb, is this Christian music?"

Stopping and looking back at Larry, Caleb's smirk grew into a full-sized grin. "Yep."

"I'm not listening to Christian music all day!" Larry hollered at the young store manager who was walking away from him.

"*I'm* not changing it," Caleb yelled back at him.

Annoyed, Larry stepped back into the office. After changing the music to an upbeat channel he had found via satellite, he returned to where Caleb stood. Picking up his own stack of labels, Larry emphatically declared, "Caleb, there are other people in the building besides you. You have to respect that not everyone believes the same thing as you."

Caleb's smile did not disappear. "You disagree with the lyrics in my music. Well, I disagree with the lyrics in this music. But I guess it's more upbeat than my music, it'll help us work better. Good choice."

Was Caleb actually patronizing him? How dare he! Didn't he realize who he was talking to? As his anger levels grew, Larry continued to study Caleb.

It was as if he was oblivious to his crime of upsetting the most powerful man in the world. He was merely focused on his work. He cheerfully bobbed his head and moved his arms to the beat of the music.

Larry's anger subsided. The reason Caleb was acting so carefree and risking making Larry angry was because he was simply living his life the way he knew how; he was having fun doing a job that he enjoyed. Wasn't the fact that he treated Larry like just another friend a good thing? In the end, didn't Larry want to go on living a normal life?

Perhaps his quest for mediocrity would upset God, who had given him his supernatural strength. Perhaps that was the point.

* * *

Rebecca felt as if she was getting as much training as much as Larry was. The first week of training hadn't involved any fighting or acrobats. Instead, the tasks Larry had performed with Jordan and Rebecca during the night were similar to the tasks he had completed during the day in Grocery Avenue. His annoyance was apparent to Jordan, who analyzed every move that he made in the store. For instance, Jordan would say that he hadn't pretended to strain enough when he had pulled the pallet of turkeys off of the truck; or he would say that his arms hadn't sagged enough when he had carried a case of butter. Or he would point out how he had over exaggerated the difficulty of carrying a five-gallon bottle; he would say that normal people wore coats and shivered while unloading a truck in negative-thirty-degree weather.

Rebecca quickly tired of being the example of someone with normal strength. Her struggle didn't cease when acrobatic training started. Somehow, Jordan had found a way to involve Rebecca in every activity—even in the drills that Larry could have easily practiced alone.

When Jordan required Larry to summersault over Rebecca, she wanted to believe that it was because he wanted to give him added incentive to pull it off correctly. When he wanted her to practice balancing moves alongside of Larry, he told her that it was to give him competition and to motivate him to learn faster. Yet Rebecca suspected that something sinister was behind her involvement in Larry's training.

When Rebecca had learned that Vance Mortus required her to become close friends with Larry, she had at first thought it was to stabilize him; perhaps it was just to restrain him from becoming a power-hungry man who would want to rule the world with his strength. But Larry couldn't have looked more stable. Other than his strength, he seemed like an average North American guy who just wanted to live an average life without bothering anyone else. He had friendships outside of the one he shared with Rebecca; Caleb especially had proved able to relate to Larry, and their relationship had grown quickly and had even extended outside of the workplace. Why, then, was Jordan pressuring her to become closer to the man?

It wasn't that Rebecca minded Larry on a personal level. He was a sweet guy whose humor and sense of adventure made him easy to like. Honestly, Rebecca couldn't keep the man off of her mind, but she wasn't sure if it was because of an infatuation or if it was because she spent so much time with the invincible man. After all, anyone who knew what he could do would have thought about him a lot.

She knew that few people would experience a relationship that complicated. She had followed orders and had formed a deep connection with the man. It wasn't fair to let Larry's feelings for her grow because of a lie, so she had allowed some of her own feelings to show as well. Yet there was always something holding their relationship back. Rebecca could tell that Larry didn't want her to like him only because of his strength and that that was always eating at his mind. Perhaps that was similar to Rebecca's ever-present suspicion that guys—including Larry—only liked her because she was attractive. If Larry hadn't had special abilities, would Rebecca have been giving him that much attention? *God knew.*

* * *

He's playing them like a violin. Prefect watched as Vance manipulated Larry's and Rebecca's emotions. Human emotions were so volatile and easy to manipulate. Yet it wasn't often that the fallen angel saw a mastery over the art that equaled Vance Mortus's.

Something was broken inside of Vance Mortus. The man believed that his lack of emotions was a gift that empowered him to become superhuman in a sense. If anything, Vance was closer to subhuman than to superhuman. The Masterful Designer had created humans with emotions because He also had emotions. One without emotions was void of a trait inside the Amazing Source of Life Himself.

Humans could be manipulated through their emotions. The Lord could not be manipulated through His emotions because He was in control of all things. When the scriptures He gave to the human race described Him as reacting emotionally, it was because He had wanted to present to the race a response that they could relate to.

It's unfair how much the Righteous One cares about that despicable race. Could He not have shown such empathy for Lucifer, whose understanding is finite just like the humans' understanding?

Prefect appreciated Vance's defect. He did not feel the joy that others felt—the joy that comes from being accepted by the one who had created him. He was another human rebelling against the Most High. Vance Mortus was a capable ally.

Chapter 16

"Don't you boys have anything more Christmasy?" Jenny asked from the kitchen. An orchestral theme song from a superhero movie filled the air: a strange combination with the lingering smell of pumpkin pie smell in the holiday decorated Slater residence.

"It's tradition to listen to this music while paying Risk," Ryan said without looking up from the game board. He was one of three men gathered around the coffee table in the living room.

"It's tradition to listen to Christmas music on Christmas Day," Rebecca added a rejoinder of her own. She was helping Jenny load the dishwasher and the fridge after a generous turkey dinner as the boys set up the game.

"I'm sick of listening to Christmas music," inserted Larry as he glared across the table at Caleb.

Caleb returned the look with a knowing grin. Every day for the past month, the young store manager had tortured his staff with the Christmas music radio station, and he had taken a certain pleasure from it. It was the only time of the year during which he could play "Christian music" with minimal repercussions.

Larry knew that any irritation he felt toward Caleb wouldn't last. He and the other people in the household were the closest thing Larry had to family. Sentimental feelings overwhelmed him when he realized that it would be the first Christmas he had spent without any of his original family members.

Rebecca too had admitted that it would be the first time she had spent Christmas away from family. *Rebecca.* Larry was grateful for her the most. A giggle from her general direction gave Larry an excuse to look at the woman in question. Her dangling Santa hat earrings matched her red turtleneck wool sweater, but the festive glow emanating from her smile was the beauty that appealed to Larry the most.

Witnessing Rebecca's cheeriness meant a great deal to him. Although she hadn't mentioned it, Larry knew that she was thinking about and worrying about her parents during the season.

Caleb interrupted his thoughts. "Larry, roll to see who goes first."

Complying, Larry reached for the dice. "So Jordan wasn't able to join us."

"You asked him?" Rebecca asked, surprised. She delivered a glass bowl of mixed shelled nuts to the table with more grace and class than a trained waitress.

"It's Christmas," Larry passively replied as he snatched a Brazil nut from the bowl. Larry wasn't hungry—he just found it fun to crack the hard shells in his hand without a nutcracker.

"Jordan doesn't seem like the kind of guy who celebrates Christmas," Rebecca said. Larry knew what she meant. Despite Jordan's constant humorous jokes and the patience he had for Larry's mistakes, he still seemed like someone who was all about work and who didn't make room for trivial things such as holidays.

"Well he should. Everyone should celebrate Jesus being born," Caleb inserted.

"If they believe it," Larry quickly added. He was used to Caleb's tendency to preach, and normally he just ignored it so that he would stop. On that night, though, he was in a good mood, and he had additional patience for his "new older annoying brother."

"Look at the gifts God has given you. Surely it's not a stretch to believe that Jesus walked the earth." Larry wondered if that would draw any questions from Jenny, who, as far as he knew, still didn't know about his strength.

"So who starts?" Rebecca said. She was less willing than anyone else at the table to engage in a religious debate. However, she didn't understand as much as Larry did what Risk at the Slaters' residence meant. When one sat around the sacred map covered in plastic pieces, one was a member of a forum of experts. Risk was less about moving pieces and more about discussing theology and making corny jokes about how everyone wanted to invade Afghanistan.

"You do," Ryan said, holding out a handful of upside-down cards. "Pick a mission."

"Who says it has to be God who gave me my gifts?" asked Larry. "What if…What if it was some neutral spirit who randomly gave me these gifts for the fun of it?"

"Maybe it was Santa Claus," jested Caleb cynically. "The truth is, there are only two sources for gifts that, uh, wouldn't be possible in a strictly natural world. One is God, one is Satan. I believe we both would rather believe that your particular gifts come from God, don't you?"

Despite Caleb's attempt to avoid using any specific terms for the "gifts" he was referring to, he had still made it easy for Jenny's curiosity to be piqued. Nevertheless, Larry was no longer in the mood for a debate. It was time to switch to a corny joke.

Referring to his game piece color, he declared, "I hope no one has 'destroy blue,' because I'm invincible!"

* * *

Tsk, tsk, tsk. Rubber bullets were being shot in rapid succession. The bullets were rubber not for the safety of the target, but for the safety of the walls and the floor.

Larry leaped, rolled, and zigzagged to avoid getting hit. Still, more bullets collided with him than missed him, as Rebecca was an excellent shot.

"Great form. It looks like you're ready for our next exercise," Jordan said. He was walking out from an adjacent room. He claimed that he had been observing

Larry from different camera angles, but Larry suspected that he had secretly been commanding an army. "Next we'll go over some nonlethal ways to knock out your opponent."

Earlier, Jordan had explained that Larry would be going through some combat-related drills because "you never know what will happen in life, and it's best to prepare for the worst." However, it seemed like they were spending a great deal of time preparing for the worst and not as much time preparing for the mundane. *Oh well, at least that last one was fun.*

"It sounds like you're training him to become a CIA agent," Rebecca said.

"While that's not my intention, Larry would be a fine asset to our agency. But would you even want to work for us, Larry? After all, we've done nothing but make you work since we met you."

A few weeks before, Larry would have objected to the notion. All he had wanted was to live an average life free of manipulation and secrets. However, he was beginning to see the advantages of being a CIA agent, especially if it meant that he would work with Rebecca. Not only would he have made an exceptional CIA agent, but he would have also been able to keep a lot of people from going through the pain that he had gone through. The more he thought of it, the more the thought of being a CIA agent excited him. It would surely beat the dullness of working at grocery store.

Shrugging, Larry replied, "You never know."

* * *

"Shut up!" Rebecca grumbled sleepily at her ringing cell phone. One disadvantage of sleeping during the day and training with Larry at night was that the rest of the world slept at night and phoned people during the day. The fact that it was New Year's Eve hadn't altered her sleeping habits. All it meant was that more people would be staying up later.

Rebecca lazily rolled to her side on the same bed that she had slept in during her first night in Terrecastor. The Slaters' hospitality was truly phenomenal.

"Hello," Rebecca did her best not to sound groggy as she answered the call. Four hours of sleep wasn't nearly enough.

"Is this Rebecca Hiltman?" the unfamiliar, feminine, solemn voice asked.

"Yes?"

"I'm afraid I have some bad news for you, Rebecca."

"What is it?" Rebecca forced herself awake and braced herself. Even as she asked the question, she felt the answer in the pit of her stomach. *My parents.*

The lady's next words confirmed Rebecca's biggest fear. *"I'm a member of your parents' church. We have reason to believe that your parents have been taken."*

Despite the fact that she had known that that would be a possibility, the statement collided with Rebecca like a wave of fire. She attempted to prevent herself from having a serious emotional breakdown and forced herself to stay objective.

"What makes you believe that they were taken?"

"Your parents were working with a local Christian to start a church in a small town. They were having some success. But the speed the church was growing concerned your father. When people started to go missing from the church, they made arrangements to leave. In an e-mail, your father told us to expect them in a week and not to mention anything to you because they didn't want to worry you. That e-mail was sent almost two weeks ago, and we still haven't heard from them. We don't know that they've been taken—perhaps they're hiding. Either way, it seems like they're in great danger, and we thought it would be best for you to know. I'm sorry. I know this must be hard for you, Rebecca."

"Thank you for letting me know. Contact me if anything else comes up."

"You'll be our first call. We'll be praying."

"Thank you. Bye."

"Take care."

After hanging up, Rebecca's mind went into overdrive. Fighting tears with the hope that her parents were still alive and well, she began to brainstorm ideas for how to save them.

Larry could help save them! No, she couldn't ask him, even though she knew that he would have helped her without hesitating. Despite the great deal of confidence she had in the abilities his training had afforded him, she knew that if he became involved, her family's plight could turn into an international crisis. It wasn't worth the risk.

* * *

A hidden figure was eavesdropping on Rebecca's phone calls. No pity arose in the man as the young CIA agent received word that her parents were in danger in Iran. No empathy was stirred when she gave a heartbreaking account of the events to her best friend, Jenny, who agreed to do her best to help her. No surprise arose when Jenny's first call was to the director of the CIA.

"Hello, Jenny, something tells me this isn't a call to wish me a happy New Year," Director Adam North said.

"Hey, Adam, you're right. I wish this were just a call to say hello. Unfortunately, I'm calling to ask you a favor."

"Since you ran off to Canada, I believe it is *you* who owes *me* favors."

"Well, perhaps I'm doing you a favor right now. There's a good chance that you're going to have another agent go AWOL on you," Jenny revealed.

"Rebecca?" guessed Adam. She was the only other member of the CIA who knew the details behind the Larry Tanner ordeal.

"Her parents disappeared in Iran, and knowing her, she'll go after them if she doesn't get any help from us."

"Ah, and where Rebecca goes, Larry will want to follow," Adam stated. "Vance Mortus has claimed control of everything Larry Tanner related. The CIA has very limited resources in that part of the world, but perhaps Vance would be willing to aid us in this matter. After all, I'm sure he wants to keep Larry out of trouble as much as we do. Isn't that right, Vance?"

Adam had acutely analyzed the situation. Vance had the technology not only to listen in to encrypted phone calls but also to join them. "Tell Rebecca there's nothing you can do. I have it under control."

"Well I guess that settles that. Happy New Year to you, Vance," Adam said, knowing that Vance didn't bother with pleasantries or holidays.

* * *

After his conversation with Adam and Jenny, Vance made a phone call to Larry and then one to Rebecca. *His plan is proceeding flawlessly.* Prefect knew what that meant. Larry would be dead in less than twenty-four hours. The demon foresaw it.

Chapter 17

Larry was confused about why Jordan had asked if he wanted to help rescue Rebecca's parents. Despite Larry's confidence in his abilities, he couldn't believe that Jordan would want him to exercise them in Iran.

But he didn't have to spend any time thinking of a response. There was no way he wouldn't help Rebecca. He knew the pain of losing one's parents, and he didn't want Rebecca to go through the same thing.

"How did you know about my parents?" Rebecca asked. She was sitting next to Larry in a helicopter that was being piloted by Jordan. They were on their way to a special private jet that Jordan had said would take them directly to their destination.

"I work for an intelligence agency. It's part of my job to know things. Suffice it to say that an engineering company was concerned about a missing consultant of theirs. They brought it to the attention of the agency, and the agency brought it to my attention since it involves Rebecca," Jordan answered. "I pulled some strings and used some of the CIA's resources to determine where your parents are."

"You found them?" Rebecca exclaimed.

"Yes, they're being kept in a well-guarded complex controlled by an Islamic extremist organization."

"Why didn't the CIA just send some people to get them out if they know where they are?" Larry asked.

"Unfortunately, Rebecca's parents aren't worth enough to the American government—they won't risk that kind of operation. One, there are a lot of guns there. Two, there would be international consequences if it became known that the States was partaking in this sort of covert mission in Iran.

"But with Larry, I believe we have a strong chance of successfully infiltrating the complex. We are going in without any official permission from the CIA, so we have no backup. Rebecca, Larry and I will do our best to keep you alive, but I can't promise your safety. If you want, you can just leave this to me and Larry."

This last sentence introduced a new level of anxiety in Larry. "Why don't you both just leave the mission to me? There's no need for either one of you to put your lives at risk when I can take care of everything myself."

"I'm going on the mission," Jordan insisted. "I'm the only one of us who knows Arabic, and I'm the only one with who has experience with this kind of rescue operation. I'm assuming that Rebecca wouldn't want to be left out of the mission. She wouldn't want to regret not doing anything to rescue her parents. Am I right?"

After a short moment, Rebecca responded. "Yes."

No! Larry thought. Despite his best efforts, he couldn't think of anything that would dissuade Jordan and Rebecca from their decision to be present in the mission.

"Perhaps you'll change your mind when you see our ride," Jordan stated as the helicopter started to descend.

The clearing that Jordan lowered the helicopter into barely existed. But the small break in the trees that Larry hadn't even seen contained more than just a place to land. There was a camouflaged structure about the size of a three-car garage next to the small patch of grass that the helicopter rested on.

Jordan walked over to the building and performed a series of motions similar to the motions needed to get into the training facility. Filled with anticipation, Larry followed Jordan and Rebecca into the secret hangar.

After switching on the lights, Jordan introduced them to the mysterious vehicle in front of them. "People call this masterpiece 'The Shadow.'" It was a fitting description for the crescent-shaped contraption. Two bullet-shaped pods flanked a larger third pod, which made the pitch-black jet look unlike any aircraft Larry had seen before. The thin aircraft spanned roughly fifteen feet and looked more like a bizarre glider than a jet.

"Cool," Larry acknowledged.

"Should stay off the radar," Rebecca surmised.

"Easily," Jordan added. "Its design isn't associated with any country, so even if we are spotted—which we won't be—our nationality will remain a mystery."

"Looks kind of tight," Larry observed. He figured that the metal cocoons wouldn't have been able to hold anyone who was overly obese.

"Yes, they are not built for comfort. You will spend the entire flight lying on your stomachs." Jordan opened the center pod and pulled out a trio of black full-body suits. They were thicker than scuba divers' suits but less bulky than astronauts' space suits. "Put these on over your clothes."

Full-face oxygen masks had been fitted to the heads of the suits, and the suits had webbing between the arms and legs. Larry and Rebecca looked like frightening oversized flying squirrels. Jordan explained that the watch-like devices on the suits were altimeters that could determine how far away the ground was. Larry assumed that the humps on their backs were their parachutes.

"Rebecca, have you ever done any BASE jumping?" Jordan asked.

"Not yet," Rebecca admitted. Larry wasn't exactly sure what BASE jumping was, but if it was anything like skydiving, he was sure that Rebecca would be up for the thrill.

"Then we'll stick to a straightforward fall," Jordan explained.

"I don't see why I need a suit," Larry said. "I don't need oxygen or a parachute."

"Two reasons," Jordan said. "One is that we want to keep your identity a secret. In your case, the most important part of the suit is the tinted mask that will simultaneously hide your face and give you night vision. Then there is the radio communicator built into the hood of your suit. It will allow you to speak to us regardless of where you are."

"Cool," Larry responded.

Rebecca wasn't as occupied with the impressive equipment. "I'm assuming I'll be getting a weapon."

"It's in the bag of supplies that will be riding with me in the center pod," Jordan said as he began to open the pods Larry and Rebecca would be riding in. Then he called out, "Last chance to use the washroom!"

"Where?" Rebecca asked. Larry kept on forgetting that part of a normal person's bodily need.

Once Rebecca's bladder was at a more comfortable level, Jordan started to pull open The Shadow's doors. "Climb backward into the pod so that you end up with your body facing the hatch and your head turned toward the center of The Shadow. Have your hands to your side like you're pretending you're Ironman. My pod in the center is the largest because I'll have the toughest job throughout the flight."

"If you're jumping out too, who's going to fly this?" Larry asked as he followed Jordan's orders.

After shutting the door on him, Jordan answered his question via radio. *"This thing will be flown remotely by a partner of mine. Dane, say hello."*

"Good day, passengers. Welcome to The Shadow Airlines. I will be your pilot for the flight."

"Hello, Dane!" After just one sentence, Larry knew that he would rather talk to Dane than to Jordan.

In a manner that was much more serious than The Shadow's pilot's manner had been, Jordan said, *"If you think it's tight in there now, just wait a moment. You will feel a blanket of wires press against your back. Rebecca, you will be unable to move. Larry, you will be able to move because of your strength, please don't."*

"Okay."

"Rebecca, are you in place?"

"Yes."

Almost silently, a layer of wires pressed Larry forward. His mouth was the only part of his body that had any free space in which to move. The semisoft pad that his head was pinned against was the only thing in his compartment that was remotely comfortable.

"This is a heck of a seatbelt."

Although he hadn't felt any movement, Larry had the weird sensation that his orientation had changed.

"We're airborne," Jordan commentated.

"Wow, I didn't feel a thing," Rebecca responded.

"You won't feel much more for the remainder of the trip. You are strapped to a board that has the best shock absorbers man has ever seen. The turns, bumps, and g-force will be absorbed—all for the quality of your inflight experience."

"How long is the trip?" Larry asked.

"For the majority of the time, we will be traveling at Mach three, so the trip will be a short two and a half hours. The time will go by even faster because we will be going over the mission the whole time," Jordan answered.

Mach three…three times the speed of sound. This is insane.

"You must have a fancy oxygen system hooked up," Rebecca said. *"Even though I'm wearing a mask, I find that I'm able to breathe without my air supply just fine."*

"You are correct. Fighter jet pilots wear masks to feed them oxygen. The fact is that we are passing enough air to provide the right amount of oxygen. A complex system of dampers allows in the correct amount of air and slows it down so the air pressure doesn't kill our eardrums. In about an hour and a half, we will be breathing in pure oxygen from our tanks. That will purge the nitrogen from our bodies and prepare us for our jump. We will be doing a HALO jump. I'm assuming you are familiar with the term."

"High altitude, low opening," responded Rebecca.

"Correct, which means we will get incredibly close to the ground before opening our chutes. That will increase our speed in aiding Larry, who will reach the ground first. That also means that you will open your chute when I say to.

"We will be dropping next to a mansion isolated by desert. If Rebecca's parents are still alive, they'll be kept inside one of the cells hidden in the mansion."

"What are the odds that my parents are still alive?" Larry hadn't anticipated such a reserved response from Rebecca. Obviously, she was doing her best to hold herself together.

"I'm going to be honest with you, Rebecca. Things aren't looking good. It is not uncommon for this group of people to keep their prisoners alive. However, if that is the case, your parents will probably in poor condition."

Larry hadn't thought that it was possible for him to become even more emotional. Rebecca, the one he cared about the most, had just been told that her parents were probably either dead or being tortured. A current of anger surged into the whirlpool of grief and anticipation swirling around inside of him.

He wanted to say a word of encouragement, but what could he have said? "Don't worry, we'll find your parents"? Or "We'll avenge them"? Or "Your parents are fine"? "I'm here for you"? Nothing seemed appropriate for the situation.

"How many men are we up against?" Rebecca said at last. She had such courage.

"Intel says that it could be anywhere between six and fifteen."

"That seems like a lot of men just to guard a couple prisoners," Larry noted.

"We suspect that they're producing explosives for their organization. That's why the CIA already had its eyes on them and why it was able to quickly identify them as the ones who captured the Hiltmans," Jordan explained.

"But we have me, and I count as an army of men."

"Yet they can always call for more help. However, if Larry looks like he's dodging the bullets, the enemy might think they're only against one guy and not bother radioing in backup. Larry, you will be the diversion. You will go in and take out as many of them as you can. Rebecca and I will go in afterward and search for her parents."

"Got it."

"And above all, follow my orders. It doesn't matter what is going on. You might be the strongest man in the world, but I am the one in charge. I have the experience. If I give an order that doesn't make sense, follow it anyway. I'm on your side, and I want the best outcome possible. Trust me—bad things happen when people don't follow orders."

"Yes, sir," Rebecca verbally saluted. Larry was slow to echo her.

Chapter 18

"We're nearing the drop zone. Brace yourselves." Had Larry not been so focused on the mission at hand, he might have noticed that Jordan Bolmer had made a joke. There was no way that a normal person could either brace himself or move in any way while he was strapped in by The Shadow's seatbelt.

Before Larry could realize what was happening, the hatch underneath him swung open and he was sprung downward.

Determined to reach the ground much sooner than either Rebecca or Jordan, Larry thrust his arms in front of him and allowed his body to fall vertically. *Perhaps I would be more aerodynamic if I had my arms at my side instead? Maybe, but this way feels too awesome to change.* With his close-fitting skydiving apparel, he didn't feel unlike Superman speeding through the air in his super-suit.

Despite the fact that it was night, his visibility was surprisingly good. Moonlight reflected off of the top of the clouds that he would soon enter.

Underneath the cool and wet clouds, the view was much less pleasant. The ground was a shadow that didn't seem to reveal any more of its secrets the closer Larry fell towards it. He could barely make out the building that he assumed was the complex he would invade.

Perhaps it isn't the greatest idea to hit the ground hands first. Wanting to hit the ground running to avoid wasting any valuable seconds, Larry started to change his position. The ground was approaching at sixty-five meters per second, and it was much closer than it looked; it was too late to hit the ground feet-first.

Thud! It was a belly flop like no other.

If anyone had seen him land, he would have been dumbfounded when Larry launched himself off of his stomach and into a sprint. Sand trickled into his cracked mouthpiece as he made his way to where he heard an incessantly barking dog.

He was not quite sure how to disable the guard dog without outright killing it, so he gave the leaping canine a powerful kick to its head.

Had it been light out, Larry might have been impressed by the proud-looking mansion that decorated the side of the large rocky hill it was perched on. For the moment, Larry bounded over a bush and into the shadow of the building's arch-supported canopy in the hope that no one had seen what the dog had been barking at.

At first, Larry couldn't see the door, and he briefly considered crashing through one of the windows protected by cast-iron bars or even making his way through the sun-bleached stone wall. *That would surprise them! If only I wasn't simultaneously trying to keep my strength a secret.*

The door was revealed to him, as was an armed man who had stepped out of it a few feet away from him. As if he were simply a plastic training dummy that had been set up by Jordan, Larry summersaulted forward and met the man's chin with his fist.

After stopping only long enough to ensure that the unconscious man at his feet wasn't dead, Larry sprinted inside of the mansion. He didn't bother to cautiously peek around the corners before he zipped around them. He was determined to explore as much of the building as he could before Rebecca and Jordan arrived. If his careless scampering about attracted all sorts of attention, then so be it. Any attention on him would be attention not on Rebecca and Jordan.

Perhaps if the lights had been on, he would have been impressed by the mansion's décor. The large brilliantly painted scene of a mountain lake looked like nothing more than a dark spot in the corridor.

Crash! He didn't doubt that the large porcelain vase that had lost its argument with both the corner of his hasty hip and the unmoving floor was priceless. But the noise it made when it broke did little more than punctuate his loud stampeding footsteps.

I would have had that fragile thing protected by a glass case. Perhaps even just some glue on the bottom of it to keep in place, Larry thought before an eruption of shouting and movement sounded from elsewhere in the mansion.

It didn't take long for the frenzy of excited residents to make its way to where Larry was unsuccessfully exploring.

The frontrunner of the pack yelled something in Arabic at Larry. *Probably asking me who I am,* Larry guessed as he leaped at the armed man in response.

Must keep moving. He didn't stop after his fist hammered against the first man's temple. Instead, he rolled to the side to avoid the bullets that the second and third men were shooting at him from the dark corners of the large foyer that he had stumbled into. *As long as they don't hit my night-vision goggles.*

Moving like a man who didn't know whether he was mad or drunk, Larry zigzagged toward a visible animated machine gun at the base of a curved staircase. After hopping right on top of the frustrated firearm, Larry tapped the man who was holding it on the back of his head. He did it just hard enough to rattle the man's brain. His poor noggin had been no match for the tip of Larry's pointer finger.

Someone turned on the lights, which caused a blanket of green to blind him for a quarter of a second before the goggles adjusted and switched off the night vision. When that happened, he had been in midair performing a beautiful backflip onto the railing of the staircase. He then held himself up upside down as if he were an acrobat doing a handstand on a balance beam. Maintaining decent form, he pushed off and landed on the balcony on which a scared, underdressed Arab was frantically yelling and shooting.

Sorry man, I would let you surrender, but I'm in a rush. He sympathetically knocked the man out.

He had no set strategy other than speed in mind, so he began to search the floor he was on.

Besides the gunmen he had encountered, he discovered no more than what he would have expected to find in an extravagantly built isolated mansion in the middle of a country that he had never been in before. There were massive bedrooms and ornate dining rooms, along with sumptuous library: all vacant of additional residents.

Gunfire from the floor beneath him told him that Rebecca and Jordan had arrived. Larry spoke into his radio. "Hold on—I'm coming down."

"Good idea," Rebecca said quietly in the midst of the staccato of fired bullets.

Larry returned to the foyer and hopped down to the ground floor. "Where you at?"

"Over here," Rebecca said. Her voice was audible both through the radio and in person. She sprinted past Larry. She was followed by Jordan and by the angry sound of sporadic gunfire. *Way to kick the hornet's nest.* Larry sprinted toward the swarm.

A line of six charging men greeted him. After almost bumping into the first man, who was built like an ogre, Larry decided to get creative in order to avoid getting shot. With one hand, he grabbed the man's thick cotton tunic, and with the other, he sent a shockwave of force up through his massive jaw. Holding the unconscious giant upright, he powered forward and trampled the second one in the line.

Three bewildered men hugged the wall and let the boulder pass. Unfortunately for them, behind the human shield was a swinging fist that had even more inertia.

The last man in line had retreated and had used his the extra seconds to take careful aim.

Pakatak! Larry's brain registered the feeling of bullets hitting his leg before it registered the sound that the gun that sent them.

Reacting quickly as he had learned to do during his repetitious training, Larry cried out loudly as if he were in pain. He dropped the beast of a man and hid behind him. As he held his leg and moaned, he hoped that the gunman would approach him to finish the job.

The man started to run away. Larry turned around to see Jordan and Rebecca emerge from their hiding spots behind the corner.

"Larry, follow him, but don't overtake him. I want to see where he thinks he's safe," Jordan barked. Larry complied and took off after the man, purposely letting his prey think he had a chance of escaping. Not bothering to hide the sound of his own footsteps, he kept in range of the fleer's frantic footfalls.

A few hallway twists later, Larry saw the man slam the door to a room. "I got him cornered in a room."

"Keep him awake if you can. I want to question him," said Jordan. *"Remember not to use any English within earshot of these people. The less they know about our real identities, the better."*

If they don't already know. Larry glanced down at his hole-filled uniform. *Hopefully, I was moving too quickly for them to notice.*

Before he crashed through the room's locked door, gunfire erupted inside of it. Upon entry, Larry observed that the bullets hadn't been intended for him. A mangled mess of metal that roughly resembled a laptop sat on a desk in the relatively sparse room. Larry looked at the man he was chasing. He quickly pulled out a grenade. The man yelled something unintelligible at him.

"Stay back," Larry spoke quickly and quietly into his radio. Perhaps the man in front of him had made out those two words and had recognized the language, but he was more concerned with his friends' safety. He guessed the man would have no problem releasing the grenade despite the fact that he was in close proximity to his target.

For a moment, the frightened man stared at Larry, whose cracked black goggles and tattered black uniform probably did little to keep him from looking like an intimidating, unstoppable demon.

Up until that point, the only casualty of the mission had been a dog, and Larry did not intend to increase the count. He took a very slow step backward, hoping that his step would dissuade the man from throwing the grenade.

The grenade was released.

Chapter 19

Larry threw himself on top of the grenade.

There was a competition between the pressure of the grenade's explosion and the force of Larry's clenched fingers. His hands easily won, and the few escaping grenade fragments were safely directed towards an unsuspecting marble floor.

At least one life had been saved—or had it? Larry wasn't sure what Jordan would do when he found out that the man had witnessed Larry safely absorb the explosion of a grenade.

"Say 'ah' if it's safe to proceed," Jordan directed.

"Ah." The Iranian was immobilized by shock.

Jordan raced past Larry, grabbed the dumbfounded soldier, and threw him to the ground. He landed on the man's back and began to speak to him in Arabic. Fluent Arabic. Larry didn't understand what his trainer was saying, but he understood that the words came without a degree of uncertainty.

The man sobbed out a few phrases in anguish.

Pointing at the laptop, Jordan yelled another phrase at the man. He was probably trying to ascertain the significance of the device and why he had felt compelled to mangle it with bullets.

The man clamped his teeth together in a display of noncompliance. He then hollered in pain as Jordan simultaneously dug his knee further into the man's back and pressed his fingers into pressure points of his neck. In a low malicious tone of voice, Jordan growled a few Arabic phrases at the man.

After a bit of thinking, the man nodded. Jordan got off of the man and helped him to the feet. He spoke much kinder words to him.

Motioning for Larry and Rebecca to follow him, Jordan walked out of the room behind the shaky Iranian. The four made their way down the hallway to a steel door that Larry had passed earlier but had not noticed because it was disguised as a part of the patterned wall. Their prisoner opened a secondary door by typing a combination of numbers on a keypad. Another heavy door swung open.

The lack of decorations and the sandstone walls made it apparent that they were no longer in the mansion. A row of seven doors with small barred windows lined the left side of the wall.

While Jordan knocked out the Iranian, Rebecca took the lead and sprinted to the first door of the makeshift prison.

"Mom! Dad! Where are you?" Rebecca yelled.

"Help her. I'll watch our backs," Jordan said.

Larry needed no further encouragement.

There was no verbal response to Rebecca's calls, but there was a shuffling noise behind one of the cell doors.

"Open this one!" Rebecca commanded. "Carefully!"

Larry yanked the door hinges right out of the stone wall and removed the door.

Rebecca's excited face turned sullen when the room revealed an individual dressed only in dirty brown trousers. The Arabic man with a scar-filled torso obviously wasn't one of her parents.

"Who are you?" Larry asked despite the fact that the prisoner probably wouldn't understand him.

"Aashir, who are you?" The wide-eyed man responded in rough English.

"No one special," Larry said before easily setting the heavy cell door against the opposite wall.

"Open the rest of the doors!" Rebecca insisted.

Complying, Larry went to the next door and proceeded to remove its hinges.

"There's no one else here," Aashir stated.

"What do you mean? My parents *have* to be here!"

"They're not here anymore." Aashir said.

"Try the rest of the doors, Larry!" Then to Aashir, Rebecca demanded, "Where are they?"

"I wish I knew," Aashir admitted solemnly as he weakly leaned up against the wall. "They were moved two days ago."

Rebecca studied the Arabic man who was struggling to hold himself vertically. The look of the thin bearded man scared her. After a brief moment of hesitation, Rebecca asked the question that Larry had known was on her mind.

"How are they?"

"I don't know. We weren't allowed to talk. They were both beaten at times, but not horribly. At least not as bad as the others were. But they were kept fed and alive, which is more than I can say about my other friends."

"We'll find them," Rebecca croaked softly. She was doing her best to keep herself together. She repeated herself louder and more clearly. "We'll find them!"

Larry was at a loss as to what to do or say. The woman he loved was trying to hold herself together. He wanted to put his arm around her and to comfort her, but he knew that if he did, she might completely break down in tears. At the same time, it would have been almost inappropriate to support Rebecca, who was healthy, when the badly abused man was barely able to stand.

Jordan cut in with a series of commands. "*We need to get moving. We don't know how many reinforcements these guys called in before we took them out. Dane, land The Shadow in front of the mansion. It should be safe for the moment. Larry, carry your acquaintance to the entryway. Rebecca, see if you can find some water for all of us. I'm going to see if I can do the world a favor and quickly disable their explosives manufacturing.*"

"What about my parents?" Rebecca said as she went to grab some water.

"If I don't find anything else," Jordan responded as he came back into physical earshot, "we can go retrieve the scrap of the laptop in the room where Larry hugged the grenade. It likely held something important. Other than that, I may be able to pull some CIA strings in order to determine their location.

"Larry, do you mind taking down this door before you go?" Jordan stood next to a wide steel door across from the cells where they had found Aashir.

"No problem." When he removed the steel door, he revealed a warehouse full of crates and a symphony of mechanical whirring.

"I will figure out a way to bury these explosives and will meet you at The Shadow shortly," said Jordan.

Larry nodded and motioned for Aashir to climb onto his back. Complying, Aashir said, "Thank God for your mercy."

"God has nothing to do with it," Larry said as he navigated the mansion.

"God created you. He created me. He had something to do with it," Aashir stated simply. The reason that the man had been locked in a cell in that part of the world became quite apparent to Larry; Aashir would have gotten along well with Caleb.

"Did He also have something to do with your current state? How much longer do you think you would have stayed alive in the hands of those men?" Larry weaved his way around the still bodies of the men who he had he had knocked out. Their own god hadn't protected them very well, had he?

"I am more alive than you."

Larry was taken aback. How could anyone who had seen his strength make that claim? "More alive than me? I am always wide awake and have inexhaustible energy. I cannot die! I'll have a brilliant future doing whatever I want. Until a few moments ago, you had a dreary life and were trapped in a cell in a place where no one else would have been able to find you. You are *not* more alive than I am!"

He didn't doubt that Rebecca and Jordan would lecture him about revealing his secret, but for the moment, he didn't care. He was sick of religious jargon that made no practical sense. Yes, God probably existed because otherwise, he would actually need to eat to survive. But the God that Christians described didn't match the one he had seen. A loving God loving wouldn't have caused his *whole* family to die. A loving God wouldn't have made one injustice after another.

A groan entered his ear. *Oops.* Distracted by his angry thoughts, he had unintentionally been increasing his pressure on Aashir's legs, which he was holding against his back.

"Sorry."

"My son, God created us to worship Him. Until you know this, you will not be able to truly live." It was another senseless sentiment.

"Didn't you hear me? I cannot die!"

"You are dead in your sin," responded Aashir. "Until you give your life and life sentence to Jesus, you will not be able to fully experience the joy of living with Him."

"What joy? God let a shark tear into my brother and kill him. God made sharks too, right? God let my dad die of cancer. Could He not have saved him? Then when my mom gave her 'life sentence to Jesus,' God killed her too! Even Rebecca's parents followed Jesus, and look what it got them!"

"So you've got God and the world figured out because you went through some tough times? I too lost my family. My mother died giving birth to me. My father is in prison for murder. The rest of my family rejected me when I converted to Christianity. Now, my new family are being tortured to death in front of me to inflict pain on me because I refuse to stop preaching," Aashir continued to speak slowly and carefully.

"Then you kind of brought some of this down on yourself," Larry pointed out. It was a cruel statement. Larry wasn't sure why he was letting his emotions run loose, especially while they were in the middle of an important mission. He was sure that he would have time to talk cordially with Aashir after the stress of the whole situation had subsided.

Aashir was making Prefect uneasy. The man had thrown away his life for the sake of The Merciful God. In return, the Christian's Loving Father in Heaven had made him a formidable enemy to Prefect's cause.

Prayer was the most powerful weapon a human had against the forces of evil, and at the moment, Aashir was in the middle of it.

Prefect expected the Almighty Holy Spirit to fill Aashir and to put words in his mouth or a verse in his head.

Discouraged, Prefect looked into Larry's future: it remained unchanged. Larry would still die on this day.

Even though Prefect could not sense any phenomenon happening as a result of Aashir's prayer, the fallen angel was still worried. The All-Knowing Spirit sometimes didn't directly come down because his faithful servant already had sufficient tools to do His will.

Larry's hope that the discussion had ended vanished when his passenger started to preach once more. "God, who had every right to be more selfish than you, chose to give up his own family to torture and death. He did that out His love for you. It is now time for you to quit being so selfish and to give your life to the only one who deserves it."

"Are you saying that I don't deserve my life?" Larry asked, clearly both angry and confused.

"Nobody is worthy of their life."

"Then why can't I die?" Larry asked emphatically.

Aashir was silent, likely because he realized that the conversation was going in circles.

Oh no! Prefect sensed the tiniest bit of inspiration trickle into Aashir from the generous Spirit of Love.

"I'm certain that God isn't completely stopping you from dying. I doubt you've tried everything," Aashir said.

What haven't I tried? I was shot at, and I skydived without a parachute. Everything I consume disappears, so that rules out a chemical overdose of any kind. What else is there? I stood in the campfire for the fun of it and didn't get burned. Suffocation? Tried that already, and my body doesn't need air.

"Pretty sure I tried everything."

"I have heard that fully healthy adults have died after losing all will to live. Not that I want you to try it, but I can't see God taking away all possible exits. But he often makes the exits hard to take. Just ask Jonah."

Why am I talking about this? I no longer want to kill myself! My life is getting better!

He *had* had suicidal thoughts in the past, even after meeting Rebecca, who had revitalized his will to live. When he had first explored his abilities, he had not cared about whether he actually survived. Part of the reason he didn't care was because he was rebelling against God, who he felt had ruined his life.

It was true that at no point had he "lost all will to live," but at the moment, Larry didn't want to travel down that path. It had been a while since he had seriously contemplated trying to kill himself. He had friends who cared about him and a future full of possibilities. There was no way he would reach the point of destitution that Aashir had described. Why would he have even mentioned it?

At that point, Larry and his human cargo stood outside of the mansion staring out into the emptiness of night. *Where is The Shadow?* Larry looked around. Nothing. *I suppose it would be impossible to find that machine in this darkness unless I knew exactly where it was.*

"I think I can make it on my own from here," Aashir informed him, which prompted him to lower the man to the ground. Aashir leaned against the outside of the mansion's wall and breathed in deeply. It was likely the first big breath of fresh air that the man had had in a long time.

"I still have yet to have someone tell me why I should live for a God who lets all this...garbage happen to people." He had posed the same question to Caleb, who had given him some confusing spiel about the sovereignty of God. Caleb's explanation had seemed self-contradicting and Larry had remained in the dark.

"First, you complain that God isn't giving you enough freedom. Then you say God gives us too much freedom."

"Huh?"

"The 'garbage' happens when men do their own thing—when they take advantage of their freedom. You can say that when God seems to take away our freedom, He's doing it out of His mercy."

His statement was clearer than what Caleb had said, and it *did* make sense in a way. But that didn't mean that Larry was going to acknowledge the point. He would need some time to think through what Aashir had said.

For what seemed like five minutes, Larry stared into the darkness, struggling with the idea of God. For some reason, Aashir's words were eating at him; despite his best efforts, he couldn't get them out of his head. He tried to focus on the mission and on helping Rebecca deal with the fact that her parents weren't there. Still, words from Aashir, Caleb, and who knew what else persisted in his mind. *What makes you think you know better than God, Larry?*

A strange sound similar to the whirring of a gas burner smoothly interrupted the silence. It lasted only a few seconds, and then the silence resumed.

"The Shadow has landed." Dane revealed.

"Where?" asked Rebecca, who had a flask of water and was making her way to where Aashir stood.

"On the northern side of the mansion," Dane replied.

"Which way is north?" Larry inquired of Rebecca. She pointed to Larry's left after handing Aashir the water.

Instead of bothering to run around the corner of the mansion and look where had Rebecca pointed, Larry bounded onto the roof of the mansion.

On his radio, Larry heard Rebecca talking to Aashir. *"How did you know who my parents were? When I asked you where my parents were, you seemed to know who I was talking about. You don't know what I look like, and you said you weren't allowed to talk to them."*

Larry had a hard time making out The Shadow, which was hiding in the shadow of the mansion. But it was there. He leapt back onto the ground so he could hear Aashir's response to Rebecca more clearly.

"...were helping me teach in a local church. Your father led one of the town's leaders to the Lord. That was both a blessing and a danger, as the town leader didn't stay quiet about his faith. That is what eventually led to my imprisonment and to the suffering of many in our church." His voice had been revitalized by the water and was stronger.

"They should have left the moment people started going missing," Rebecca said.

"They had planned to. I'm not sure why they didn't," Aashir admitted.

"Because my father is bullheaded," Rebecca stated firmly.

"They are brave and loving," Aashir said.

"Time to go!" Jordan announced as he rushed out of the door holding the remains of a laptop.

"What are we going to do about Aashir?" Rebecca asked. "There's only room for three people in the jet."

A figure was hiding behind a boulder over a kilometer away from the mansion. Looking through the scope of his sniper rifle, he could make out the three intruders, Aashir, and the almost-invisible jet that they had planned to leave on.

They wouldn't be leaving unharmed if he had anything to do with it.

He aimed at the female.

His shot was true to its mark, and she collapsed to the ground.

Chapter 20

"Agh!" Rebecca yelped.

Before Jordan got out the word "sniper," Aashir had a newly formed hole in his head from which blood was gushing.

Larry might have puked if he hadn't been invincible and frantically looking for the shooter in order to take him out.

Two brutal seconds of searching passed by, and one of them resulted in a bullet to his head.

Rebecca let loose a stream of curses.

"Cover me while I bring Rebecca inside!" Jordan commanded from his position on the ground next to Rebecca. She was moaning in pain. Blood poured from the wound on her thigh that she was covering with both of her hands.

Larry made his stance as wide as he could, and behind him, Jordan lifted Rebecca to her feet and practically carried her inside of the building. A bullet grazed Larry's shoulder and found its home in the wall not far from the open door.

"Get inside and close the door!" Jordan ordered. As Larry complied, Jordan continued. "We need to stop the bleeding."

"And the pain!" Rebecca said emphatically through gritted teeth.

"Don't worry, Rebecca. I came prepared." Jordan's reassuring words were almost as calming as the efficient manner in which he swung his backpack off of his back and scooped some gauze out of it. While he speedily bandaged her up, he soothingly kept talking. "Rebecca, stay calm. We don't want you to go into shock. I'll give you some morphine for the pain. You're going to be fine.

"Larry, find a way to turn off these lights. Take them out manually if you have to. We will make our way to The Shadow in the dark so the enemy can't see us."

"What about Aashir?" Larry asked as he sprinted around the mansion to turn off the lights. He had a feeling that he knew what Jordan was going to say, but he needed to ask.

"We don't have time to bury him," Jordan responded almost unsentimentally. *"Bandaging done. Meet you at The Shadow, Larry. Rebecca will live, but we need to get her to a hospital immediately to fix her up properly."*

"Okay." Larry found that it was easier to just punch out the lights than to go around looking for switches. When he passed by the bodies of the men he had knocked out earlier, he wondered how long they would stay unconscious. *I didn't kill them, did I?* He spared a second to take a glance at one of the bodies. *Good, he's still breathing.*

It was fortunate that Larry had located The Shadow's position before the sniper incident. It would have been impossible to make out the jet with the lights off.

Only one of the Shadow's three pods was open—his. *"Hop in when you get here. Rebecca and I are in place and ready to go."*

Larry crawled into the same pod that had restricted his freedom during the trip to Iran. He wasn't bothered by the lack of space—he needed some time for his mind to unwind and to process all that had happened in the few minutes that he had spent outside of this aircraft.

"The Shadow took some fire from the sniper, and for some reason, the controls from my side are glitching whenever I try to do anything," Dane revealed.

"I'll drive," Jordan spoke. *"Our destination is a hospital in the United States."*

"Isn't there anything closer?" Rebecca asked. She sounded drained. Larry hoped that that was because of the stress and morphine, and not because of the large quantity of blood that she had lost.

"None that will refrain from asking questions. Plus, we need to get this laptop into the hands of the CIA as soon as we can. You'll live, but we don't know about your parents yet."

You'll live. Those words coming from Jordan helped tremendously with the stress that Larry felt. Still, Aashir was dead. If they couldn't retrieve anything valuable from the laptop that Jordan had salvaged, then their mission would have done more harm than good. They needed to rescue Rebecca's parents.

"At least I was able to set a charge to collapse the mountain onto the explosives, so this mission wasn't a complete failure," Jordan said. It was almost as if he had read Larry's thoughts about the outcome of the mission. Larry wished he actually cared about the explosives.

* * *

Not a minute after The Shadow had taken off, there was a massive explosion. A flaming ball rose from the shaking ground right where the mansion had once stood. None of its inhabitants had escaped.

* * *

"I'm feeling sleepy," Rebecca said drowsily.

"Don't bother fighting it. There are some sedatives mixed in with the morphine. If you fall asleep, it will slow your heart rate and lessen the bleeding," Jordan explained.

"But…I…don't…wanna…" Perhaps it was for the best. Rebecca had begun the mission on very little sleep. Larry was emotionally drained from the last few minutes, so he knew Rebecca would be drained in every sense of the word. At least for the moment, she would be free from suffering.

Larry wished he could pass the time by sleeping; his perpetual wakefulness was more of a curse.

Like a bad dream, the events of the mission played out in Larry's head over and over again. The unconscious bodies on the floor; the disappointment when he had found out that Rebecca's parents were no longer there; the blood spilling out of Aashir's forehead. Larry wished he could wake up and find out that the whole mission had been a bad dream—that his whole life had been a bad dream.

If Rebecca had been awake, he would have had someone to talk to who could have distracted from his dismal thoughts. Jordan was awake, but he didn't have Rebecca's beautiful voice or her skill of calming his emotions.

He decided that talking to Jordan was better than the alternative. "Jordan, do you believe in God?"

"I do my best not to think about things I cannot control. I cannot control God," Jordan said bluntly. It was a standard Jordan response.

"Why do you think he lets stuff like this happen?"

"God is a control freak who is willing to do anything necessary to show that He is in charge."

Jordan's statement lined up with Larry's attitude, and it made more sense than Aashir's response, especially in the context of everything in Larry's life.

With his training complete, Larry would be free to do whatever he wanted without any outside forces interfering. He would be free of the CIA, free of the mystery organization that had contacted him on Dr. Daniels's phone, and free of the training and missions. However, he wouldn't be free of God. As long as he had his super strength, he would feel God's hand trying to manipulate him into becoming a Christian or something.

"How do you do it, Jordan?" Larry voiced the words before he realized what he was trying to ask.

Taking Jordan's silence as prodding to be more specific, he continued. "How do you go on through life knowing that the one in charge is such an arrogant jerk?"

"God doesn't concern Himself with me, so I don't concern myself with Him. I do what is best for humanity even if he doesn't."

If only Larry could have ignored God so easily. *Well, starting now, I'll try.* Doing his best to keep his mind more down to earth, Larry started to wonder what he would do next. Would he go on another mission to save Rebecca's parents?

Would his going on another mission make matters worse? Would Rebecca's parents die as a result of his presence? After all, Aashir would have still been alive if it hadn't been for his intrusion.

No, that's YOUR fault, God, not mine! Trying a different tactic, Larry started daydreaming about what he would do outside of the missions. Perhaps he would go back to school or try to connect with old friends. Then again, their presence might remind him of his old life, the life he wanted to forget. Maybe he would stick around for the most part and help Caleb run Grocery Avenue.

Rebecca probably won't want to stick around Terrecastor longer than she has to, though. Larry realized that Rebecca hadn't given him a clear-cut answer about what she wanted to do after his training was over. She always said something along with the lines of, "I don't know what I want to do, but you can go do whatever you want. The world is yours to explore!"

She had laughed when he had said that he planned to dress up as a yeti and play in the snow on the top of mountains. *I still need to go and do that.* Yet he knew that if he spent the future alone, it would become boring. He wanted to spend time with Rebecca, even if it meant doing something more mundane.

Thank God for Rebecca. No. Thank goodness for Rebecca. "Goodness." I don't know what that means, but I need to start thinking along those lines. God, You ruined Your chance of having anything to do with me, and I won't have anything to do with You.

* * *

"Change directions," Caleb declared as he laid down an Uno card on top of the discard pile. New Year's Eve was best spent with company, and since Larry and Ryan were both out of town, Caleb's family's invitation had won out over his online guildmates' invitation.

As the card game was predominantly driven by chance, Caleb had ample opportunity to wonder about how Larry was doing. His top-secret mission with Rebecca was his first escape from Terrecastor since his training had begun.

Is Larry going to be okay? Caleb wasn't sure where the thought had come from, as Rebecca and Jordan were the two people who were in danger. He blankly stared at his cards in his hand, unable to focus on them. *Larry really needs Jesus. Hope he's alright.*

Why am I still thinking about this? He's going to be fine!

His little brother nudged him. "Your turn, Caleb!"

He absentmindedly threw down a card and continued to think about Larry's welfare.

"What color?" his mom asked.

Caleb looked down at the card he had thrown. He needed to change the color, but he had no idea what to change the color to. "Um…"

For some reason, he couldn't focus on the game. Larry's name kept on hogging the brainpower that he would have otherwise used to analyze his cards. *Maybe I should pray for Larry right now.* It didn't make a whole lot of sense, but it couldn't hurt, and he knew his family would understand.

"Can we just all stop playing right now and pray for Larry?"

* * *

The majority of the flight had passed in silence. Larry was daydreaming frivolous thoughts about single-handedly taking over the world and making everyone get along by force when Jordan cursed.

It was the first time Larry had heard Jordan swear.

"Dane, open Rebecca's secondary chute!"

"What's going on?" Larry demanded.

"The Shadow's damaged system glitched and Rebecca's door opened. I'm circling back then releasing you to go and retrieve her."

"Seriously?"

"I can track her using the GPS coordinates sent out by her suit, I'll guide you to her," Dane said. *"Jordan, head to the coordinates on the monitor. Both of you need to calm down and do as I say. We'll get her back."*

"Yes we will!" Larry growled threateningly. *We'd better.*

"Rebecca, can you hear me?" Jordan blared.

Larry added his own "Rebecca, wake up!"

No response.

"My system is showing that Rebecca's comm is offline," Dane calmly inserted. *"Oh, lost her GPS signal as well. How close are you to her last known location?"*

"Right on top of the coordinates."

The door to Larry's compartment opened, and for a brief moment, he soared through the open, star-lit sky.

Then there was wet darkness. Before Larry's mind could process the fact that he was falling through a cloud, he fell through its bottom. The rain-saturated air he was then traversing was only slightly less wet.

The peak of an ocean wave ended the easy part of his journey. Larry swam to the top of the rolling sea to look around.

"I don't see her!" The only source of light was the electrical discharges from the clouds he had fallen through, and the flashes lit nothing but the mountainous waves.

"The wind probably blew her off course. I'm using The Shadow's infrared camera to find her," Dane commentated.

As Larry he bobbed in place, he screamed, "Rebecca!"

The only response was the sound of water, the wind, and the thunder.

"Rebecca!"

"Have visual. Jordan, stay put. Larry, swim forward. Okay turn twenty degrees to your right…there you go."

"How far is she?" Larry yelled despite his mouthful of water.

"Pick up your speed, Larry, she's still a ways out." Larry kicked harder.

"Heat signatures closing in on Rebecca. Possibly sharks." Larry broke personal speed records.

Images of the shark bite that had killed his brother, Jason, swam through his head. *I swear, God, You have a sick sense of humor. I hate You so much. If you let Rebecca die...*

His anger and acceleration escalated.

"Image showing conflict between Rebecca and the sharks."

Chapter 21

If anything exciting was going to happen in Terrecastor, it would happen on New Year's Eve. It would be the busiest night of the year for the local police force, and Jenny was doing her rounds around town to make sure that everyone was celebrating in a safe and legal manner.

Too bad Rebecca isn't here. She would have fun on a day like today. Hope she's okay. No, she will be okay. Vance would have to deal with an unstable Larry if something happened to Rebecca. I hope Larry's alright. And Ryan driving on these roads. Hope Larry's alright.

Jenny's private cell phone buzzed. *One second.* She deftly pulled into the only empty parking space in front of one of the town's two liquor shops. She checked her text messages and saw only three words from Caleb: "Pray for Larry."

Probably not a bad idea. Bowing her head, Jenny started to pray for both Rebecca and Larry.

* * *

"I don't know what to make out of these images. Can't make out Rebecca anymore. Turn five degrees right, Larry. Yeah, you should be able to see her in three…two…one." Somehow, Larry was able to make out Dane's voice despite the storm and his own splashing.

He barely saw the pack of sharks before he swam right into the center of them. They were frantically feeding on something.

"No!" Larry screamed. He swam in around in the. midst of the great white sharks, making certain to damage them as much as he could as he searched for a trace of Rebecca. He could make out strands of meat, but he couldn't find any pieces larger than a screwdriver.

"I'm sorry, Larry. At this point, there's nothing we can do."

Cursing Dane, cursing God, cursing the sharks, and cursing his life, Larry stopped swimming. After grabbing the monstrous jaw that had clamped onto his leg, Larry ripped the mighty beast apart. "That's for Jason!"

And this is for Rebecca! One after another, Larry slaughtered every shark he could get his hands on.

Even after he could no longer find any sharks moving of their own accord, his fury continued to burn.

After swimming to the surface, Larry bellowed as loudly as he could. "Aaagh!" The storm raged on indifferently.

Larry dove, wanting to put as much distance as he could between him, the mess of slaughtered sharks, and the tumultuous surface that represented the storm of anger, frustration, and sadness he felt. He propelled himself farther and farther from the sky with ferocious kicks.

The ocean floor arrived quickly. It was as if God was saying, "You can't run from me." He was disappointed when even the pressure of the water at that depth wasn't enough to squeeze the life from him. *Figures.*

* * *

Ryan felt his pocket vibrate. He was about to check the text message despite the fact that he was driving, but he decided to keep focused on the road when his headlights reflected off of the eyes of an animal.

It was a deer, and not a very smart one. Instead of staying still on the side of the road or even risking a mad dash across the road, it had jumped in the path of Ryan's truck where it remained, running away from the fully loaded semi.

Fortunately, Ryan had seen the creature in time to shift down and keep from hitting it. The frightened deer ran a distance on the snowy road, stumbling and almost falling down completely in the process. It looked as though one half of his body wanted to juke to the right while the other half wanted to escape to the left. After fifteen seconds of embarrassing itself in front of the metal beast that had chased it, the deer finally leaped off the road.

"That was weird," Ryan said as he shifted back up to speed. *Not as weird as when I collided with Larry and he was perfectly fine. I wonder how he's doing right now. I kind of feel like praying for him. God, I pray for Larry. I pray for his salvation. I pray that he sees You are the only one worth living for. I pray that You save him and use him to do amazing things in Your name. That would be awesome, eh?*

* * *

His body prostrate on the seafloor, Larry wept. *Why God? What did I ever do to deserve this? Why do You torture me?*

Why did You let Jason die? You should have sent a shark to attack me instead of him that day! Jason had more potential than me. He could have done more with his life. Who knows, he might even have followed You if you had given him this strength instead of me. He was a better person than I am.

Same with Dad. He did everything right. He was a perfect father, ate healthily, and loved Mom. Why did You tear him away from us? Why?

You could have at least let me keep Mom. She was serving You, just like Rebecca's parents. What more could You want from them?

Just when I was finally getting somewhere in life. I had a job, I had friends, and I had Rebecca.

What do You want from me, God? To follow You? Are you kidding me? No. You are not worth following. You had Aashir! He followed You! He followed You even though You are a terrible leader.

I hate You! I hate You with my entire existence! Why don't you just let me die? I don't want to walk in this world anymore. I don't want to make more friends for You to kill off. I don't want to be a living testimony of Your cruelty.

The words Aashir had spoken entered his mind: words that explained that God probably hadn't taken all of possible avenues of death away from him. Perfectly healthy people had died after losing all will to live.

This is the path that I choose, God.

Larry started to swim forward. Even after he had reached a speed faster than any sea animal or vessel could travel at, he continued to accelerate. When he finally was satisfied with his momentum, he gradually changed his trajectory to an upward one, all the while continuing to accelerate. He pierced the firmament called sky at a faster speed than a missile would have. As his ascent slowed to a stop, Larry arched backward so that his whole front faced the lightning-blanketed heavens.

"God, take this life from me!" Larry hollered as he fell backward.

There was a flash of light brighter than anything Larry had ever seen before.

Then he was in darkness darker than the bottom of the ocean.

Larry's heart stopped beating by the time his body hit the water.

Chapter 22

Prefect's oracle had come to pass. Larry was dead. The demon saw no pulse or brain activity in the bald man's body.

It was too early to celebrate another soul won. The Grandmaster Of The Universe had not yet allowed Larry's spirit to separate from his body. The Holy Spirit's protection of Larry's body was still in place.

A human soul only stayed within its deceased physical shell when the Merciful Wellspring of Life knew that the human would be brought back to life through physical or supernatural means.

Larry had already been living thanks to divine aid, and it would take the same power to bring him back to life once more. The Blessed Redeemer was being unusually generous with that detestable human.

No fair, thought Prefect as it slipped away to a part of the physical realm in which it would be more useful. *Larry deserves to die completely.*

* * *

As if the storm was being orchestrated by Vance Mortus along with everything else, it dissipated to make room for a helicopter under his command.

"Hello, Larry, can you hear me?" Vance Mortus said with Jordan Bolmer's Dutch accent. If Larry had been anyone else, Vance wouldn't have bothered with those words. He could tell by the way that Larry's body was bobbing on top of the calming ocean waves that he was essentially dead.

Vance had kept track of Test Subject Fourteen via a transmitter that had adhered to the inside of the subject's ear. It was a technology that not even the CIA had access to. Larry had known he was wearing a fancy radio, but he had had no idea that the communication device could withstand the thousands of pounds of water pressure that he had subjected it to during his spontaneous dive. It wasn't the only functioning transmitting device attached to Larry's attire. In situations like this, it was unwise to not be over-prepared.

It wasn't an accident that Larry had worn the advanced technology that had been designed by Vance himself. Vance had manipulated Larry and had caused his mental breakdown in order to kill the threat to international security.

A lesser mind, such as the mind of the brilliant Dr. Daniels, might have answered the question of how to kill Larry Tanner in a different way. He might have said, "Easy—send him into space without his knowing it. Even if he doesn't die, he won't pose any threat to humanity." Certainly Mortus could have done so proficiently with The Shadow.

One variable—a very consequential variable—had made the space solution unsatisfactory.

When the average human mind couldn't comprehend an observation as being physically possible, it wasn't uncommon for him to attribute the event to the supernatural. It would have been a faulty assumption, as science continued to prove the supernatural as merely natural.

Vance didn't have an average human mind. His was a mind that perceived all of the variables and reached the most logical conclusion that was void of any biases or superstitions. The conclusion that Vance Mortus had arrived at was that the supernatural was real.

Perhaps at some future date, humans would have sufficient tools to analyze "supernatural" phenomenon and explain them scientifically. At the moment, however, Vance Mortus didn't have a problem with the word "supernatural" because he had observed things that had defied the known laws of the natural realm—things such as Larry's abnormal strength and invincibility.

In order to understand the way the world worked in its entirety, it was necessary for Vance Mortus to take all of the forces in the realm he existed in into consideration; in order for Vance to do his job in the most efficient manner, he needed to understand the truth behind the influence of the supernatural.

The world was littered with contrasting viewpoints about the supernatural. Humanity as a whole was confused about the realm that overlapped its own. However, Vance was adept at analyzing the facts about the supernatural and coming to a conclusion closest to the truth. His world belief wasn't mere religion based on faith. His was reality. He believed in the most logical explanation based on the observed evidence.

The truth was that there was a god-like being who inhabited a higher dimension than the one that humans were currently predominantly occupied with. By using the tools available in that dimension, that god had undertook in the formation of humans on the planet Earth. He had most likely been aided by other spiritual beings that lived in that dimension.

Of all of the spirits that lived in that realm, the one referred to by Christians as "God" was the most powerful and therefore was the leader among the spirits. Second in command and magnificence was Lucifer. Lucifer had seen how self-centered God was and had become jealous of all the attention his superior was receiving.

After amassing a large number of sympathetic followers, Lucifer had attempted to overthrow the god. After all, it was only fair for all of the spirit beings that were worthy of praise to receive it and to not let a leader deny them of it. However, not only did God have a larger following than Lucifer had, but He also had craftily hidden some of his power from Lucifer, which had given His former second-in-command a false idea of His true power.

Lucifer's rebellion had failed, and he had been forced to carry out a sentence in a torturous realm separated from heaven. Because God had not yet prepared Hell,

Lucifer still had some freedom before he was to serve his sentence, so he journeyed to Earth. There he planned to turn God's beloved humans against Him out of spite. God was unsuccessful in stopping Lucifer from deceiving humankind. However, God did manage to curse Lucifer and his followers and bind them to earth's realm. In that realm, Lucifer and God both led armies and fought over the most valuable resource: the human soul.

When Vance had been presented with Larry's case, he hadn't been certain whether it had been God or Lucifer who had bestowed Dr. Daniels's test subject with divine protection. Either way, there was a divine entity interested in keeping Larry alive. Regardless of which divine entity was in control, it probably wouldn't have been easy to exile him into outer space. Larry hadn't received supernatural aid because the giver had been willing to let another human being able to physically put him out of commission.

Vance could have been battling either deity. Of the two, he would have preferred to take on Lucifer, yet there were tools in place that would allow him to take on either one; either way, the supernatural forces in the physical realm had to follow some rules.

Because humans had a spiritual component, they by right had a degree of freedom. Anything physical God or Lucifer could manipulate or change because the physical was temporary and relatively insignificant. However, just as Lucifer had made the choice to rebel against God, all humans could also make the choice to take a political position on the spiritual realm. God and Lucifer could make compelling cases and could reveal their powers, but in the end, humans had the spiritual right to make the choice of who to follow.

God and Lucifer could deny Vance's choice to physically move Larry to a favorable location. In fact, in a sense, one of them had done that with Oliver Weston, who, through a divinely inspired hallucination, had tipped Test Subject Fourteen off about the true role that Dr. Daniels had played in his condition. However, neither deity could deny Larry's freedom to choose to die.

Even if it was a decision made while being manipulated. From the very start, Vance had manipulated Larry. He had played off of Rebecca's natural desire for excitement and Larry's natural desire for a meaningful connection with another human being to bring them close together.

He had pulled some strings that had enabled Rebecca's parents to travel to Iran. It had simply been a matter of manipulating a local group of extremists into capturing Rebecca's parents. The extremists had believed they had been following their devout Islamic leader who had given them commands via e-mail, which is why one of them had filled the laptop containing the e-mails with bullet holes.

The Hiltmans were being held in a safe location by Vance's own men, one of whom was the sniper who had ended Aashir's life.

Rebecca was still alive in the belly of The Shadow. Rebecca was one of the biggest threats to the security of Dr. Daniels's secret research. Her emotional state made her an unstable liability. She would be controlled, but not necessarily eliminated. If Larry returned to the land of the living, Rebecca would be useful as a playable card.

A heat signature began to grow underneath Larry. After focusing on the infrared image, Vance ordered the men in the helicopter to ready their weapons. A lesser mind wouldn't believe what it was seeing, but the nature of the heat signature he was witnessing was unmistakable. He was observing something that shouldn't have existed.

No beast of the ocean was its equal. Not anymore. It was the last megalodon alive.

The twenty-five-meter-long monster calmly closed in to its next meal. A submarine would have been just a submarine sandwich in the shark's massive jaws, but its current meal was a mere man. It didn't know why it was going to eat the man. All of nature was God's to control, and it was part of nature. God had told it to eat the man, and so it would obey.

If the shark had had any kind of intelligence or free will, it might not have been so eager to follow those particular orders. The last time the megalodon had swallowed a man, the prophet had managed to stay alive in its stomach. That had led to a gag reflex like no other in history. Fortunately for the large beast, it had no insight into the outcome of its next meal.

Agent Two-O had been trained to develop a steel mind. The training had involved teaching him to emotionlessly enter into unique situations and to analyze and react to those situations without hesitation. He was in a business that required him to handle all kinds of surprises.

Despite his training, Two-O wasn't perfect. Perhaps if he had had Vance Mortus's disposition, he could have reacted without hesitation. But the moonlit mouth of the megaladon momentarily mesmerized the man and he missed microseconds of moving ammunition into the monster.

The whirlybird's autocannon shells were not enough to slow the beast; Two-O had failed to react appropriately to the situation. Only when the giant shark's jaws wholly surrounded Larry's body did Two-O start firing the helicopter's missiles.

It would have been ridiculous to think that any member of the animal kingdom could have survived being blasted with just one thermobaric Ataka Missile. Yet even after firing a couple of the missiles that had been designed to take out a tank, Agent Two-O found himself wondering if he had managed to kill the beast.

"Four-F, plant a tracker on it," Mortus commanded Two-O's partner in the helicopter. Agent Four-F was already geared up in a wetsuit and dove in after the shark that was unhurriedly making its way downward. Two-O couldn't be sure whether it was swimming or sinking. He was sure, however, that it would probably be the only dinosaur that he would ever be ordered to fire on.

Chapter 23

Devon had a new name: Test Subject Twenty-Seven. It might have been a bit more degrading than "Patient Twenty-Seven," but at least it wasn't "Inmate Twenty-Seven." He was content. He felt that by allowing his body to be used for research he was making up for having unintentionally robbed Grocery Avenue.

And the voices were gone. Those horrible, degrading, hell-raising, demonic voices were gone.

Devon was alone, but for the moment, he didn't mind it. It gave him a chance to think uninterrupted.

It was too bad that he wasn't good at thinking. That's probably what had led him into his current situation. *I wish I was smarter.*

If Devon had been smarter, he could have had the grades to go to college with his friends. Instead, he had stayed in Terrecastor after high school and had worked under his uncle at Grocery Avenue. His uncle, like the majority of his family, had been critical of him and had told him that he could do better than working in a grocery store and that he should do something more with his life.

The alcohol had helped stave off all of the negativity that had surrounded him. He had been happiest when he wasn't sober. That eventually led to his going into work drunk one day and getting fired. He hadn't become sober that day.

That day, Devon almost ended his life. He remembered sitting in his home in his uncle's basement with enough pills in his hand to blissfully take him out of this godforsaken world. *Only a miracle can save me now,* Devon had thought at the time. Then he had used drunken logic and had thought, *Hey, maybe the Internet has a miracle for me.* He had stumbled over to the computer and had sloppily pecked out the letters: m-i-r-a-c-l-e. The search engine had led him to a page that hosted a program called "Give Yourself a Miracle."

The website had changed Devon's life. It had taught Devon about "the law of attraction" and about how positive thinking produces positive results. At first, it had seemed ridiculous to think that he could change the world around him with the right focus and mindset. But since he had had nothing to lose, he had decided to try it out.

Replacing negative thoughts with positive ones had made a huge difference. *I am a young, capable man. Who says I can't do something good with my life?* As if it had been reading his mind, the world had handed him one thing after another. He had received a job as a garbage collector. Forcing himself to keep positive, he had then earned him a second job doing odd jobs around the town of Terrecastor.

Motivated by his success, Devon had decided to apply to an online drawing course through a legitimate college. The law of attraction had worked again, and he was accepted. Soon he was having the time of his life designing graphics. Devon had indeed given himself a miracle.

Then Devon had delved into the spiritual realm. Perhaps that was when it had all gone wrong.

The Give Yourself a Miracle Program had explained to him that "God" was in him because "God" was just a collaboration of all things and emotions. He believed that that was why he had been able to change the things around him with just a positive attitude. He had learned that he could accomplish more by tapping into his "higher consciousness," or "the divine."

He had started meditating in order to reach his higher consciousness, and it had brought him clarity of mind, which had tremendously improved his problem-solving abilities. He was convinced that this meditation also had brought him Cecilia.

The cute young lady who worked at the Terrecastor post office had entered into the same online drawing course that he had, which had led him to believe that they were fated to be together. Devon had taken advantage of his newfound confidence and had found ways to insert himself into Cecilia's life.

Comparing drawings had eventually led to comparing thoughts, an activity that had fuelled Devon's love for her.

He hadn't cared that she had had a boyfriend. After all, Devon was everything the boyfriend wasn't: he was dependable, calm, and mature. Then there was the way Cecilia smiled when she talked to him, the way she laughed at his jokes, and the way she got into deep conversations with him. Obviously, Cecilia would have been better off with him.

That's what he had been thinking before he began one particular evening session of connecting with the divine. Devon had found that using a pendulum was an effective way to tap into his higher consciousness. He would hold the trinket on a thin string, and ask "yes" or "no" questions. The trinket would swing back and forth or left and right, depending on the answer. That night, Devon had consulted with the divine about whether he should ask Cecilia to go out with him. The answer he had received was "yes."

Unfortunately for Devon, Cecilia had given him the opposite answer. Devon had been heartbroken, but he hadn't been devastated until Cecilia shut him out of her life completely. Not knowing where he had gone wrong, Devon had delved deeper into the spiritual realm to look for answers. Soon, he was auto-writing (letting his hand move a pencil/pen on its own), having out-of-body experiences, and levitating. Of course, he communicated with the spirits. To him, they weren't really spirits; they were manifestations of energy and, like him, part of the universe—part of the divine.

Devon was no longer at the top of the hill called life. He was all the way on the bottom of the other side. Devon couldn't focus on his jobs because of all of the amazing and distracting supernatural things that were happening to him, so he quit. Like the last time he had been unemployed, Devon found himself surrounded by suicidal thoughts. Except they were more than mere thoughts—they were voices. They said things like, "You are worthless," and, "You should end your life," and, "No one cares about you."

It had been hard for him to believe that those voices were merely manifestations of the negative energy in the world, especially since he had stopped dabbling in the spiritual realm after their arrival.

He had almost followed through with their suggestion of killing Cecilia and her boyfriend, perhaps because a part of him believed that if he listened to the spirits, life would start going his way again. After all, that's what had happened before, wasn't it? But how could life have gotten better if the voices were also telling him to kill himself?

The voices were finally being held back by medication, and Devon could see the lies he hadn't seen before. He wasn't worthless—he just needed to keep a positive mindset. If he did, he could once more get to a successful place.

But how can I get to a successful place if I'm stuck inside of this facility? No, I can't be thinking along those lines. My situation only has as much power as I give it.

Devon didn't know what time it was—he only knew that it was late. One of the side effects of his medication was "drowsiness," so he was confused about why he was having difficulty falling asleep.

Perhaps it was because it was New Year's Eve and part of him wanted to stay up for tradition's sake. Perhaps it was because being cooped up in the prison-like facility made him feel restless.

Enough about prisons. I need to be here.

To help himself focus on positive thoughts, Devon closed his eyes and began to meditate, feeling safe because he knew he would be protected by the meds. There was nothing "spiritual" about it, Devon told himself. He was simply releasing endorphins into his brain by allowing his mind to go to a happy place.

Meditating proved to be difficult, as the meds had an additional side effect of taking away his clarity of thought. In order to battle his mind's fogginess, Devon decided to get into the lotus position. Sitting on his mattress with his legs crossed underneath him, he closed his eyes and made small circles with his hand by pressing the tips of his thumbs to the tips of his middle fingers.

Soon he was imagining himself on the edge of a perfectly calm lake. The water was crystal clear, but it was hard to see through it because the sunlight reflected off of it like it was a giant mirror. The reflection of the lake revealed the image of a snow-covered mountain that powerfully poked through the horizon and beautifully imposed itself on the canvas of a blue sky covered in gentle white clouds.

Next to Devon in his fantasy was a blank canvas on which he would paint the serene scene. He would paint the spruce trees congregating around the lake; he would paint the heron standing patiently in the lake's shallow water; he would paint Cecilia, who was peacefully humming softly and teasing the green grass on the water's edge with her bare feet. No—not Cecilia. His happy place did not require the presence of another.

"Be at peace," the softly-spoken words sent chills down his spine. The voice that had spoken them had sounded like his own, yet he had not opened his mouth.

Devon reflexively opened his eyes and was shocked to see a man had silently made his way into his cell. The shock had less to do with the silence of the entry and more to do with the man's appearance.

Devon was looking at himself. Well, himself minus the beard, the long hair, and the imperfections like the bags under his eyes that had been caused many sleepless nights. The sight of his "perfect" self was both intriguing and creepy.

"Fear not, for I am the manifestation of your higher consciousness," announced the visitor emanating light that filled his dark cell.

"Not funny." Devon had read about people whose higher consciousnesses had visited them, but communicating with spiritual beings was what had caused all of Devon's problems to begin with. Because he was on medication, it was easier to accept and deal with the probability that the man was some sort of test that the research facility had come up with. Either way, he was not interested in talking to the one in front of him.

"I know about the ones who have bothered you before. They tormented you with lies and made you do horrible things. I am sorry for what you have gone through, but it would be best if you did not see me in a bad light, for I am here to help you."

"I don't need your help."

He doesn't have any option but to accept my "help," Prefect thought. The Will had allowed it to use more of its powers than it had used when it had invaded Larry Tanner. Devon would obey Prefect: the archdemon foresaw it.

"Yes, you do. Think about it. If you can trust me, then you can trust me when I say you need me. The people here are not planning on letting you free to live the life you want to live. You can see me, so if you can't trust me, then you can't trust your own eyes, either." The apparition smiled, revealing teeth that were straighter than Devon's but otherwise identical.

For whatever reason, Devon decided to reach out and touch the man to see if he was physically there. Devon's fingers disappeared into the man's body without resistance.

"If you were dreaming this, you would be able to feel me. But instead, you feel the air around you vividly, you feel the mattress underneath you, you see things with a clarity that isn't possible in dreams."

"Go away. I don't care what these people do with me. I don't want to live as someone who talks with a ghost that looks like me."

"Because I care about you, I will not go away. I want you to reach your full potential and to get the most out of life."

Devon lay down on the mattress, closed his eyes, and covered his ears. He just wanted a normal life free of voices in his head, demonic possessions, and "spirit guardians" that wouldn't leave him alone. He did want to be freed of the sickly white cell that was only furnished by a bed, a counter, and a toilet. But he was safe from the voices there, and the world was safe from him.

"In five seconds, you will have visitors." He heard the voice clearly even though he was covering his ears.

Five seconds later, he heard the click of his cell door opening. *Big deal. The guard probably heard me talking. My subconscious probably predicted that that would cause him to come in and check things out.* Devon sat upright to give the incoming guard the impression that there was nothing wrong him. He would then talk to the guard like a healthy, sane, civil human being and casually bring up the topic of the apparition.

A tall female scientist flipped on the lights to his room and entered along with a guard. She was friendly when she greeted him.

"Hello, Devon. Can't sleep?" She was probably the poor woman who had been stuck with the evening shifts. Devon had heard her talking before but had never met her before.

"Good evening," Devon said as casually as he could. He was trying hard to ignore the version of himself that was smiling smugly behind the scientist. "No, I can't sleep. For some reason, my medication isn't working properly."

"What's wrong?" the spirit said, mimicking a concerned female.

"What's wrong?" the scientist asked. Devon noticed the male guard slightly stiffen.

"I'm still not hearing voices in my head, but for some reason I'm having this hallucination." Devon assured himself that he had succeeded in sounding more like a patient describing a flu symptom than like a mentally disturbed patient going on about how crazy he was.

"Right now?"

"Right now?"

"Yes." He wouldn't tell her that his "hallucination" was also predicting what she would say. *Maybe she's a hallucination too. This sucks.*

"What are you seeing?" The words were rushed in order to finish before the scientist could say them.

"What are you seeing?" *You know what, still no big deal. Even if she was real, I could have predicted what she would say so far.*

"I see a man who looks similar to me standing and smirking right behind you."

"I don't see anything," his spirit twin said as both the scientist and the guard glanced in the direction that he had nodded in.

"I don't see anything."

"I know. Like I said, I'm hallucinating. I'm not crazy. I don't actually think he's real," Devon with a shrug.

"Oh, I'm real."

"I didn't say you were crazy. I'm sure we—"

Devon didn't catch the last bit of what she said because the spirit said, *"Watch this!"*

The apparition snapped its fingers with its thumb and pointer finger ending up forming the shape of a gun, which he pointed at the roof. A fraction of a second later, the cage-protected fluorescent light bulbs in the cell went out.

"Time to go," the guard spoke to the scientist, whose face displayed a degree of shock. She then nodded, said a quick "see you later," to Devon, and hurriedly made her way out of the cell.

"I agree. It's time to go."

Devon was legitimately scared.

"No," he said. He rebelliously lay back down in his bed. He would simply ignore the hallucination. That's what a sane person would have done, right?

If the being had truly been the manifestation of his higher consciousness, then Devon would have been in control. So what if it had pointed to the ceilings right before the light bulbs had gone out? His subconscious could have picked up on some abnormal flickering or even a high-pitched sound that could have told him that they would burn out momentarily.

"Yes." The still grinning man snapped his fingers again. Behind him, the cement wall collapsed to the ground. *Please let this be a dream.*

Chapter 24

The signal from Larry's transmitter had disappeared. It must have been damaged by the shark's digestive system because it should have been able to transmit a signal even from inside the shark. That was the reason Vance Mortus had told Agent Four-F to place a tracker on the shark itself.

However, the process of tracking and retrieving Larry's body would be left to Vance's men. Another test subject had escaped Dr. Daniels's grasp in a spectacular fashion, and dealing with this would be a better use of Vance's time.

After hearing the details of how Test Subject Twenty-Seven had miraculously made his way through locked doors and walls and meandered out of Skiontia, Vance Mortus knew exactly what to do. His staff could handle physical threats to world security sufficiently on their own, but no one could handle the supernatural like he could. He would need his demon-fighting kit for this one.

* * *

Larry's body might have been dead by clinical standards, yet he was still very much alive. Alive and in pain.

The pain was the wake-up call for Larry. Not only had it abruptly taken away his desire for death, but it had also reminded him that God cared for him. It was a strange conclusion to come to, especially because the sensation he had felt the most was a pain that had surpassed anything his body would have been able to feel if he had been alive. It was hellish pain, even though he wasn't in Hell.

He knew he wasn't in Hell, even though he had no conscious sensation coming from his body. The pain was too real for it to have been a dream, but he *just knew* things like he was in a dream. He just knew that God had allowed him to physically die; he just knew that he wasn't in Hell. He just knew that it was God's love that kept him from physical pain during the last few months; he just knew that the pain would have been even worse in Hell, even though he couldn't fathom how the pain could have been worse.

Death had overcome his body, and it tugged at his spirit like sleep tugs at a drowsy man's mind. For the moment, however, Larry had a will to live that he had never had before.

The death of his body had enhanced his ability to think, as he had been free from all of the distractions of the physical world. Despite the pain, he was somehow able to process the information that he had struggled with when he had been alive.

Larry's epiphany was comparable to seeing light, breathing air, and drinking cool, refreshing water for the very first time. It was more vitalizing than becoming healthy after a lifetime of being sick. The new life in his world of pain had come when he had understood and accepted the truth about Jesus.

Jesus had left his place in paradise to come down to Earth, which by comparison was more unappealing than the pain that was tormenting Larry's being. Jesus had suffered through this humiliating position and had died for Larry because of His unselfish love for him—him, who was just as undeserving of His love as the rest of humanity.

Larry had been selfish and mad at God, and God had blessed him. Not only had God offered him life, but he also had protected Larry's physical life. All Larry had done in return was look at the despair wrought by mankind's fallen state and blame God for it.

Finally, Larry did what he had been stupid to not have done much earlier. He talked to God, a physical mouth not needed to relay the words.

"God, I am sorry for my attitude and my sins. Thank You for dying for me and protecting me. I pray that You will allow me to go out into the world once more so that I can serve You as I was meant to."

All at once, the pain disappeared, and Larry's strength reappeared. He opened his eyes—his physical eyes, this time—and saw that things were still dark. Wherever he was stunk worse than anything he had ever smelled before, but he didn't care. He was alive!

But where am I?

His eyes presented him with darkness, and the only clues his body could give him were the horrendous, putrid smell and the feeling of his clothes sizzling. *Why are my clothes sizzling? Acid. Dark…acid…hellish stink…I think I was just swallowed by a fish like Jonah. A whale, probably. Don't know why a whale would eat me, but what else would have swallowed me whole?*

Regardless of the nature of the fish that swallowed him, he wasn't keen on exploring its digestive system. He needed to get out.

The slimy walls were resistant to his grasp and stretched when he pulled or pushed them. But his grip was too intense and his tearing force was too strong. The organic barrier could not to keep him trapped.

Crawling through flesh, he made his way into a different dark environment. *The ocean.* It felt good to let the salty fluid in the water replace the even more disgusting fluid that had invaded his nostrils and mouth.

But what was I in? As excited as he was to get back to the surface and then to land, he felt compelled to explore the exterior of the beast he was in. It was humongous, and because he could only use his sense of touch to identify it, he was at a loss as to what kind of species it was—until he got to the teeth. Rows upon ferocious rows of giant teeth decorated the beast's massive jaws. *A shark.*

The beast hadn't responded to his toothpick-sized meal's exploration of his body or teeth. *Maybe I should have just let him vomit me out. I think I just killed the last living dinosaur. Oh well, can't be helped. I've got a life to go live now!*

But what kind of life should I live? The answer came readily. *I wasn't given this gift to keep it a secret. The best thing I can do is to use it to help others find the joy that I have. I guess I'll be getting famous after all.*

Larry swam to the surface. He exuberantly shouted, "Look out, world! I'm alive!" He laughed out of pure happiness.

No more was the sky lit by angry lightening, no more did massive waves loom around him. The external storm had ceased along with his internal one.

Stars twinkled in the night sky. It was beautiful! Acknowledging God's majesty had allowed Larry to perceive His creation with a new sense of awe.

The stars had their practical use as well. After locating what he believed was the North Star, Larry identified the general direction of west, where he guessed he would find land first.

Larry had only been swimming for a couple of seconds when a thought came to him. It seemed silly, but he wanted to try it. Kicking himself upward so that more of his body stuck out of the water, Larry began moving his legs at an astounding speed. Water was forced downward, which resulted in an upward force—and the force was so great that it propelled the majority of his body above the water.

Larry started to run. On top of the water. Larry was running on top of the water. *I can't believe it! This is so amazing!* Pushing against both air and water, Larry started running on top of the ocean at a much faster speed than he had ever travelled at on top of land. *I'm going to reach land in no time! Not that it would really bother me if it took a while...This is so fun!*

* * *

Ryan's eyes darted across the area that his headlights lit. The deer that had raced in front of him had motivated him to focus more on his surroundings. He turned up the volume on his music to help his mind's stay alert.

A grin appeared on his face when the next song began. It was the song that had been playing when he had run into Larry. The worship song had sentimental value for him.

"I want to worship you with the places I go..." As he sang, he couldn't help but look out for any bald men who might be about to run right into his path.

The person who Ryan saw and braked for was far from bald. The hitchhiker had a shoulder-length mess of curly hair. The young white man wore a gray hoodie and faded blue jeans. Ryan doubted that he would have stopped for the man if he hadn't met Larry a few months ago and if the same song that had played then hadn't been playing at that moment. *Lord, I'm trusting I'm doing the right thing. Please don't let me get mugged.*

As the man hopped in, Ryan greeted him warmly. "Hey, man, where you headed?"

"Anywhere with food is cool. I'm flippin' starvin'." The man tossed his backpack to his feet as he sat down. Ryan wondered if the bag was full of weed because the man reeked of it.

"Um, I don't think anything will be open at this time of night. But, uh"—Ryan reached into his own bag, which was sitting in the space next to his seat, and pulled out a couple granola bars—"this might hold you over until morning if you want."

"That's tight. Thanks, bro," the man said, graciously accepting his offering.

"My name's Ryan."

"Ollie."

"So what brings you to the middle of nowhere in the middle of the night?" Ryan asked as he shifted the truck into gear.

"Doin' the whole life-on-the-road thing for a bit. You know. I want to go places."

Simply baffled, Ryan thought, *Lots of people want to go places and do things, but not here, at this time of night.*

Admittedly, Ryan's own excuse for bringing in the New Year on the pavement was less than normal.

A mysterious customer had paid for a load of lumber to be dropped off at specific coordinates. He had spent an extra sum of money to have the lumber delivered immediately. Ryan was the only driver who hadn't made any plans for New Year's, and so he and his truck had been assigned to the task.

"So where we goin'?" Ollie asked.

"Some place a little north of, um, I forget the name." Ryan pulled out his GPS and tapped on the screen to see where they were in relation to where they were going. Nothing happened. The screen was frozen.

Then the feminine GPS voice spoke. *"Recalculating."*

"Recalculating? But I didn't go off of the route you were showing me," Ryan voiced his confusion.

"Why don't you just use a map?"

"Because for some reason, my boss only had a land description as an address, and I don't know how to look those up using a map. Do you?"

Ollie shook his head, "Sorry, bro."

"Make a U-Turn."

"What?" Ryan tapped at the GPS screen. If he could have seen the destination, maybe he would taken Ollie's advice and tried to just use a map instead. Zooming out, he saw the destination was not too far from Terrecastor. "This can't be right."

After retrieving the piece of paper on which he had recorded the coordinates, Ryan matched the numbers on the paper to the numbers on his GPS. Then he double-checked it. Triple-checked it. *Maybe this nine is actually an eight. Nope—that's definitely a nine. Maybe I had it punched in wrong the first time. No, I didn't change anything. I'm so confused.*

"Where does that thing want us to go?"

"Terrecastor," replied Ryan, baffled. "I drove all of these hours to the middle of nowhere, and it wants me to go to a place fifteen minutes away from where I started."

"Terrecastor," Ollie repeated, looking thoughtful. "Is that where we're going?"

Ryan turned off the GPS system and then turned it back on. He reentered the numbers. The destination remained the same. "Yeah, I guess so. Back to Terrecastor."

Shifting the truck into gear, Ryan said, "It makes no sense, but I don't see what else I can do. Worse comes to worse, the client will phone back, and we'll ask for actual directions instead of a number."

"Well if your little computer hadn't sent you the wrong way, you wouldn't have found me," Ollie pointed out.

"Yeah," Ryan affirmed. Picking up Ollie had happened against the odds. Ryan had never given a hitchhiker a ride before. If he had been in a different frame of mind, he could have easily passed by the man, especially since he was on company time. Coupled with his buggy GPS system, it certainly seemed like he had been meant to pick him up. "Kinda looks like God wanted me to give you a ride."

Chapter 25

It was party night on the Palm Bay Beach! There were both underage kids and immature adults—everyone had been invited to the free-for-all New Year's Eve party. A ferocious bonfire lit the youths' drunken revelry. Blaring music filled the warm Florida air, and it was accompanied by laughing, screaming, shouting, and singing.

A sandy-haired man held a crowd's attention as he performed break-dancing stunts. Many of the people who were not cheering him or the guy doing a keg stand on were intoxicated and hypnotically dancing near the fire. Their trance was briefly interrupted when a queasy sophomore split their ranks to expel some excess alcohol into the ocean. A stinky guy in rags emerged out of the dark water beside her. The man's putrid scent only worsened the girl's heaving.

Larry quickly leapt out of the water and onto the crowded beach.

"Ew, who is that?" was one of the responses the sight of him drew from the crowd. Most of the partiers, however, were oblivious to his presence. *So this is my grand entry.*

He knew that it wouldn't be hard to get the attention of the rest of the crowd. Larry headed to the speakers and pulled its plugs.

The dancing and laughing were replaced by a large wave of hostile protests. *Good, and now that I have your attention...* Larry leapt into the middle of the bonfire.

Girls and guys alike started screaming. Some of them took out their cell phones, cameras, and iPods: anything to capture the image of the crazed man.

"Silence!" bellowed Larry. Fortunately for him, when a man inside of a fire speaks, people tend to listen. The screaming died down, except for the inevitable chanting of "oh my god."

"So the last of my clothes have burned off. Anyone have a spare set?" The perfectly logical words coming from a man wearing nothing but ashes were likely not expected by the onlookers.

"Who are you?" exclaimed the blond-haired break-dancer.

"Who I am is not important. What is important is that God loves you and sent His son Jesus to die for you. And that He wants to be in a relationship with you. Something else that is important is for someone to get me a towel or something so I can cover my nakedness."

A young bikini-clad teenager held out a Florida Panther towel and said, "You can have this one."

"Okay, everyone turn around. I'm going to come out of the bonfire now," Larry said. Once more, he appreciated the authority that someone standing in the middle of a bonfire has.

"Do y'all want to see another miracle?" Larry called out to the crowd who were now staring as he awkwardly tried to figure out how to tie a towel around his waist.

There was a chorus of not-quite-sober "yeahs," so Larry tried to think of what to do next. At first, he thought of holding himself upside down using only his pinky, but being as he was only wearing a towel, this feat could have an undesirable after-effect.

"Has anyone got a coin? Please don't expect to get it back." A second later, he was pelted with loose change. "Thank you, ladies and gentlemen. Good thing I'm invincible, or that might have hurt.

"That wasn't the trick, though. Watch closely." Using his thumb and pointer fingers, he squeezed one of the larger coins he had retrieved. Holding up a bent quarter, he said, "You can try this yourself. Someone with normal strength wouldn't have been able to bend this."

Larry grabbed a handful of the loose change and squeezed it all at once in a single closed fist. He then outstretched his open hand and rotated three hundred sixty degrees so that all of the people circled around him could see the deformed pieces of metal.

Despite the light coming from the bonfire and the glow coming from the luminescent accessories that some of the partiers were wearing, it was still quite dark where Larry stood, and he knew people were having a hard time seeing the result of his trick. He looked down at his towel. If he were going to do anything really big and amazing, he would have really preferred to do it while wearing actual clothes.

"You all gave me money, and I ruined it. Now I have nothing to buy a set of clothes with. Can any of you give me a set of clothes? Be warned—you probably won't get the clothes back."

Before Larry had finished talking, people were throwing shirts, shorts, and articles of clothing that were meant for more feminine bodies at him. "Okay...um, I'm hoping you were wearing something underneath this." Larry put on a pair of tropical-themed swimming shorts that were roughly his size.

"Alright, are you ready to have your minds blown again?" Larry hollered.

"Yeah!" "Yeah!" "Do it!" "Put a shirt on!" "Yes!" "Woooh!" The crowd responded energetically.

Larry grinned, tightened the strings on his shorts, and did a handstand. On his hands, he walked his way over to where there was a Hawaiian T-shirt on the ground.

"I've never done this before," Larry said while holding himself up with one hand and shaking the sand out of the shirt with another. "But if I'm not able to actually put on the shirt like this, don't act like you can do better."

He managed the feat and ended up holding the shirt up with one hand and the rest of his body up with one pinky. The crowd cheered.

"Okay, so much for the lame trick. Now for something really exciting. I'm going to count down from five. When I say one, I need you all to cover your eyes. Don't worry—I'm not going to do anything you wouldn't approve of. I just don't want you to get sand in your eyes, because then you won't be able to see me finish the highest jump a human has ever done. Can I borrow a glow stick?"

Several glow sticks of varying colors were chucked his way.

"Don't try this at home." Biting the end off a few of the brighter ones, Larry gave himself a glowing shower. He was relieved that the luminescent ooze kept on shining once free of its plastic prison.

"That was so you don't lose me in the night sky. Yes, I'm actually going to jump that high. I'll aim for the ocean so I don't land on anything breakable. I recommend you all back up. Ready? Okay. Five…four…three…two…one…" Larry sprang upward. The wave of sand that shot up under him came nowhere close to his peak height of one hundred seventy-three meters.

He yelled in exhilaration for the full duration of his trip—partially to let the crowd know where he was in the sky, and partially because he was having a blast.

Satisfied with the splash that he made both in the ocean and in the minds of his viewers, Larry began to reveal the point of it all once he stood on the shore.

"Do you all want to know how you can do that?"

"Yeah!" "Wooo!" "Who are you?"

"Well it's too bad. You can't do that. It wasn't a trick—it was real. However, I'm going to tell something even more amazing than all of that!"

There were more screams of enthusiasm. *A bit of a noisy group considering how speechless they should be right now. Ah well, most of them are probably drunk. Hope there are at least a few sober people out there, because I don't want them to miss the next part.*

"More amazing than anything we can do here on Earth will be the experience of being in the presence of God! You can be with Him if you give your lives over to Jesus. You will know unending joy that will outlast any kind of fun thing you are currently into. That is the reason you were made. That is the reason I have come to you—so that you can know Jesus!"

Larry wondered what he should say next. He wished he had known more about God and Christianity. However, he knew enough to proclaim the good news to the world.

"God loves you. It doesn't matter who you are. It doesn't matter what you have done in the past. It doesn't matter what you have done this very night. He loves you, and that's why He sent His son to die for you. He wants to be with you! All you have to do is accept Jesus as your God and savior."

Originally, Larry had planned on stopping his preaching there. Yet he kept on talking. He felt compelled to speak the words that were coming to him unexpectedly.

"I am not an angel. I am a man who God has given very special gifts to. But even if I were an angel, this doesn't mean you should listen to me. Even if I could fly, this still doesn't mean you should listen to me. In the past, people saw amazing things and started religions because of it. In the future, you may see even more impressive feats. Just because something is a miracle doesn't mean it's from God.

"Now," Larry grinned. "Who wants to see how many of you I can carry at once?"

* * *

Agent Four-C located Larry. His discovery of the man had come too late, and soon millions would see images and videos of the revived superhuman online. He considered formulating a computer virus that would eat up any online evidence of this man's presence. However, this would be akin to dropping a bomb on the beach where Larry was being filmed. If people thought something big was happening, covering it up would just confirm any suspicions.

The best option was to swoop in with a helicopter, convince Larry to hop on, fly away from the group of partiers, and hope that nobody in this group had enough integrity to be believed by any large amount of people. The videos and pictures posted online weren't so convincing that someone who had not been present had to believe they were real.

By the time the helicopter hit the wet sand, Larry had already thrown his fans to great heights and into the ocean (only after they had promised to start going to church), ate burning pieces of wood from the bonfire, held himself off of the ground with his tongue, and performed countless midair flips and summersaults. Additional lights had been set up on the beach so that it would be easier to see his stunts.

Some people in the crowd had momentarily looked over to the helicopter, but its arrival was relatively boring compared to the spectacle of Larry Tanner. He wasn't concerned with the arrival of the helicopter, and so they weren't either.

"Raise your hand if you think this is all a trick," Agent Four-F heard Larry call. No one raised his or her hand. *Not good,* thought the agent as he ran from the helicopter to the stage where Larry then stood.

"Good!" Larry beamed. "For this next not-a-trick, I'm going to need a volunteer with something sharp."

Immediately, there was a chorus of declarations from the audience. A variety of knives were waved in the air, as well as some very hopeful ballpoint pens.

Agent Four-F was still covered in the scuba gear that he had worn when he had followed the giant dead shark. As one of the agents who were nearest to Larry Tanner's current position, the task of retrieving the invincible man had fallen to him. Even though his diving mask hadn't been designed for use on land, it would help conceal his identity when his figure became famous. The fame would come by way of his handgun. He was going to be Larry's volunteer.

The sound of a bullet being fired into the air encouraged screams from the crowd.

As he had expected him to, Larry took the bait. "We have a winner! Come up here, helicopter scuba man with a gun!"

The crowd did not need extra motivation to make way for the intimidating man in black who was confidently striding toward Larry Tanner.

"Keep that gun facing me. We don't want anyone getting hurt," Larry commanded.

Good, he recognizes me as dangerous. I need his attention.

"Okay, sir. Now I want you to hold the pistol to my eye—right up against it so you won't miss."

Agent Four-F complied and moved his gun and his head closer to Larry. He spoke quietly so only Larry could hear. "Larry, Jordan needs help with another dangerous invincible man."

Larry's widened eyes told Agent Four-F that he had received the message.

After taking a brief moment to process the information, he loudly said, "Okay, now shoot!"

Four-F let loose a lethal projectile into Larry's unblinking eye.

"For those of you who think the gun was fake," Larry said before scooping up a flattened bullet from his feet and holding it in the air for all to see. He then tossed the piece of metal to a nearby shirtless lad. "This thing will be worth something. If you sell it, be a good boy and give the money to Jesus.

"In fact," Larry continued, "as I have said before, you should all give your very lives to Jesus. He is the reason for my life and strength, and He can be the reason for your eternal happiness.

"I have some bad news…This show has come to a close. I am needed elsewhere. Thank you for your attention, everyone."

Larry's response was one more testament to the genius of Vance Mortus. He was the one who had given Agent Four-F the words he had said to Larry.

The easiest way to convince a man with Larry's mindset to abandon his show was to give him an opportunity to put on an even greater show. Introducing another invincible man not only fed Larry's desire to showcase his strength, but it also made him curious. Larry wondered who the mystery invincible man was and why he was dangerous. He wondered if he would still be special if there were others out there like him. What would it mean for Larry's newfound purpose in life?

By taking part in Larry's show and pulling the trigger, Agent Four-F had shown him that he wasn't just making up the story to stop him from revealing his strength to the world.

In the midst of pleading cries from the crowd for him to stay, Larry spoke to Agent Four-F. "Hold on tight."

At that moment, Agent Four-F experienced a sensation he had neither experienced before nor wished to experience again. Larry scooped him up and carried him like a newlywed groom would carry his bride, and then he leaped over the crowd toward the helicopter. They landed safely.

Larry waved to the crowd, pointed to the sky, and followed Four-F into the flying machine.

"What's going on?" Larry asked as he sat down.

"To be honest," Agent Four answered after removing his diving mask, "I don't think I've really known what's been going on since the moment you first stepped onto the scene."

Chapter 26

Just as a hypothetical sentient two-dimensional object could not fully understand the nature of a three-dimensional object, it was impossible for even the most knowledgeable physical being to comprehend the spiritual. The wise among the physical beings understood where the limit to what they knew lay and didn't try to fill in the gaps by assuming anything further. Vance Mortus was the wisest among those beings.

Mortus clearly understood where data ended and hypotheses began. Life couldn't be lived without relying on hypotheses: the hypothesis that because one could perceive, what one was perceiving is real and applicable; the hypothesis that because one lived, life was worth living; the hypothesis that since one gathered data using reason and logic, one should continue to do so; the hypothesis that data gathered in the past should stay constant enough that it could be trusted in the future; the hypothesis that a relatively absolute truth was obtainable and should be striven for.

Vance hypothesized that regardless of who had initially given Test Subject Fourteen his strength, Larry Tanner had become a pawn on the side of God, and Lucifer had responded to the hero with a pawn of his own.

There was a battle going on between the two powerful spiritual beings, and Vance Mortus was right in the middle of it. So was all of humanity. And since Vance was a human, he was going to battle on the side of humanity. It was the most logical thing to do.

Vance Mortus would remove all of the physical threats to humanity, regardless of their sources.

One of the threats to the security of humanity was Devon Olson. In his case, demonic presence was evident. Since Vance had discerned which side of the spiritual battle Test Subject Twenty-Seven was on, he simply had to decide which weapons to use.

Both God and Lucifer had provided humans with physical tools that could be used to deal with the presence of Lucifer's demonic servants. God had done so because He had wanted to protect His beloved humans from the spiritual forces of evil that wished them harm. Lucifer had done so because he had wanted mankind to rely on his power, and not on God's. Vance had in his arsenal ammunition from both sides.

The sun had not yet graced the northern Alberta sky with its morning light when Agent Two-O lowered the helicopter that he and Vance Mortus occupied. Although it was almost identical, it wasn't the same helicopter Agent Two-O had piloted in his memorable engagement with the megalodon. They had taken a jet to speed up the journey from the southeast coast of the United States. They then sat in a military aircraft that was more suited to their upcoming confrontation.

"Target confirmed," Vance Mortus said once they reached Test Subject Twenty-Seven's location. His image on the helicopter's infrared camera hadn't been difficult to identify. In addition to the his physical measurements, which were already known to Vance, the nature of his walk through the forest marked him as someone who knew exactly where he was going—with the branches of trees getting out of his way before him.

"Close in."

"You won't win." The voice would have been blood chilling if it had been heard by anyone other than Vance Mortus. It was rare to hear a demon's words so far away from the human vessel, but Vance already knew his foe held a high position in the hierarchy of Lucifer's followers.

Vance positioned himself on the floor of the helicopter next to an awaiting wooden board. Comparable to but in many ways different from an Ouija board, Vance's homemade tool was covered in characters only a learned etymologist would have understood. It was through the board that Vance would communicate with the spirit. He began to chant.

Vance could sense the spirit's presence but was not successful in opening a communication channel with it.

"Engage," Vance commanded. Two-O aimed the nose of the helicopter at the target and opened fire with the machine's autocannon.

The rapid spray of bullets combined with the wind of the whirlybird's rotors caused woodchips and leaves to dance about Devon Olson, who stood unharmed and watched in bemusement as bullets stopped midair and dropped before reaching him.

"Land," the demon spoke again.

"Request permission to land." An irregularity in the wavelength of Two-O's voice revealed to Vance that his pilot had heard the voice too.

"Ascend," Vance responded. He took out an aerosol can filled with a concoction of holy water and mandrake root extract and began to spray the interior of the helicopter with it. That would have scared off lesser demons. Vance didn't expect that it would fully work against his adversary, but he did it to lessen the demon's influence in the space.

"Land, or I will land you." The helicopter shook to emphasize the words of the demon.

"Land," Vance said. He immediately started to chant and make motions in the air. His leather bracelet, which was decorated by human bones, began to rattle on his wrist.

"Good, now get out."

Mortus gave no indication that he was going to comply with the order. Because Vance was fully focused on his ritual and hadn't given any order to the contrary, Agent Two-O exited the helicopter. His boss would be fine on his own.

Test Subject Twenty-Seven started making his way into the chopper where Vance sat with his eyes closed and making motions with the amulet and cross that hung on his neck. Even after Devon had entered the helicopter, Vance didn't budge from his cross-legged position.

"Sir, I'm going to have to ask you to move, or else he will move you himself." Devon's voice sounded much different than the demon Vance had heard earlier.

"You want to be free," Vance stated matter-of-factly. He held out a cross pendant to Devon. "I want you to be free. Let me help you."

"No!" the evil voice boomed. Vance could not place its origin, if not from inside his own head. *"At first, you flattered me, calling on one of my own names as the power to drive me away. But now you are being annoying and disobedient."*

Vance tried to respond, but his voice was unable to escape from his mouth.

"You will not be able to negotiate with me. Here's how it will work. I tell you what to do, and you will do it. It's not a command. it's stating how things will go.

"I know you, Vance. I know how your brain works. You are the most logical of the humans, and so I know you will make the most logical of choices. You want Larry Tanner neutralized. So do I. Here's what you will do."

The voice proceeded to give Vance a very detailed list of instructions. The words ended with *"now get out."*

Vance recognized that he currently did not have the resources to deal with the demon, and so he complied and exited the helicopter. He then found himself with the ability to speak again, which he exercised with the humblest words he had ever spoken.

"How did you beat me?"

"You aren't God."

Chapter 27

"You're wondering"—the demon said while it flipped the switches and pulled the levers to lift off the helicopter— *"if that man could have helped you. You are wondering if I would have left you alone if you put that cross on. He looked like a medicine man, did he not? A powerful shaman."*

Prefect chuckled. *"The man couldn't decide whether he was a druid or a priest."*

"They tried to kill me," Devon noted. "Maybe he would have killed me if you had left."

"Maybe. Maybe if he had been a truly good man, he would have been able to protect you. We'll be testing that theory out before too long. Your next meeting will be with a friend."

* * *

Caleb didn't have to be at the store until late in the morning because of the holiday, and so he had hoped that he would be able to sleep in. Yet he felt like he had barely slept when an unfamiliar mechanical sound woke him up. He was too lazy to try to ascertain the source of the sound and lay in bed, trying to go back to sleep.

No sleep came, even after the sound that was coming from outside subsided.

Then fear hit him. It was the same sort of fear Caleb sometimes felt during a nightmare and immediately afterward, but the fear was more intense. *What am I afraid of? Angels are watching over me.*

Then came a sound that made his nervous heart skip a beat. *Knock knock.*

After he came to the conclusion that the sound was undoubtedly someone knocking at his door, he groggily made his way to see who it was.

"Hey, Caleb," said the man on the other side of the door.

"Hey," Caleb croaked, trying to register what he was seeing. Devon Olson, his former coworker and the man who had tried to rob Grocery Avenue, was standing in his doorway. He was wearing a hospital gown and looked about as sleepless as Caleb felt. The uneasy feeling that Caleb had in his gut increased.

"I need to talk with you."

"Okay, come in," Caleb said. It was far from the strangest thing that had happened in his life.

"Actually, I was wondering if you could give me a ride somewhere while we talk." Devon sounded timid and nervous.

"Um, okay. Do you mind if I get changed first?" It was an awkward question to ask someone who was wearing attire less suitable for an Albertan winter than his pajamas were.

Devon looked to his side and then looked back at Caleb. "Go ahead. I can wait."

Caleb paused for a moment and then said, "Do you want something to wear? It looks like it's a bit too cold to be wearing something like that."

Devon looked down at his garb, to the side again, and then back to Caleb. "Maybe just a coat."

"Good thing I have more than one winter jacket," Caleb said as he opened his entryway closet. "Come in and find something that fits. I'll be right back."

As Caleb threw on some clothes, he couldn't think of a reasonable explanation for Devon's presence—at least none that involved both a talk and a ride. *Why me? Doesn't he have other friends who could give him a ride? What's with the hospital gown? Did he escape from a mental institute? Is he not supposed to be here?* Fear and anxiety weighed down his fatigued mind and hampered his ability to think.

Caleb returned to see Devon hanging up a coat in the closet. Shrugging, Devon said, "None of them fit. It's okay, the cold doesn't bother me. Plus, we'll be in your car."

"Where are we headed?" Caleb put on a jacket that would have probably easily fit Devon.

"Only fifteen minutes away or so, I think. I'll give you directions. We're headed around the lake."

Caleb didn't notice the helicopter in the field behind his trailer until he was almost at his car. "What's that doing there?"

"I'll explain on the way," Devon answered.

Caleb was about to ask if he was doing something illegal, but if the answer was "yes," things would have gotten a lot more awkward, and Devon could have become less cordial. *I'll tell Jenny about it later.*

Once his car was in "drive," Devon asked, "Caleb, what do you know about demons?"

"One can't know too much about demons," Caleb began. "I know that they are real. I know that they are dangerous. I know that they aren't as strong as Jesus."

"Is Jesus with you?"

"Yes. Why? Are we going to a haunted location?"

"Caleb, *I'm* haunted."

The feeling that he was having a nightmare while he was awake finally made sense. Caleb began to silently pray. He prayed for personal protection from the demons that haunted Devon. He prayed that God would expel any demons in or around Devon.

"Are you sure that Jesus is with you?"

"Yes."

"Did you just pray?"

"Yes."

"Well it didn't work. The demon is in the back seat smirking."

Chapter 28

Having company during the return trip to Terrecastor made it feel like it was going by more quickly. Ollie's presence made for some entertaining conversation. Although Ryan had been unable to ascertain the reason that Ollie had been in the middle of the forest, he had learned a fair bit about Ollie's past and about his outlook in life.

"Sometimes you gotta just take life for all she's got in store for ya," Ollie stated. "Like, you only get one. You might as well enjoy it, right?"

"I *am* enjoying my life," Ryan admitted, "But I look forward to my next life even more."

"You one of them people who think we get reborn over and over again as different people or something wack like a hippopotamus?"

Ryan chuckled and wondered how hippopotamuses fit into the belief system of reincarnation. "Not exactly. I mean my next life in Heaven, with Jesus."

"You one of them born-again folk?"

"Yeah, that's one way to put it."

Ollie looked like he was thinking intensely about something. "Can I ask you somethin' without you thinking I'm nuts?"

It's a bit too late for that. Ryan grinned. "Well, some people say I'm nuts, so the worst that could happen is you would be in the same boat as me."

"Do you believe in dreams?"

"What do you mean? What kind of dreams are we talking about?"

"I mean when you dream dreams, man! When you catch some a few z's, and all of a sudden you're in another world. Like your tripping out on some weird 'shrooms or something," Ollie said emphatically. "Do you believe in those things?"

"I guess so," Ryan said as he tried to make heads and tails out of the question. "For the most part, dreams are just made up by the mind depending on what you spend time thinking about. Sometimes, they're also affected by the last thing you ate."

"Cuz man, I've been having some really tripped-out dreams. Do you think, they're like, they could be real?"

"Depends what you dreamt. It doesn't happen very often, but God does use dreams every once in a while to reach people."

"I think God wants me to build a church."

Wow. This conversation is getting very real very quickly. This is why You wanted me to pick him up, isn't it?

"What makes you say that?"

"It's 'cause of my dreams. They feel like they mean somethin'. Ever since I met that strong man."

"What strong man?" Ryan couldn't help but think about Larry Tanner.

"Well, this one night I was tripping out on some real messed-up weed, and I saw this man talking to a doctor. Next thing I knew, I was talking to him for reals. Ever since that night, I've been dreaming about that man jumping super high like a superhero. Then I had this other dream—a dream where this other man is building something. These dreams came to me every time, man. I mean, not when I'm on some high, but when I'm legit sleepin'. A few hours ago, I finally saw this other dude's face. It was me!"

"Wow. Cool. So you saw yourself building a church?"

"I know my buildings, man, and even though it don't make no sense, it has to be a church!" Ollie exclaimed excitedly. He looked at Ryan. "Do I need to become born again to build a church?"

Ryan didn't know what to say to that. "No, but it definitely helps."

"Can you tell me how to become born again?"

As far as Ryan was concerned, the man couldn't have asked a better question. "I would be happy to."

* * *

The sunlight had already breached the horizon by the time Vance Mortus drew close to the rendezvous point. He had done everything the demon had asked him to, as well as one additional thing.

It was not unlikely that his rival had anticipated his extra precaution. After all, Vance wasn't a difficult book to read. No chaotic emotions clouded Vance's thought process: he would always make the most logical decision in every situation. Since his opponent was a supernatural one, it had been able to see what the most logical decision was and prepare for it.

Vance hadn't entertained the idea of doing something against his nature to throw off his opponent. That would have entailed doing something illogical. The logical thing to do would be to further the cause for humankind. If that meant that his actions were what his supernatural adversary had wanted him to do as well, then perhaps this deity hadn't been his enemy after all.

The rendezvous point was a short distance north of Terrecastor Lake. It was a small clearing that was the resting place of a twelve-foot-high stone that resembled a giant foot. Vance looked through his binoculars at the distinct landmark. Discolorations on it told Vance that it had held some spiritual significance to the Native Americans.

Next to the rock stood Devon and Caleb. They were engaged in serious conversation. Vance read their lips while he waited for his prearranged entry.

"You can be free from the demon, Devon. You just need to try!" Caleb seemed so sure of his words. Yet he wasn't the one haunted by an image of himself. He hadn't seen what Devon had seen.

In the car, Caleb had audibly commanded the demon to identify himself. The demon had complied and had said, "Prefect," although only Devon had heard it.

"So much for you just being a manifestation of my higher conscious, Prefect," Devon had said antagonistically.

"But Devon, I have shown you my power, have I not? You are invincible because of me. And you can become even greater through my power," the demon had responded while maintaining his smirk.

It's not like I have much of a choice, Devon thought. In response to Caleb's claim that he could be free, he said, "How? It came to me while I was still on my schizophrenia medication. It stayed while you prayed. How do you suppose I could try to be free?"

"You need to pray! You need to ask Jesus yourself. Why would it leave you if you are unwilling to let it go?"

"What do you mean 'unwilling'?! Do you think I *want* this creep around me?" Devon pointed to Prefect, who was casually sitting on the top of Giant's Foot Rock, a familiar landmark that Devon had been prohibited from climbing as a child.

Caleb looked to the top of the rock. "It's up there?"

Devon nodded.

A slight smile appeared on Caleb's lips. "Do you know what *did* happen after I prayed?"

"What?"

"I felt at peace. I know that there's an evil around you. But I felt courage from God at that moment. Just to show you that the God I serve is greater than the demon who sits up there, I will climb this rock."

"Tell him not to," Prefect said seriously as it looked intensely at Devon.

"Don't do it," Devon said out loud.

"Why not?" Caleb stood on top of the base of the foot.

"Because this is my spot, and no one is allowed up here but me."

"It says that it's his spot and that no one else is allowed up there."

Caleb started to make his way up the incline of the foot. Devon watched Caleb's disobedience with almost passive interest. Then he felt a force around his neck.

"Stop!" He cried hoarsely.

Caleb didn't stop. The force around Devon's neck intensified. He struggled to breathe. "Stop…it's choking…me."

Fortunately, Caleb was close enough to hear his words despite his inability to give them a great deal of volume. Caleb stopped and looked at Devon.

Then, with great authority in his voice, he declared loudly, "In the name of Jesus, I command you to stop choking Devon."

Instantly, the force around Devon's neck left, and he was able to breathe freely. "Please, Caleb, don't climb up there. It will just hurt one of us if you try."

Prefect turned its attention from Caleb to the sky.

"Behold, our guest of honor."

Chapter 29

The descent was nothing short of beautiful. Larry had seen sunrises before, but it was the first one he had seen as a Christian. On that morning, it was more than just a sunrise. It was a masterpiece. It was God's dynamic painting with His sky as a canvas. Reds, pinks, and violets blended perfectly as the sun's light reflected off of the top of clouds. Even the sun itself held some supreme beauty and was a brilliant symbol of God's own loving light that had displaced the darkness of the world.

As he free-fell feet first past the clouds, he was greeted with one more scenic view. Whites, greens, and grays were arranged in a distinct pattern in the form of snow-capped trees covering the snow-capped ground. *Amazing!*

Allowing his knees to absorb the full impact of his speeding body hitting the frozen ground, Larry's dramatic landing sent cold crystals into the air around him.

There were two men straight ahead of Larry. One of them was Caleb, who stood on the lower portion of a large rock. The other was Devon Olson, the man who he had prevented from robbing Grocery Avenue a few months ago. He had just learned that Devon Olson was his invincible nemesis.

"Hey guys, what's happening?" Larry good-naturedly greeted the two with a smile. Both of them looked satisfactorily impressed by his grand entry.

"I'll answer that question," an authoritative voice filled the air.

Caleb looked with shock at an empty space on the top of the rock that he stood on.

Devon looked down at his own feet. They were beginning to levitate off of the ground, but Devon's only expressions were curiosity and resignation.

"What is happening is that we are going to have a show of who is more powerful. You or me."

Unsure of what to do at that point, Larry just stood and watched Devon slowly rise higher as the deep voice reverberated from an unknown source.

"Devon is going to stand next to me at the top of this rock, and we are going to have a game. I know you are familiar with this game. It's called 'King of the Mountain.' You used to play it as a kid. Caleb started to play it just now, but he hasn't got very far yet. But I don't want to play with him. I want to play with you, Larry Tanner."

Immediately, Larry resisted playing along. As Devon's feet fell to rest on the top of the rock, Larry ignored the voice, half to irritate its owner and half because he had some news that he was dying to share.

"Hey, Caleb. Want to hear something awesome?"

"Yes," Caleb replied with cautious interest. Soon he wouldn't look so tense.

"I'm a Christian now!"

A large smile appeared on Caleb's face. "That *is* awesome!" The smile turned into a laugh. "So awesome."

"What is really awesome is the fact that that means absolutely nothing!" the voice bellowed out. *"Caleb tried to use his connection to his savior to try to get me to leave. I didn't leave. And I won't leave. Not until you try to make me."*

"Well if you won't leave," Larry said. "You can have fun just standing there for all of eternity. I intend on doing some traveling."

Caleb joined in. "Prefect, in the name of Jesus I forbid you to prevent Devon from leaving. Come on down, Devon. We can't let the devil have his way."

Before Devon could make a decision one way or another, the demon bellowed, *"I will have my way. Here's why. If you don't win at the game that I wish to play, then Rebecca will die."*

"Rebecca is already dead," Larry said solemnly.

"No, she's not," Caleb said. He looked away from Larry to something hidden from his view by the rock.

Larry leaped toward Caleb in order to see what he could. As if he had hit a giant invisible protective barrier, Larry stopped midair and fell to the ground. Shock overwhelmed Larry as he lay on his back in the snow. He had been cast into a sea of confusion, but not just because he had been knocked backward. For a moment, he had reached a height at which he could see Rebecca walking into the clearing with Jordan.

That's right, I never did see her body. I saw flesh being ripped apart by sharks, but I didn't know it was hers. I was relying on what Dane was telling me. Why did he lie to me?

"Get down, Caleb," Jordan commanded. Caleb complied and hopped down from the rock to make room for Jordan and Rebecca to climb on top of it.

Larry felt the kind of happiness that he had hoped to bring Caleb by telling him of his conversion. Rebecca was alive!

It pained Rebecca to not be allowed to speak to Larry. She wanted to comfort him, to encourage him, or even to just say hello. But she forced herself to stay silent.

When she had awoken from her sleep, she had been tied down to a stretcher. She had still been wearing the black jumpsuit, minus a small section of it that had been removed from her thigh where a fresh set of gauze covered her bullet wound.

At that point, she had learned that the CIA had used the laptop to discover where her parents were being kept. However, before she could see her parents again, she needed to fully cooperate with Jordan and the CIA and help them with Larry Tanner and the new threat that had arisen. After she completed her role in the situation "with the strictest complete obedience," she would be rewarded with a rescue effort to get her parents back that would be backed by the full force of the CIA.

For the moment, Rebecca complied.

She saw the happiness her presence had brought Larry. She knew it was because he had previously thought that she was dead. For the first time, she regretted the relationship she had built with Larry. Jenny had warned her. She had warned her to not be too enthusiastic about the mission, and she had warned her of the danger of Vance Mortus. Finally, Rebecca saw the repercussion of her actions, even though she had only been acting on orders.

She wondered what would happen to Larry Tanner. What would happen if she played her part? Would they try to kill him again? They had almost succeeded once, and they could probably succeed again. Rebecca wanted to save her parents, but was it worth sacrificing the life of her friend?

What would Jenny have done? *The old Jenny or the new Jenny?* It didn't matter. The answer would have been the same: Jenny would have stayed professional. Of course, she would have tried to save Larry's life. It was the right thing to do. But she would have followed her orders for the greater good. That's what this was all about, wasn't it? The greater good. It was hard to think that broadly as she looked into the happy but questioning eyes of her friend.

I wonder if he thinks I was aligned against him from the very beginning.

"Rebecca is innocent," Jordan said, reading Larry's thoughts. "But I am not. From the very beginning, I was acting under instructions to manipulate you and to break you for the sake of humanity."

So what if my relationship with Rebecca was based on a lie, Larry thought. Before that day, Jordan's revelation would have caused Larry's thoughts to be a myriad of confusion and negative emotions. But at the moment his thoughts funneled into a clear and simple statement. *Before today, my whole life was based on a lie. Now I see the truth. God loves me. He loves everyone, including this man who tried to kill me.*

"I forgive you." It felt good to say it, but it felt better to mean it.

Jordan seemed unmoved by Larry's sentiment. "Right now, a demon is a threat to humanity, just as you are. It assured me that if I obeyed it for the next little bit, it would agree to leave this physical realm awhile. For that reason, I *will* kill Rebecca if you don't do as it says."

"Demons lie," Caleb firmly put in.

"As long as Larry plays along, it won't matter whether the demon is honest, because I won't shoot." Jordan revealed a gun that he then pressed against Rebecca's solemn unmoving head.

A simple glance into Jordan Bolmer's emotionless eyes told Larry that the man was very serious and capable of doing what he had threatened to do.

"Okay demon. I'll make you a deal," Larry said after a moment. "I'll play this 'King of the Mountain' with you. When I make it to the top, you need to promise to never cause me any trouble again."

"If you make it to the top of this rock, I promise to never bother you again."

"With the all-powerful God that is within me as witness, I will hold you to your promise," Larry declared authoritatively.

Casually and confidently, Larry strode forward. Then he bumped into the wall.

"It will be kind of difficult for you to reach the top of this rock if you can't even get to its base," taunted the evil spirit.

Curious, Larry placed his hand against the invisible wall that stood in his way. "Hey, Caleb, come here. Can you feel this?"

Caleb jogged over and stood next to Larry. He waved his hand in the air next to where Larry's hands were blocked by an invisible force. "Nope."

"Interesting." Larry placed both of his hands against the supernatural force field and pushed. Even though he felt nothing but air against his skin, the resistance made him feel like he was pressing against a solid wall.

Bringing both his body and his legs into the effort, Larry began to add more pressure to the barrier. He pressed harder and harder. His feet began to slide backward on the snow, as there the invisible wall did not give. Larry dug his bare feet into the snow and ice to give himself a better grip. It didn't help.

A new idea came into his head. "Caleb, try pushing me through."

Caleb moved behind Larry and pushed him. Then he tried pulling Larry from the other side. When that failed as well, Caleb softly spoke to Larry.

"Have you been praying?"

"Yes!" the evil voice boomed. *"Go ahead! Pray! See if you will be granted the strength to be able to even compete with my power."*

Perhaps the demon was egging him on because it wanted him to refuse, to continue to try on his own power, and to continue to humiliate himself. The reverse psychology wouldn't work. *God, I know You are more powerful than this demon, even if I alone am not. Please grant me the strength to defeat it.*

Even though he felt as though nothing had changed, Larry renewed his attempts to reach the rock. He punched, kicked, and leaped at the wall without making progress.

"Perhaps Caleb would like to continue his prayers out loud."

Caleb, who already had his eyes closed, began to speak out loud. He spoke slowly and solemnly, but with an encouraging measure of confidence and firmness.

"Lord Jesus, I do not know what is going on here, but you do. I know that in the end your will is done and that you win, no matter what outcome we witness here on earth. I pray that regardless of what happens during this particular showdown, that all who witness it will be able to see your power and glorify you. Lord, I thank you for Larry Tanner's commitment to you, for there is no truer joy than becoming part of your family. I pray for—"

"Enough!" Prefect bellowed. The whole point of telling Caleb to pray out loud had been to have him verbally call upon the Divine Savior to grant Larry the

power to prevail against Prefect's invisible force field. From the foresight The Will had allowed it, Prefect could see that this cry for strength wouldn't help Larry on his quest. Yet that prayer wasn't the one that Caleb had voiced, and it had resulted in a change in the foreseeable future.

Prefect knew that time was not a loose cord. It would not be changed when the supernatural imposed itself on the course of the physical realm. It was not a loose cord because all-knowing God was outside of time and saw it as solid, impervious cord. In the viewpoint of the Almighty Keeper of Time, everything that was to happen had already happened. Prefect did not share that absolute perspective, but from its own broad viewpoint it saw much more than the humans did.

The number of angels on the battlefield had multiplied. Although none of the fallen or God-following angels were as powerful as Prefect, their increasing numbers were making Prefect anxious. Some of its angelic enemies had already prevented it from causing Caleb any physical harm, and Prefect had taken its frustrations out on Devon. The growing presence of the supernatural beings was unsurprising to Prefect. Although its target audience was humans, spiritual forces were always observing. The grand display of human history was for their benefit as well.

Encouraged by Caleb's prayer, Larry applied himself once more against Prefect's barrier. Just as Prefect had known, that didn't work.

"I'll make you another deal," Prefect spoke to Larry, but all present would hear the announcement. *"We could continue this battle for eternity, you not being able to harm me and me not being able to physically harm you. But I know you would much rather spend your time doing other things. So would I."*

Larry continued to listen without interrupting. Prefect was proud of the attention its authoritative voice commanded. *"So here's what we'll do. You'll pray to your Jesus to take away your power, and I'll agree to refrain from causing any harm to you or to anyone you know."*

"He could be lying," Caleb reminded his friend.

"You fool! How could I lie about this? If the God you worship can see what happens next, will He not see if I am lying and therefore refuse to grant your prayer request?"

Deep in thought, Larry stared straight ahead of him. Prefect knew that he wasn't praying—or at least that he wasn't praying the prayer that it had proposed in its deal. Not yet.

In order to speed up the prayer that would eventually come, Prefect added some additional motivation. *"Just a quick reminder that Jordan will pull the trigger if you decline my deal. Your problems won't end with Rebecca's death, as there is no shortage of hostages that I can use against you in this world. I will have my way."*

"I accept the terms of your deal. But you will not have your way. At least not in the very end," Larry gave in, although it was in a manner that annoyed Prefect almost as much as Caleb's faithful prayer had. If Larry had known what would come next, he wouldn't have said those words with as much conviction.

"*Say the words,*" Prefect prodded. "*Say them out loud.*"

"Dear Jesus," Larry prayed. "As much as I don't want to say these words, I say them with full sincerity. Relieve me of this precious gift of strength and invincibility that You have blessed me with."

Larry's prayer was immediately answered. Prefect could see it. The others saw it too, for Larry's arms immediately crossed around his chest and he began to shiver.

Prefect had not been lying when it had said that it would not harm Larry or anyone he knew. Vance would do it instead.

"Your mission is complete," Vance said to Rebecca as he removed his gun from against her head and her from his grasp. Just as Vance had predicted she would, Rebecca used her freedom to run toward Larry, who was accepting Caleb's jacket.

Larry wouldn't have time to enjoy either the warmth of Caleb's jacket or Rebecca's embrace. The bullet from Vance's gun made sure of that.

Chapter 30

"Third time's a charm," Prefect voiced. *How charming it is indeed.*

Rebecca screamed and cried.

Caleb froze in horror and shock.

Devon's own horror was accompanied by anger.

Larry did nothing but lay back in the snow that was being dyed red by the blood from his forehead.

That time, Larry would stay dead.

Prefect watched as Larry's spirit, which was far from dead, drifted away from its mortal shell. *You were wrong, Larry. My will was done. My will be done.*

Vance stood motionless and emotionless. He didn't need to say anything. Prefect knew what he was thinking. *Yes, Vance, we had a deal, and I broke it. I promised I would leave when Larry was dead, but I didn't. That doesn't surprise you. You knew my betrayal was an option. But you can't do anything about it.*

As much as Vance Mortus's unique mind separated him from the rest of humanity, one thing joined him with his fallen race. Pride. He had been thoroughly self-deceived and had believed that he made all of his decisions based on purely objective logical reasoning. For all of his mental calculating power, he hadn't been able to realize that his pride had guided his actions.

It was pride that had allowed Vance to believe that it was logical to compete with both sides of the supernatural war. He should have launched Larry into space when he had had the chance. His failure to do so had resulted in Larry's grand entrance onto the global stage.

Prefect would make its own entry, and nothing would get in its way. The demon physically manifested itself in the form of a ball of light. It chose to dim itself so that it wouldn't blind its human audience. Its beauty would be awe-inspiring and appreciated.

"Behold, I am Prefect! The world will know my name and fear me! The world will hear my voice and heed my words!" Prefect morphed into the figure of a giant man. Light continued to emanate from its perfect image. The demon had used that form to start a number of religions, as it made it look very much like an angel of light and a true servant of the faithful God.

Unsurprisingly, it was Caleb who responded first. The others—with the exception Vance, of course, who maintained his emotionless visage—were too overcome by awe and shock.

"You are an agent of lies, and lies cannot survive in the face of truth," Caleb said.

"You speak as someone who claims to know the truth." Despite the fact that Caleb was just one individual and Prefect had a whole world to deceive, pride kept it in place, and it defied the follower of Christ. *"But do you really know the truth? You thought*

you had power over me. You thought you had the power to protect your friends. But look what happened. The God you have faith in isn't listening to you, His so-called loved child."

"Why should God listen to me? I am not worthy. But you cannot fight the truth. The truth is that Jesus defeated you and your kind on the cross. The battle has already been won."

Prefect summoned a cyclone of wind. The gust circled the clearing, and the display of Prefect's power bended the trees. *"Strong words from someone with so much doubt. I can see it in you. Does it really look like God is winning? Perhaps this God of yours isn't who you believe He is. Perhaps He is—"*

"Enough!" Caleb interrupted Prefect just as it had interrupted his prayer earlier. "In the name of Jesus, I command you to be silent!"

The ground shook with Prefect's laughter. At first, it was annoyed that Caleb had interrupted it, but when Caleb tried to silence it, it gave Prefect more material that it could use to magnify its magnificence. The command would have worked on a lesser demon, but Prefect could not be silenced by this mortal. The awesome Lord of All had preordained that Prefect would be present near the end of days and that it would aid Lucifer in deceiving the nations. As such, it had been granted the power that the lesser demons lacked.

Vance saw that it was not a battle that Caleb could win. Yet the demon had to be stopped. He raised his fist in the air as a signal.

Prefect saw the bullet the moment it pierced through the wall of wind around the clearing. *Do you really think that since I took on a human form, something physical could harm me? I thought you were smarter than that, Vance,* Prefect thought. This time, Prefect would exhibit a more impressive way of stopping the bullet than it had displayed during its last showdown with Vance. The fallen angel reached out its hand and dramatically caught the bullet.

Prefect was surprised when the speeding projectile did not stop in its grip and instead stopped inside the illusory flesh of its hand. Still, there was a way to showcase a victory.

"Not only can I stop bullets in midair, but I can also heal wounds I have allowed myself to obtain for instructional purposes." No blood followed the bullet out of its hand as the hole it created closed for all to see.

It had been subtle, and there was no doubt that anyone but Vance would have missed it, but he had seen the surprise in Prefect, not so much because Prefect's beaming face had changed, but because of the short pause it had taken before it had explained that it had "allowed itself to get injured." Not only that, but there had not been a dramatic lead-up to the catch. Prefect's arm had simply appeared where it had needed to be with no travel time. That had been contrary to Prefect's usual arrogant and dramatic style.

His adversary might not have been aware of Jenny's presence.

Jenny knew that she was not the only sniper near the clearing. At least one of their guns was trained on her lest she have a desire to go against their commander's strategy. That was why she had not prevented Jordan from shooting Larry. That, and the fact that she hadn't expected the shot to be a fatal one.

She had honestly been surprised when Jordan had enlisted her help. As experienced as she was, she didn't have any abilities that his team didn't already have. Then she had learned that it wasn't her abilities that Jordan had required, but rather her personal conviction. Her faith in Christ was something that none of his men had. For whatever reason, Jordan had thought that her belief could make her bullets different from his men's bullets.

Her past training allowed her to maintain her composure after witnessing what had transpired in the clearing. She was already familiar with the violence of men, and she already believed in the supernatural, so its manifestation hadn't shaken her off of her foundation.

No part of her training and beliefs had told her that a bullet shot by a Christian would make a difference. *I suppose anything is possible with God.*

After the bullet had hit the fallen angel, Jenny had known for certain that God was with her.

Considering the plethora of trees that did its best to shield the clearing, Jenny lay in a remarkably effective vantage point on a hill two hundred and fifty yards away from it. From the lying position that Jordan had assigned to her, she could easily make out the handful of people next to the large rock on which her shining target stood. At least, of course, until the wind had started.

Even though she had been safe from the gusts the archdemon had summoned, the force of the tree-bending miniature storm had filled her vision with snow dust, small branches, and leaves, all of which had been obstacles to her bullet. If those factors hadn't made the shot impossible enough, there was the issue of the intense wind speed.

The only way I'm making this shot is if God Himself guides my bullet, Jenny had thought. With that in mind, Jenny had sent up a prayer before taking the shot. It was like there had not been a single obstacle between her and her target. It had hit. God had been with her.

Thanks, God. If You want, You can help me with my next few shots as well.

Prefect's arm fell to its side when a second bullet hit it in the shoulder.

It's as if this body I'm displaying were a real physical body, Prefect thought in horror. There was no way that anything as lowly as a bullet should have been able to do anything to it. *Unless You are behind it.* If a bullet could temporarily disable its arm, what would a bullet to its head accomplish?

Outwardly, Prefect displayed no fear. *"As much as I would love to stand here and display my magnificent healing power, I have places to go and more audiences to entertain. Fear not, you'll see more of me soon."*

Prefect wanted to fade out of the physical realm so it would be safe from any God-empowered bullets. The Will wouldn't let it. Yet The Will allowed it to keep its magnificent human form, complete with its control over its environment.

The wind that Prefect was sustaining came to an abrupt stop as it leaped down from the top of the rock and let the large stone temporarily hide it from the unseen shooter. Prefect sprinted into the forest as if it needed to rely on its muscular legs to propel it.

A wave of bullets followed Prefect into the forest, and they all fell short at its command. Prefect knew that none of the bullets had originated from the original shooter.

Trees uprooted themselves in front of Prefect, who was not willing to deviate its course because of physical barriers if it didn't have to. No human—save Larry if he had still been alive—would have been able to match the speed of Prefect as it sped away. Then again, no human should have been able to make the shot that had pierced its mortal disguise, so Prefect continued to run. It would stop for nothing, and nothing would get in its way.

* * *

Ryan was very careful to use simple terms when he explained what it meant to become and live as a Christian. Ollie listened with a concentration that seemed uncharacteristic. Although he looked confused at times, he didn't interrupt. Ryan finished by asking him if he had any questions.

Ollie took Ryan by surprise when he answered, "Nah, man. I got it." The simple, passive statement caused Ryan to think that Ollie probably *didn't* get it. At the very least, Ollie's response was anticlimactic. There weren't any tears or any conviction-filled arguments. He didn't even widen his eyes to indicate that for the first time in his life, he was seeing things clearly.

"You got it?"

"Ya, man," Ollie answered. He smiled after short silence. "I'm a Christian now."

The words were not an excited proclamation but rather a calm, firm statement. Those words, coupled with Ryan's belief that they were sincere, gave him indescribable joy.

"That's awesome!"

"It's legit," Ollie agreed. "Now all I have to do is find where I need to build the church."

It was at that moment that something clicked inside Ryan Slater's mind. There were two unlikely pieces of the puzzle that might possibly fit quite nicely together. After thinking about the mysterious consignee of his load, Ryan asked, "Hey, Ollie, would your full name happen to be Oliver Weston?"

Surprise registered on Ollie's face. "Totally! Did God tell you that?"

At first, Ryan was going to say "sort of," but he ended up going with a response that he felt was more appropriate given the circumstances.

"Yes, He did. I'm also carrying the lumber you will need to build your church."

"Are you an angel?"

"No, but I have an idea about where God wants you to build that church."

They were nearing the location that Ryan's GPS was showing as their destination. Ollie's eyes were wide with excitement. "We're almost there, dude! I can feel it."

Ryan smiled, but said nothing, not wanting to discourage the man, because he understood the very real possibility that his feelings were unfounded.

"Approaching destination, on right," the GPS spoke. If the GPS was correct, their destination would be right where a silver car was parked on the side of the road. *Looks like Caleb's car*, Ryan thought.

Even more convincing than Ollie's "feeling" that there was something special about their destination were the extremely bright rays of light emanating from trees.

"What is that?" Ollie asked.

Whatever the mysterious source of light was, it was approaching them fast. Ryan slowed the truck to a stop.

Prefect saw the truck that was in its path. It didn't stop running; the truck would clear out of its way like the trees had. Of course, no one in the truck would be harmed. The Will wouldn't have allowed it.

It then became apparent that The Will wouldn't allow the truck to move out of its way.

It was time for Prefect to return to its prison.

The glowing figure disappeared just as it connected with Ollie's side of the truck.

"Now *that*," said Ryan, "was an angel."

Chapter 31

Agent Three-C knew it would be uncomfortable and strange for Caleb. It was not every day that the only man who had ever pointed a gun at you and threatened to shoot came inside your bedroom to wake you up. There was certainly a whole list of people who the store manager would have preferred to be woken up and interrogated by.

"Caleb, where is Larry?"

"I don't know." Three-C could tell the man was struggling just to wake up, let alone to answer the question. Sitting up, Caleb continued. "Last I knew, he was with Jordan and Rebecca on some secret mission."

He wasn't lying. In addition to a sedative, Caleb had been subject to a drug that had made him forget the last few hours, as unforgettable as they had been.

"Well, the mission is over. Rebecca and Jordan are dead, and Larry is missing."

"Dead," Caleb repeated the word as if it would help its meaning sink in.

Although "Jordan" was in perfect health, the man Caleb knew as Colin Duprey wasn't being completely dishonest about the fate of Rebecca Hiltman. Her knowledge about Vance Mortus, the CIA's involvement in Larry's situation, and the part that Dr. Daniels played made her a liability. The simplest way to deal with it had been to kill her.

The lie that Rebecca and Jordan had died in Iran was the same lie that he had told to Jenny Slater, who had also had her memory erased. Adam North, the director of the CIA, would be upset along with Jenny about the loss of the agent, but there would be no recoil against Vance Mortus for a death that Rebecca Hiltman had walked into on her own.

It was unfortunate that the Hiltmans would meet the same fate as their daughter. Vance's team didn't enjoy killing people, but they understood that there was a cost to global security. If Vance Mortus determined that death was the best option, then death it would be.

"Well, that's what Larry told us before he went missing. We have yet to find any evidence to the contrary. Perhaps it was their deaths that caused Larry to finally snap and turn to religion," Three-C said as if he were thinking out loud. "It's going to be difficult for us to get to Larry first with the whole world looking for him, so it's imperative that you let us know if he contacts you."

Straining to process all of the new information that had been presented to him, Caleb squinted in concentration and asked one of the many questions he was wondering about.

"Why would the whole world be looking for him?"

"Maybe if you hadn't slept in, you would know."

Caleb glanced at the digital clock on his bedside table. His eyes grew wider when he saw that that it was late in the morning. It was well past the time he had been due to be at the store that he had never been late to before.

"Don't worry about Gross Ave," Agent Three-C said, reading his thoughts. "When the baker failed to get a hold of you or any of the other supervisors, he put a sign on the door saying that the place was closed for the day. It was probably for the best, as you'd likely get more questions than customers today."

After pulling out a tablet computer that he himself had designed, Three-C showed Caleb a couple of the videos of Larry Tanner preaching and performing stunts at Palm Bay Beach. Caleb's face was solemn to match the occasion, yet it betrayed some happiness when he observed Larry talking about Jesus.

"Larry was easily identifiable to the people of Terrecastor who shopped at Gross Ave on a regular basis. The media is already beginning to show up in town. They'll want to talk to you."

"What do I tell them?"

"As a professional, you can confirm that a Larry Tanner was in fact employed by Grocery Avenue. But you will say that due to company policy, you are not allowed to disclose any personal details about the man, especially to the media. Any additional questions will have to be directed to the public relations department of Grocery Avenue's head office."

"Larry started right after Gross Ave was rebuilt. People will connect the dots."

"There will only be speculation. No one will be able to find the training facility under the store. No one will be able to prove that something bigger was going on, so long as certain people stay quiet."

Even high-powered intelligence gathering agencies would fail to figure out the truth behind the rebuilt Grocery Avenue. No records of any expenditure on the grocery store would be evident in the CIA's books. Of course, people would know that a CIA agent had been in Terrecastor for roughly the same amount of time as Larry, but her organization would let it leak that she had been there both to visit her friend and to investigate an unconfirmed speculation that there was something special about Larry Tanner. No one could cover one's tracks as efficiently as Agent Three-C's commander could.

"There are drugs out there that will not leave me the option of keeping your secret." Caleb pointed out. He was sharp. It was too bad that he knew too much. When it was no longer economical to provide security to ensure that he didn't talk, he would have to be dealt with. Perhaps he was even smart enough to realize that.

Three-C decided that the best option was to deal with Caleb on his own, religious, level. "Caleb. You believe that God is in control and that in the end He will have His way. You know that there's no sense in worrying about things you have no control over. Trust us to do our job and protect you, and trust your God to take care of things even if we fail—which we won't. This situation may bigger than you could imagine, but all you have to do is keep doing the right thing.

"Which is worse, death or dishonesty? Keeping another person's secret isn't all that dishonest, but you can be certain that your failure to keep this secret will lead to death. That's like murdering, is it not?"

Caleb nodded. He was smart enough to know he was being manipulated, but he was also smart enough to realize that "Colin Duprey" was right.

The computer specialist then went on to tell Caleb what to say if he had any questions about Rebecca's involvement. He would say believable mostly-true statements that would satisfy the listener. Statements like, "It's really hard to say what level anyone's relationship is at, especially one as complex as Larry and Rebecca's," and, "If you told me that Rebecca was CIA, I wouldn't be surprised."

If he had to, Caleb would be allowed to acknowledge that he had seen Larry's strength but had kept it a secret because Larry had asked him too. It was a big deal, but not world-shaking news. After all, believers would likely do what Caleb had done and attribute Larry's strength to the supernatural. Most skeptics would think that Caleb's faith in Jesus made his perspective biased and unscientific, and so it was unlikely that his testimony would result in more than the typical short-lived isolated conversion spikes.

If Caleb was questioned about whether the situation had been bigger than Larry alone, he would say something along the lines of, "Most definitely, because God gave Larry gifts for a reason, just like God gives everyone gifts. It's not certain how big of an impact we can make with our gifts."

Directing conversations into broad religious statements would be right up Caleb's alley. His responses would be similar to Ryan Slater's responses. Ryan knew less about the overall situation than Caleb did, so fortunately for his sake, he did not pose the same security risk and would not have to be dealt with in the same way. Their Christian bias would help deter them from being the targets of people who were searching out objective hard facts.

Jenny, of course, was adept at keeping secrets, and she would be regarded as more of an asset to the security of Test Subject Fourteen's mission than a liability.

To conclude his intense conversation with Caleb, Agent Three-C handed him a paper with a number on it. "Keep this number in a safe place. If you can, memorize it and then destroy it. Call it immediately if Larry Tanner contacts you. Seconds count."

Garbed in attire that identified him as a member of the FBI, Agent Three-C then exited Caleb's trailer. After sliding into the passenger seat of the white van in which Agent Two-O had been waiting for him, he sighed. "Glad that's over."

Two-O, who had been monitoring their conversation remotely, nodded as he shifted the vehicle into drive. He knew his colleague was referring to his part in the overall mission more than to just his talk with Caleb. The two men could deftly handle missions that most thought were impossible—missions where perfection was expected and achieved—without fear or flinching. But there was something unnerving about dealing with missions in which the supernatural was involved. Vance's team could easily analyze and deal with the most unpredictable, dangerous lunatics, but the amount of uncertainties present in the missions that concerned the spiritual realm unnerved even the most elite agents.

That particular mission had been the most intense one Agent Three-C had taken part in. It shouldn't have surprised him that his leader had pulled off another victory, but he had to admit that it had had its messy parts.

"Why do you suppose Devon had to die?" asked Three-C. Two-O knew that he trusted Vance Mortus completely and had asked the question merely to collect data for future purposes. "We could have wiped his mind and sent him back to Dr. Daniels as a test subject. The public wouldn't have even known the difference."

"Think about it," Two-O responded. "Devon was a suitable vessel for a powerful archdemon before. What would stop another of such demons from taking its place?"

"Couldn't a demon like that victimize anyone?"

Agent Two-O shrugged. "Guess we can't know that kind of thing for sure, but better to be safe than sorry."

Better to be safe than sorry...Religions begin when one decides what the "safe" spiritual route is. Both Rebecca and Devon spoke under their breath as they drifted to sleep. I wonder if they were praying—making a play for the safe route. What is the safest route?

Agent Three-C would have liked to believe that following Vance Mortus was the safest route. After all, in the end, the man had won, hadn't he? Larry was dead, and there was no sign of the demon that had declared itself to be "Prefect" either. Throughout the process, Dr. Daniels's project had remained a secret. Global security had remained intact.

Yet Vance Mortus hadn't only contended against physical forces. Had the mortal actually won the game on a spiritual level as well?

In the past, Three-C had seen the spiritual as just a metaphysical layer that needed to be manipulated if one were to succeed. The showdown at Giant's Foot Rock had shaken the agent's very perspective about the supernatural; the kind of tangible things that the intangible forces had done had taken Agent Three-C by surprise. If he had been wrong about the relationship between the spiritual and physical, did that mean the rest of his worldview was off center?

Hadn't Vance Mortus' use of Jenny Slater been an admittance of sorts of his own shortcoming in his spiritual knowledge? He had lost to the archdemon in a one-on-one battle. In a one-on-one battle with Jenny Slater, the demon had lost to her bullet. She had intimidated the demon; she had succeeded where Vance Mortus had failed. That fact alone had caused Agent Three-C to reevaluate his worldview.

Until the present, it had only made sense to focus on the human aspect of the supernatural because they were humans. When the demon had told Caleb to pray out loud, the man hadn't prayed for salvation or victory. He had prayed that God would receive glory. Just maybe, the man hadn't said those words because of an incorrect worldview. Perhaps the meaning of it all wasn't centered on the fate of humans or their souls, but on the glorification of God.

Author's Note

I began writing *Freedom to Die* more than a few years ago in an attempt to amuse myself and to do something somewhat productive with my boredom. Over time, my writing goals evolved into something greater than simply self-entertainment.

Although my faith in Christ probably comes through strongly (perhaps *too* strongly for a few of you) in this book, let it be known that it was not my primary intention to persuade or convince you. I wanted, rather, to provide a new, unique lens through which to look at the relationship between the physical and the spiritual; I wanted to inspire deep thinking about what you know about reality, regardless of whether or not you chose in the end to adopt a viewpoint akin to my own.

As I wrote this novel, I tried to imagine how things would take place in reality. Yes, I introduced some very wildly unrealistic—and, I hope you will agree, fun—aspects to the book, but for a large portion of the book, I tried to just sit back and let the characters and the events sort themselves out on their own. That was especially true for the fates of the leading characters in the last two chapters.

If you found yourself confused about who the protagonist and antagonist were, know that that was not an accident. There was a definite protagonist, but seeing who it was may take a shift in perspective.

Thank you for taking the time to read this humble addition to the literary world. Even if you disagreed with certain parts of the book, my hope is that you found yourself amused, entertained, and enriched by the experience of reading it.

Sincerely,

Stephen Selke

Made in the USA
Charleston, SC
01 June 2015